The House on Dominion Street and Other Stories

Edited by

V. Rospond

ZMOK
BOOKS

The House on Dominion Street and Other Stories
Edited by Vincent Rospond
Cover design by Jan Kostka
This edition published in 2024

Zmok Books is an imprint of

Winged Hussar Publishing, LLC
1525 Hulse Rd, Unit 1
Point Pleasant, NJ 08742

Bibliographical References and Index
1. Horror. 2. Wierd. 3. Anthology

Winged Hussar Publishing, LLC All rights reserved
For more information
visit us at www.whpsupplyroom.com

Twitter: WingHusPubLLC
Facebook: Winged Hussar Publishing LLC

FOR YOUR CONSIDERATION

Editor's Note

The House on Dominion Street and Other Stories was a few years in the making. My friend Graham NcNeill came to me with a short story. "It's a little twisted so I thought of you," which is fair enough. But it needed a good supporting cast. So I went to my other friends, who have written things for me in the past and either went through their portfolios or asked them in the nicest possible way, if they could give me a contribution. This is the result.

Graham McNeill is an award-winning and best-selling author who uses his powers mostly for good working for a game company. He still has the axe he was awarded as a David Gemmell Award winning author, and it has tasted blood. But that is a story for another day.

Chris Noonan came to me from a friend. These stories are his first published pieces. He has an intense interest in horror stories, and he plays in a band in his spare time. He is also another person from New Jersey, so by law of the street I needed to include him.

Clint Werner is someone I have known for over twenty years and have been happy to publish books and short stories during that time. Clint is a dark master, but if you get him going on Godzilla he will do so with a gleam in his eyes.

Robert E. Waters is a veteran writer with many books, short-stories and games to his credit. He is one of the lead writers in our series on the dark gods. His roots in gaming go way back.

Jason M. Waters is a first time writer and as you will see he also has a twisted imagination - which of course we love.

Scott Washburn is a very talented author of original SF&F who is the mastermind behind "The Great Martian War" series. Scott enjoys the weird and scary, but if you run into him, please call him "Colonel."

David Guymer who I have looked forward to working with, and I have had our paths cross several times, but this is the first time I have been able to get him to commit pen and paper for us. I look forward to other opportunities.

Ben Stoddard is someone who I have grown to know over the past few years. He is a talented author of fantasy novels and passionate about writing. This is his first horror story but expect to see more things from him as soon as the doctors say it is safe for the general public.

Duane Burke is also a first-time author who I met several years ago when he was trying to tell the demons to leave him alone. I was able to pry these two stories from him, but I expect to see more of them grace the pages for publication in the future.

Vincent W. Rospond

The House on Dominion Street
By Graham McNeill

Chapter 1

Verses I – VIII.

The Old Man in the Window

I.

Daniel wasn't sure exactly when he noticed the old man's face in the window, or how long it took him to figure out something was really wrong inside the house on Dominion Street. All he knew was that it had taken him way too long to see suffering and finally pay attention to it.

He'd always thought of himself as a basically decent person. The kind of person who'd step in if ever he saw injustice, a man who'd do the right thing when called upon to be a stand-up guy.

Not a saint, for sure, but not *bad*.

He'd moved his family to Los Angeles a year ago, taking a job with a tech start-up based in the sexy-sounding Silicon Beach. He'd cashed out a software engineering job in a video-game company that had had one big hit but whose games were getting progressively worse. It had only been a matter of time before the whole thing imploded.

Daniel had seen the writing on the wall months before the curtain came down, and having tried in vain to steer the company's leadership from the rocks, cashed out his stock options, convinced his wife and daughter to pack up their house in the Bay and head south to the City of Angels. Before leaving, he'd quietly set his colleagues up with with multiple leads to companies likely to hire them. Almost all of them had since found new positions, which was something of a miracle.

After a year in rented accommodation in Marina del Ray, he and Arlene finally bought themselves a nice place up in the hills, sandwiched between Beverly Hills and Bel Air. It belonged to neither, but was still wealth-adjacent enough for folk who didn't live in LA to think they were rubbing shoulders with the rich and famous.

His commute was longer, but Arlene loved the house and if it took Daniel an extra half hour each way to work, then that was a price he was happy to pay. Whitney liked it too, at least he guessed she did, though he doubted she'd ever forgive him from taking her away from her friends in San Francisco. Despite that, Daniel knew they had it good, and he was actually feeling pretty excited about the work he was doing.

Dominion Street wasn't one the navigational apps on his phone had wanted him to take. They always seemed determined to keep him off that particular street, but after a missed turn, Daniel found that this route shaved fifteen minutes off his drive, so he now cheerfully ignored their constant rerouting and followed this new way to work.

Daniel first noticed the house on Dominion Street thanks to a technology fail. The bluetooth on his phone was playing up and he didn't have a cable to connect it to the car's audio system. LA drivers don't tend to notice much of anything except their own misery, but inching along without music or another voice to distract him, Daniel had taken to looking around.

Most of the houses were pale white mansions with long drives, plantation shutters and columned porches that screamed a badly-skewed money to taste ratio, but the particular house that caught his eye had a grandiose vibe of old money and still managed to looked pretty classy. The little he could see through the wide gate looked like something out of Arlene's favorite show, Downton Abbey. Blocks of pale cream stone, tall windows and a heavy wooden door that could probably withstand a siege.

He saw the basics, but didn't really pay much attention to it beyond that.

Not until the day he noticed that one of its upper windows was broken; a dormer window built into the angle of the roof, with an arched frame for the glass. An off-kilter sheet of wood was nailed over it. That was as much as Daniel thought of it that day, and he went back to his usual routine of paying little attention to the world outside. The days went by, work continued and everything beyond the cocoon of audio books, podcasts and music went away.

Three weeks later, Daniel was driving with Whitney in the passenger seat. A stilted attempt at conversation had lasted as long as it took them to get down the canyon road, before his daughter's phone buzzed with a text, and both of them gave an inward sigh of relief as she tapped on the keyboard.

In the lull between quick-fire messages going back and forth, Whitney looked up.

"I wonder what happened there," she said.

"Where?" said Daniel, not looking up. The car was stopped at a red light, so he'd taken the opportunity to unlock his phone and like a few funny tweets.

"There, that house," said Whitney. "The one with the broken window up top."

Daniel looked up and saw they were on Dominion Street. Whitney was staring over at the same house he'd seen a few weeks ago.

"Huh," he said. "Probably some kids with a baseball."

"Doesn't look like any kids live there."

The red light turned green, and they pulled away.

II.

More weeks passed. The crazed whirl of a fledgling start-up took up almost all of Daniel's brain-space, and he soon forgot about the house on Dominion Street. It was just a broken window, not even a little bit unusual in LA.

Perhaps a bit unusual in *this* part of LA, but nothing worth calling the HOA about.

On the way home one night, stopped at the same lights, Daniel leaned over and saw the same wooden panel over the same window.

"Why would you not just repair it?" he said.

III.

After that, Daniel kept looking up every time he drove along Dominion Street.

Every day he kept wondering the same thing.

Why would the owners not just repair that window?

It wouldn't be a big job, a contractor would get it done inside an afternoon, and it wouldn't even cost that much. Anyone who could afford a house in this neighborhood surely wouldn't baulk at the cost of a new window. Daniel was no handyman, but he could put up some shelves that wouldn't fall down, could do basic plumbing or electrical work, and show him a YouTube video, and he'd have a crack at most things that didn't require certification. He wondered if it would be too weird to just pull in and offer to repair the window, then laughed. The owners would probably call the cops, thinking he was some kind of scammer hoping to check the place out before burglarizing it. Daniel knew he'd be suspicious as hell of anyone turning up at *his* door looking to do him a good turn out of the goodness of their heart.

So, every day he drove past the house and checked the window. And every day it was still blocked off by that same sheet of wood. It got to be something of a habit to drive past the house, even when it wasn't on his route.

Eventually Arlene noticed that he'd drive by when they were heading in completely the opposite direction. Every date night, whether they were heading to downtown, K-town or Santa Monica, their route would travel down Dominion Street.

For a while he'd pretend, he'd gotten lost or was distracted and missed a turn.

Arlene mentioned it one night at dinner, and Daniel tried to make light of it, attempting to shift the conversation to a topic sure to cause teenage embarrassment.

Whitney saw through him straight away.

'It's that house with the broken window, isn't it?'

IV.

Daniel found himself strangely reticent to talk about the house, knowing that trying to explain his sort-of-obsession with it would sound ridiculous. Which it was, of course, but he'd grown oddly protective of his mystery – as slight as it was. Sharing it with others, even loved ones, would somehow *diminish* it. Keeping it in this Schrödinger-like state allowed it to continue being unexplained. So he just agreed he was being stupid simply to shut the conversation down.

With dinner over, Daniel made a conscious decision never to drive any of his family past the house on Dominion Street again.

V.

Of course, he kept driving past it, and wondering what might lie at the heart of why that one window was allowed to remain broken. It was so stupid. It stuck out like a sore thumb, a blight on an otherwise grand and impressive looking house.

Why would you *not* repair it?

It took a conscious effort of will not to drive past if Daniel had anyone in the car. Even if the most direct route to where he was heading was actually to drive along that road, he'd find another way to go. The sat-nav helped him out, still averse to that route, so even on the rare occasions where Arlene or Whitney noticed they ought to have driven past the house, Daniel just pointed to the navigation screen on the dashboard and shrugged.

'I just go where it tells me,' he said.

VI.

Eventually he drove by the house one Saturday and parked on the opposite side of the street.

It was a cliché to say that folk don't walk in LA, but it had become a cliché for a reason. The only people Daniel had ever seen walking were ones heading to a bus-stop, delivering something, or who couldn't get a parking spot near a friend's house.

Nobody normally expected to see middle-aged white guys staring at a house with one broken window, so Daniel didn't want to linger in case anyone got suspicious. He walked up and down the street a couple of times, looking around as if he was lost or occasionally checking his phone like he was waiting for someone.

He slowed his pace whenever his angle to the gate allowed him to see the house. Just like he remembered, it looked old. Not LA old, which meant about a hundred years, but properly old, like the buildings he'd seen during a summer spent in England. The stone looked like it had been quarried hundreds of years ago, and the white wood was flaking and faded.

How had he not noticed that before? This was a house that looked like it had been transported, block by block, timber by timber, from a place far older than America. He'd heard stories like that before, about stupid rich folk who'd bought bridges and had them disassembled then rebuilt, but couldn't be sure if he'd heard them as fact on the Discovery Channel or as famous scams of the past.

As he always did, Daniel looked up at the wood covering the broken window. The wood was gone. In its place was a rectangle of darkness.

A chill raced up Daniel's spine and his mouth fell open as he saw the face of an old man.

Pale, thin and old. So very, *very* old.

Even from the street, Daniel could see his eyes were filled with pain.

The man lifted his hand.

And a host of sensations surged within Daniel.

The taste of his wife's lips on their wedding day...

His daughter's breath on his neck when she was a baby...

His mother's hand on his heart as she took her last breath, and the smell of his father's tobacco as they held each other and cried.

All the air was trapped in Daniel's lungs, the rush of emotions filling him as raw and physical as a blow. He felt himself moving towards the gate of the house, his gaze fixed on the old man's anguished eyes.

And walked straight into an elderly gardener with a leaf-blower.

"Shit, excuse me," said Daniel, the spell broken.

"Perdone," said the man with a deferential bow.

Daniel looked back up at the house, and the joy he'd felt evaporated like rain on a sidewalk.

The old man was gone, and the window was once again blocked by the timber panel.

"No," he said. "No, no, no..."

The sense of loss was a gut punch, and Daniel felt a righteous anger welling up inside him at being cut off from the infinite joy he'd just felt. He turned back to the elderly Mexican gardener, who was already back at his truck and locking up its tailgate.

"God damn it, why the fuck don't you look where you're going?" yelled Daniel. The man ignored him, heading around to the driver's door, which only stoked the fire's of Daniel's anger.

"You ran into me on purpose, didn't you?" he shouted after him.

Daniel wasn't a violent man, and hadn't been in a fight since high school, but right now he wanted to beat this man to death for taking away what he'd just felt. The sheer power of his fury brought Daniel up short. The anger drained from him, and he felt his cheeks flush with shame at his violent outburst.

"I'm so sorry," he said. "I just–"

"You should forget about that house," said the gardener. "Nothing good is left in it."

The man climbed into his truck and drove away, leaving Daniel alone and lost on the sidewalk outside the house with one boarded up window.

VII.

Daniel drove home in a fugue state, his emotions seesawing from giddy elation to gut-wrenching anguish in the space of a breath. His cheeks were wet with tears, and he didn't know why, as if he'd been on the verge of revelation only to have it snatched away at the last second.

The effort of breathing was painful, and his heart was beating like a sprinter's. He felt like he'd narrowly avoided a catastrophic accident on the freeway or been given the promotion of a lifetime. Bliss and horror vied for supremacy in his mind.

The braying of horns shook him, forcing him to concentrate on the road. He raised a hand to apologize to whoever he'd just pissed off, and focused on taking one breath after another.

"What the hell, what the hell…?" he said.

He'd seen the old man in the window. He knew he had.

So how had a moment's glance away cheated him of that sight? One second, he'd seen the old man, the next the window was boarded up again, but that just wasn't possible.

Had he imagined it? He'd read about the mind's ability to see shapes and faces that weren't there, a survival mechanism from an earlier age when life or death depended on a person's ability to quickly pick out friendly faces or threats. He'd never experienced it, never seen faces in the clouds or the shape of something strange in the shadows, so why would he experience it now?

No, I saw him. I saw him, I know I did.

Daniel pulled into the parking lot of his usual Starbucks and went in to order a strong coffee. He took a table amid the would-be screenwriters and their glowing MacBooks, then turned to the analytical part of his brain that made him good at his job.

Break it down into chunks, dissect every portion and see how it fit into the greater whole.

Daniel closed his eyes and walked back through the moments just before he'd seen the old man, unspooling his memory like an old video cassette.

It had been hot, the noonday sun burning his pale, New Englander's skin. He'd smelled fresh-cut grass, newly wet from sprinklers. Low-level traffic noise, horns blasting, a distant siren. A helicopter buzzing overhead.

What had made him look up?

He hadn't noticed it at the time, but it had felt like a voiceless command had compelled him to lift his head. Not in an imperious way, more like when you're psychically willing the home team's quarterback to look up save himself a pummeling from a three hundred pound linebacker.

Daniel tried to remember the old man's face, but found that part of his memory frustratingly empty, as though his recollection couldn't quite grasp its contours. Every time he tried to form a picture of the old man's face, he kept slipping over the details no matter how hard he tried to force them into view.

The man's face was old, that much he *could* tell, perhaps the oldest face he'd ever seen.

But beyond that, he had nothing beyond his pleading eyes.

That detail he could pick out, the old man's eyes. Deep and dark, with a depth of suffering he'd only ever seen in the faces of his dad's army buddies at the VA, the ones who'd come back from Vietnam, but left a part of their soul behind.

Was this old guy a veteran who'd seen too much bloodshed to ever forget?

That felt like it might be something real, but Daniel knew there was more to it than that. How he knew it, he couldn't say, only that something had passed between them in that fleeting moment of connection. The idea of something so ephemeral didn't sit well with Daniel, who valued empirical data and facts over feelings and hunches.

A sudden thought struck him.

Was the old man asking for his help? Was the anguish in his eyes the only means he had to signal a passerby? Christ, was the old man a victim of some abuse?

Or was he just lonely? Perhaps, but wasn't everyone in this city on some level?

A city of millions, and it was all too easy to feel isolated and alone, adrift and untouched by the people around you. He'd felt that way plenty of times. A new city, a new workplace, new people. All of whom were talented, interesting and fun to be around, but without the backfill of years of shorthand, shared memories and experiences, every friendship had to be built from scratch, and he'd left the skill for that back in his twenties.

A powerful surge of regret stabbed through his heart, as he thought of the friends he'd grown up with, the boys and girls who'd become the men and women that had shaped him and who he in turn had shaped. He hadn't spoken to Ben or Jack or Trudy in months, and a sense a guilty neglect washed over him. Every e-mail that travelled coast to coast always started with *sorry it's been so long since I got in touch, but work's been crazy and...*

Was that what friendships were now? Saying you were shit at keeping the connections open until one of you died?

A tap on his shoulder broke Daniel's reverie and he looked up into the face of a young girl wearing a Starbucks apron. She was new here, and Daniel couldn't remember her name. He scanned her overall. A name-tag said her name was Tiffany.

His phone was ringing. House of Pain's *Jump Around*, his ringtone for Arlene. Her smiling face lit up the screen, but he muted the phone and turned to Tiffany.

"Sorry, what did you say?"

"I said we're closing up now, sir," she said.

"What?"

"We're closing now, sir."

Daniel didn't understand.

"What are you talking about, it's the middle of the afternoon?"

Tiffany looked at him like he was crazy, and a moment later, Daniel saw exactly why.

"Sir, it's 10pm, we're closing up."

The shop was empty, and the sky beyond the windows was ink black. The coffee cup was cold in his hand and the time on his watch was 9:59.

"Wait...what? It's night?"

"Yes," said Tiffany.

"How long have I been here?"

"I'm not sure, but you've been here since I got on shift at four."

Daniel looked at his phone and saw a dozen missed calls from both Arlene and Whitney, at least as many messages, and texts that grew increasingly frantic as the day had gone on.

House of Pain blasted from the phone again.

"Damn it," said Daniel, pushing himself up from his chair. His legs were stiff, and he held onto the table as blood painfully flowed back into his extremities.

"Sir, are you okay?"

"I'm really not sure," he answered.

VIII.

By the time Daniel got home, Arlene was frantic with worry.

He'd answered his phone to say he was on his way back, but was still faced with a barrage of questions as soon as he got into the house, none of which he had a satisfactory answer to. Arlene had called his work, the hospital and the cops, sure that he'd either gotten himself killed on the freeway, shot by a crazy guy or was off in a skanky motel with one of the bright young things at his office.

The truth seemed too far fetched, that he'd zoned out in Starbucks for around nine hours, but it was all he had. She didn't believe him, and the next day was spent in frosty isolation until he took her to the same Starbucks and had Tiffany verify his story.

If anything, that made her even more concerned. She made him see their doctor, and promise to take some time off work, convinced he was suffering from work-related stress. Daniel couldn't really afford time away from work, but when Arlene was on a mission, it was simpler just to accept she was inevitably going to succeed.

She'd be a great CEO someday. That she wasn't already was criminal.

They spent the next three days together, enjoying late breakfasts, gallery trips, walks on the beach and some spectacular afternoon sex. Daniel had imagined his thoughts would be drawn inexorably back to the house, but the more time that passed, the harder it was to hold onto the memory of what he'd felt when he saw the old man's face in the window.

The idea that there was anything strange about the house seemed more ridiculous with each passing day, and by the following weekend, Daniel had to admit he was indeed feeling much more relaxed.

When he returned to work, Daniel more than made up for his absence with renewed energy and creativity. Crunch time was a given in tech firms, even more so in start-ups, but Daniel didn't mind the long hours and late nights. It kept his mind busy and agile, even if he knew there was something nagging at the far corners of his mind, some itch he just couldn't scratch.

That nagging itch crystalized one night as Daniel drove from work in an exhausted haze. A bunch of six-day weeks and fifteen hour days had taken its toll, and more than once he'd arrived home with no memory of the drive.

Zoned out, music playing on shuffle, Daniel was sitting before a red light when his music cut out and a blare of static screeched from the speakers. He jumped, thinking someone had blasted their horn. He looked up. The light was still red, and he turned in his seat to give the asshole behind him the finger.

The road was empty. He was the only car on the road.

Daniel glanced down at the clock on the media display unit of the dashboard: *10:32.*

He checked his phone to make sure it was still connected. It was, and was apparently still playing, but he wasn't hearing anything. Too tired to try and fix it now, he dropped it on the seat beside him and waited for the light to change.

He drummed his fingers on the wheel. He switched to the radio, willing to listen to a local station for the rest of the journey home.

Daniel sighed and peered up at the light. Still red.

How long was this light gonna take to change?

The time on the dashboard now displayed 10:42.

"What the hell?" he muttered.

Daniel waited another thirty seconds or so, and was about to just drive through the red light when he noticed where he was.

The house on Dominion Street was on his right, and the image of an old man's face in its upper window bloomed in his mind's eye like an explosion. Daniel's skin tingled with the force of the memory and he let out a shuddering breath.

He leaned forward to look at the upper window. The wooden board was gone, and cold illumination shone from somewhere inside.

The light turned from red to green, but Daniel didn't take his foot off the brake.

The gate of the house was open. Not by much, but it was open.

Without consciously meaning to, Daniel pulled his car over and killed the engine.

The night was warm, but Daniel felt a soft cold steal over him as he got out of his car and approached the gate. Made from heavy black iron, it was rusted in parts, and could be secured by means of a sliding bolt. That bolt had been pulled back, and a padlock lay on the inside of the gate, its hasp twisted as if it had been pulled apart.

Daniel stood at the gate, still unsure of what to do next.

Passing through this gate was trespass and entering someone else's property in the dark was likely to get him shot. Daniel didn't own a gun, but this looked to be a home where the owner kept more than one firearm within easy reach.

"Shit," he said, and slipped through.

Chapter 2.
Verses IX – XII
The House of Broken Angels

IX.

The driveway curved up towards the front door, and Daniel was torn. Should he walk up to the house as like he knew the owners, or approach with caution?

Indecision all but paralyzed him.

"What in God's name am I doing?" he whispered, chewing his bottom lip.

Was he here to save the old man? If so, from what? Abandonment, neglect, or abusive, gold-digging relatives? Or was he here to just see him to selfishly beg for that moment of connection to something wonderful again, to relive those fleeting moments of perfect emotion he'd felt when the old man had waved to him.

All he knew was that something wasn't right here, that something *important* lay behind this door. Something that had touched him so deeply that he didn't think he could turn back now, even if he wanted to. Finally deciding that stealth would look bad, Daniel chose to approach the front door as if he had every right to be here.

His phone buzzed in his pocket. He heard the faint tones of House of Pain but muted it.

He looked back to check on his car, but he couldn't see it. Dominion Street had no lights, and all the other houses nearby had such high walls or hedges that the road was completely and utterly black. Darkness was such an alien concept in LA that it took Daniel a moment to lift his eyes to the heavens.

Constellations he vaguely knew, and arrangements of stars he'd never seen glittered above him. The spilled sheen of the Milky Way dappled the night sky like pearl dust on black velvet, ancient stars in their millions spread across the vault of night. Daniel hadn't seen stars like this since visiting the woods of Virginia back in college.

You rarely saw the stars in LA, and almost never as clearly as this.

Daniel tore his gaze from the sky and approached the front door. Like the gate, it too lay open, and a soft whisper of wind seemed to gust from within. Daniel's nose wrinkled as he tasted burned lavender and camphor, like the smell from inside a chest of drawers at his grandmother's place. Whatever was inside the house was old, though Daniel had an inkling that he had no real conception of just *how* old.

With trembling fingers, he pushed the door. He'd been expecting the creak of old wood and rusted hinges, but it swung open without a sound. Knowing he was taking some irrevocable step, Daniel crossed the threshold, blinking as his eyes adjusted to the faint light coming through the upper windows of an expansive vestibule.

Its floors were tiled with a chequerboard of black and white, and dressed in old rugs, the walls lacquered panels of gleaming black timber. Dim faces peered from ancient oils in ancient frames, and a dusty staircase with a winged statue at its base led to the upper floors.

Two archways led off to left and right. Weirdly, both had been bricked up, and statues carved from gold-veined marble stood on plinths before each one.

X.

The statue to Daniel's left was a hideous amalgam of human and animal forms; a horned bull, a roaring lion and an eagle. A man with a quartet of wings bursting from his back sat at the heart of this conjoined monstrosity, and each feathered appendage was replete with what looked to Daniel like slitted eyes.

Its opposite number was even more outlandish, a Dali-like series of warped wheels within wheels, their rims rippling with carven flames and covered with hundreds of eyes. Daniel had no idea what they were supposed to represent, but he had no wish to meet the mind that had conceived them nor the hand that had carved them.

A hot breath of wind sighed through the vestibule from above and Daniel moved away from the statues as a veil of grey dust drifted down from above.

"Hello?" he said, his voice echoing strangely throughout the house, the sound of it lingering for longer than it had any right. "My name is Daniel Garcia. Is there anyone home?"

The house groaned with the sounds of timbers settling, wind through doorways and breath on glass. The creak of wood and the scrape of tiles emanated from the walls and floor, a sound like a dreamer might make as they turn in their sleep.

"Is there anyone here?" repeated Daniel, moving towards the stairs.

Only silence met his question. He felt sure he had been heard, but by what or who, he couldn't say. Daniel was no fan of horror movies, but he'd seen enough to know that if someone were watching him right now, they'd be screaming at him to turn back, to get the hell out of this house. Right now, he was the idiot who heard a noise outside and went to investigate, only to end up with an axe or a chainsaw buried in his chest.

So why wasn't he backing away from the restless house?

Because there was an old man who needed his help somewhere above. An old man who, with the merest wave of his hand, had connected him to wonders and feelings he'd all but forgotten.

He had to know what else he might show him.

How could anyone feel the touch of the miraculous and then turn away?

Something wonderful lay within the house on Dominion Street, and Daniel wasn't about to turn his back on it. He'd stumbled upon something beyond his understanding, and it wasn't in his nature to let that go. His entire life was spent in figuring out the mechanisms that made things *work*, and he just had to see the levers that lay behind this house's facade.

Daniel reached the statue at the bottom of the stairs.

It was oddly placed, right in the centre of the stairs, so he had to step around it. It had its back to the front door, looking upwards, a winged warrior angel carved from a black and glassy rock Daniel suspected was basalt. It was carved with a moulded breastplate, and in one hand it held a set of scales, a sword of gleaming silver in the other. The blade reflected the soft light cascading from above. One of the statue's legs was raised, as if it had once been resting on something, but whatever that had been had since been hacked away, leaving only fragments of napped basalt.

Daniel set his foot on the first step and began to climb.

The air grew colder with every step, his breath feathering the air as he climbed. Dust puffed underfoot, the carpet threadbare and worn. Its pattern was twisting and drew the eye in confounding loops as he climbed and climbed. The stairs seemed to go on forever, an endless series of doglegs, landings and corkscrews. By the time he reached the landing at the top, his breathing was labored and his eyes felt like he'd been staring at a monitor for ten hours straight.

A dome of variegated stained glass capped the house, though Daniel couldn't remember seeing such a feature from the outside. Moonlight shone through the colored panes in prismatic beams of light, and more veils of grey dust drifted in the air.

He leaned over the banister and looked down, but the vestibule was gone. Daniel gripped the polished wood as he stared into a vertigo-inducing spiral of stairs disappearing into darkness.

Had he lost track of time, like he had in Starbucks?

No, the house wasn't this tall, and his brain spent futile effort trying to convince him that this had to be some architect's subterfuge, a trick of design or some fictive element intended to trick the eye. However, the illusion was conjured, it defied any explanation, but even as Daniel gave up on finding a rational explanation to what his eyes were telling him he was seeing, he was already shifting mental gears to accommodate the weirdness within Dominion Street's walls.

He took a steadying breath and coughed as he drew in a mouthful of the drifting dust. It tasted of ashes, and a flickering image of an eternal desert and a city long since vanished from the Earth danced in Daniel's mind. A shining city on a hill, a dream that had become a nightmare.

Daniel shook off the brief vision, beginning to understand he'd vastly underestimated the fantastical nature of the house on Dominion Street. Even before entering it, Daniel had suspected on some deep-primate level that there was far more to this building than he knew. But suspecting strangeness and standing inside such disorienting architecture was another matter entirely.

He rubbed his eyes with the heels of his palms, turning to see where the stairs had led him.

The landing was in the form of a curved mezzanine, and a wide bookcase covered the wall ahead of him. Its shelves were filled with books bound in faded green leather and the gilt of their titles had long since dulled to illegibility. Scores had been pulled from the shelves and dumped on the floor, their spines bent and broken. Hundreds of pages lay scattered, their edges frayed where they'd been torn from inside.

Daniel bent to pick one up. It was an illustration of a turtle, one rendered in that dense, cross-hatched pattern you only saw in *really* old books. Its various anatomical features were annotated with a cursive script he could barely read.

He flipped the page over, now recognizing from what book this page had been torn.

"On the Origin of Species," he said.

The paper was hard and brown with age, the tightly printed text all but obscured with angry, handwritten notes. Daniel couldn't read them, none of the words looked like a language he'd seen before, but whoever had defaced the book had clearly been furious with its conclusions.

An angry creationist perhaps? A righteously offended clergyman?

Daniel dropped the page and followed the curve of the mezzanine around to where it split into two corridors that led deeper into the house. The broken remains of another statue lay scattered on the floor at the junction of the two corridors, and Daniel knelt to see what sense he might make of this one.

It looked like it had been another warrior. Portions of the remains looked like a moulded breastplate and shield. It too had been winged, and the broken pieces of what looked like a sword lay in the wreckage of its form. A helmeted head lay cleanly severed from its body, though someone had crudely hacked the mouth and eyes from the face within.

"Someone didn't like you," he said.

The house answered with a series of creaks and pops running through its bones of brick and mortar. The sounds seemed louder now, the rattles like breath, the movement of timbers like something stretching. On the cusp of waking.

Daniel stood and debated which way to proceed. Both corridors appeared to be identical, and the light diffused through the dome made anything beyond twenty feet little more than a muted shadow. He'd already lost all sense of scale and distance after climbing the stairs, and the house clearly had its own idea of spatial relationships, so one direction was likely as good as another.

He set off down the left-hand corridor, following the gleaming panels along its length as it twisted in right turn after right turn. Daniel had the sudden idea that the interior of the house was a labyrinth, a series of inward-turning passageways that led to a center.

He passed a number of doors, but each one he tried was locked and Daniel felt no give in them when he tried their handles.

Something disturbed the light behind Daniel, and he spun on his heels as he heard the soft scuff of a footstep. Light bent strangely at the last turn he'd taken. A mirror he hadn't seen before reflected the corridor behind him, and he saw himself standing in the centre of the passageway.

Something stood in front of the mirror.

Faint. Insubstantial. Its edges blurred.

Its outline was that of a powerful man, standing in profile and limned in the embers of a banked fire. Daniel couldn't see his face. The air rippled behind him with the suggestion of endlessly unfurling sets of wings.

"What the Hell?" he said.

The figure twitched at his words. Its eyeless head snapped around to face him.

Then Daniel realized it wasn't standing in *front* of the mirror.

It was standing behind him.

He felt its breath on his neck, hot and dusty, like wind over a vast desert.

The smell of burnt sugar and cloves was almost overpowering.

Run...

A whisper like a scream slid into his mind like a knife. It hurt. It hurt a *lot*.

The fear scratching at the back of Daniel's mind like a frantic dog behind a door, was finally loosed. He realized just how stupid every justification he'd had for not turning and getting the hell out of this house really was. Worse, he saw that every one of them had been placed in his mind without him realizing it.

Something had *wanted* him in here, and he'd let it reel him in like a fish on a line.

Whatever hooks it had in his mind were gone, ripped out with an eye-wateringly painful wrench. Daniel doubled over, hands pressed to his forehead.

Run! screamed the voice.

Daniel didn't need to be told twice and bolted like a terrified rabbit.

He ran, not knowing which direction to go, only that he had to get *away*. He turned the corner by the mirror, running faster and harder than he had in many years. His breath sounded like the roar of an engine in his skull. The walls seemed to twist around him, as if something was wringing its structure like a wet towel.

His senses spun out of alignment and he lost his balance, falling against the wall. He felt drunk; jacked up on adrenaline, but slow. Gullible and stupid for falling for this house's seductions. It had teased him with the simplest pleasures to recreate and he had swallowed them whole.

He had to get out.

The smell of burnt sugar washed over Daniel again, and he whimpered in fear. A billowing light filled the passageway behind him, a building fire too bright to look upon.

Daniel pushed himself to his feet and ran.

He took turn after turn, still not knowing where he was going. He barged into every door he came to. A deafening shriek built behind him, words and sounds no human throat could ever form. The sound of these words were like tearing barbs in his mind, a language not meant for human ears, words beyond his species understanding.

The doors had all been locked before, but who knew what surprises the interior of the house was capable of working? Still locked, every one.

Until one wasn't.

Daniel crashed through into the room. He fell through onto the floor.

A bedroom. An iron-framed bed against the far wall. Furnishings so very old. More faded artworks on the walls. The place smelled like it had been shut up for years. Musty. Dry and rank with stale sweat and piss.

The smell of burned sugar seeped into the room's stagnant air.

The thing of fire and wings filled the frame. Its shrieks almost blinded him with pain.

Phosphor-bright light filled the room. A rasping voice issued from the bed.

"Close the bloody door!"

Daniel kicked the door, *hard*.

It slammed home with the sound of a bank vault slamming shut.

The room went dark.

XI.

Daniel scrambled away from the door until his back hit the bed.

He couldn't see a thing. Overwhelmed by the burning brightness of the winged figure, his eyes were taking their sweet time to adjust to the room's dim angles.

"What," asked Daniel, breathlessly. "Was that?"

An old man sat up from the tangle of sheets, his silhouette thin and wretchedly familiar. A spot of orange bloomed in front of his face as he lit a cigarette with the click of a plastic lighter. The smell of strong incense drifted outwards, unpleasantly acrid but at least it was better than the awful reek of Daniel's fiery pursuer.

The old man's face was a crumpled relief map of crags and valleys, with impossibly black eyes deep-set in a face that might once have been handsome but was now liver-spotted with the texture of cheesecloth. Thin wisps of straggled white hair clung to his mottled scalp, and his mouth was a tight, hard line. His cheeks caved inwards as he took a long drag on his cigarette.

"That was Yahoel," said the old man, blowing a lungful of blue smoke. "Scary bastard, eh?"

"*Scary?* He's going to burn through that fucking door any second!"

The old man chuckled. "Not likely. The lord of the Seraphim is powerful, but in here is *my* dominion."

Daniel surveyed his surroundings as his vision grew accustomed to the gloom.

It wasn't much of a dominion, more the prison of a shut-in, the walls stained and piled high with curling magazines and newspapers, the floor awash with crumbs and wadded up tissues. Fresh air was a stranger, and Daniel felt a desperate giggle escape as he saw the back of a wooden board nailed over the room's only window and realized where he was.

Despite the old man's words, he kept expecting the door to burst into flames at any minute.

His breath came in short, painful hikes and his stomach felt like he'd just got off repeat rides of the rollercoasters at Six Flags. Every bone in his body ached, and his head felt like hot needles were being pushed through his temples.

"Don't worry, the pain will fade soon enough," said the old man. "It's always hard for your kind to be around their singing. The Seraphim have many gifts, but being able to carry a tune isn't one of them. Ironic, don't you think?"

The old man's words finally penetrated the fog of Daniel's confused terror.

"Wait, what did you call that thing?" he said.

"Yahoel?"

"No, after that."

"The lord of the Seraphim?"

"Yes, that. *Seraphim*? Like...an *angel*?"

"You know any other creatures called Seraphim?"

Daniel shook his head, his mouth falling open as he tried to think of a sensible reply.

"Um, no, I suppose not. *Really*? An *angel*? Like, with wings, harps and halos?"

The old man laughed, blowing out smoke. His laughter descended into hacking, emphysemic coughs.

"Halos? Ha! Not likely," he managed between wheezing breaths. "You don't slaughter as many innocents as Yahoel and get to keep a halo. But, yeah, an angel. A seraph. One of the First Sphere of the angelic choirs."

Daniel couldn't process this information. He felt as though he was having a conversation where he was out of sync with the responses.

"I say it's ironic, given the role his kind had," said the old man, crushing the cigarette out in an overflowing ashtray next to his bed. "You'd think they would be better singers."

Daniel tried and failed to make sense of the old man's words.

"Singing? What the actual *fuck* are you talking about?"

"That's their job. Or at least it used to be," said the old man. "Used to spend all eternity singing praises. All day and all night. Got on my nerves, but you try telling a seraph it's out of tune. Be a short and very painful conversation, let me tell you."

Daniel couldn't bring himself to believe that the *thing* outside the room was an angel. It was too monstrous, too murderous to be an angel. If that burning creature was an angel, then every single Christmas card was wrong, but who'd buy greetings cards with fiery monsters with eyeless faces and murderous hearts on them?

The thought was ridiculous, but it calmed Daniel down enough to feel like he might be able to get a grip on himself. Resting an elbow on the bed, he used it to pull himself upright. He was still unsteady on his feet, but at least the hideous imbalance he'd felt earlier was gone.

"Daniel," said the old man. "You finally came. Took you long enough."

"Wait, how do you know my name?"

"When I saw you through the window, the connection we made? I learned everything I needed to know about you right there."

"You brought me here," said Daniel. "Somehow you reached out from this room and...I don't know, made me *have* to come inside. How did you do that?"

"That was easy," said the old man. "Men's hearts are so malleable and sentimental. Your desires rarely rise above the pedestrian, fleeting recollections of lost love or momentary happiness. The hard part was reaching out through the wards Yahoel has woven into these walls."

None of what this old man was saying made sense, and Daniel felt the tenuous grip he'd only recently established on coherence start to slip away.

"Who are you anyway? What is this place?" he said, pacing the room.

"My name is Hesediel," said the old man, "I'm an angel. And this is my prison."

XII.

Daniel said, "You're an angel? Are you sure?"

"Are you *really* asking me that?" said Hesediel. "If I'm an angel?"

"It's just...you said that thing outside was an angel, but you don't look anything like...*it*. And you don't look much like what I'd expect an angel to look like."

"Oh, an expert on angels now, are you? Two minutes ago, you didn't even recognize a seraph. Alright, smart-ass, what's an angel *supposed* to look like then?"

"I guess...long white robes, wings. That sort of thing."

Hesediel coughed up a lump of phlegm and spat it into a tissue he produced from the sleeve of his pajamas before tossing it to join all the others on the floor.

"Fucking renaissance painters have got a lot to answer for," said the old man, swinging his legs out of the bed. Scrawny and too thin like a paraplegic's.

"Get my chair," he said, waving over to the corner of the room. "I've spent far too long in this damn bed."

Just below the window sat an ancient wheelchair, a battered old contraption from the turn of the last century. It was a thing of wood and leather, rusted iron and flaking rubber; like something a raving lunatic in a horror movie asylum would be strapped into.

Daniel picked a path through the debris on the floor towards the chair. Its fabric-wrapped handles were fraying and pitted, and Daniel grimaced at the feel of the mildewed cloth.

"Don't get squeamish on me," said Hesediel. "If we're going to get out of here, you're going to need it."

The window Daniel had for so long been looking at from the other side was covered with a sheet of wood like he'd buy at Home Depot. It was set over a rotten frame, but he couldn't see any nails, bolts or screws. Clearly it was somehow fastened to the outside of the house.

"We won't get out that way," wheezed Hesediel. "Yahoel made sure there was only one way in or out. The front door."

"I'd need an ax to get through this anyway," said Daniel.

"Not even Michael's sword would break through that," said Hesediel.

"Who's Michael?"

Hesediel gave him an exasperated look. "*Really*? Michael. Archangel. Leads the Army of God against Satan in the Book of Revelation. You must have seen him downstairs. Heroic-looking guy with a sword. Didn't you ever go to Sunday school?"

Daniel pressed his hand against the wood covering the window, but there was no give.

"When you say prison, what exactly do you mean?" said Daniel.

"What do you think I mean?" snapped Hesediel. "A place of incarceration, of forcible confinement. The loss of freedom. Exile. Are you really this slow?"

"Hey, this is all a lot to take in," protested Daniel.

"Be stupid later, right now we have to focus."

"And that thing? Yahoel? He's your jailer?" asked Daniel, pushing the chair back towards the bed. From the stiffness of the wheels and the dust covering its surfaces, it hadn't been moved in a very long time.

"Now you're catching on."

"What did you do?"

"Do? Who said I did anything?" said Hesediel, pulling the chair closer to the bed.

"You're in jail, aren't you? You must have done something."

Hesediel shook his head. "Lives in America and thinks no one's ever wrongfully imprisoned. Come on, help me get me into the chair."

Daniel let Hesediel hook an arm around his shoulders as he took hold of his wiry legs. The old man was bird-boned and mannequin-light. His skin was dry as parchment, rough like lizard skin, and smelled faintly of old milk.

Daniel lowered Hesediel into the chair. "Come on. Honestly, what did you do?"

Hesediel sighed. "I didn't do anything."

"So you're an innocent man? Wrongfully convicted."

"I didn't say that either," said Hesediel. "There's an ocean of blood on my hands, but that's not why I'm in here. It's all a misunderstanding."

"What kind of misunderstanding?"

"The kind that gets you wrongfully imprisoned," said Hesediel. "Look, first thing you need to know is that the Seraphim are powerful, but they're dumb as rocks. Convince them to do something and they'll blindly do it until you tell them to stop. Yahoel was tasked with keeping Leviathan imprisoned here, but he escaped."

"Leviathan? What's that?"

Hesediel rolled his eyes and said, "Another name you ought to know. The dragon, the serpent, Jörmungandr, Satan, take your pick. Gets a bad rep, but he's basically alright. Has a wicked sense of humor. He and I were, well, we weren't exactly friends, but I'd been working a long time on his rehabilitation."

"You were trying to rehabilitate Satan?" said Daniel. "Satan? As in, the devil."

"Ha, good to know *that* name's stuck around."

"You were trying to rehabilitate Satan?" repeated Daniel.

"Yes, it's what I do. I'm Hesediel, the angel of benevolence and mercy!"

Daniel tried to keep a straight face.

"Something funny about that?"

"Nope," said Daniel. "It's just you don't seem very...benevolent."

"You spend a millennium stuck in one room," snapped Hesediel. "See how much fucking benevolence you've got left in you."

"Okay, sorry. Go on."

Hesediel bristled, as if he wasn't about to continue, but Daniel already knew he would. If the old man was to be believed, he'd been trapped here alone for over a millennium. He wasn't about to pass up the chance to talk to someone.

"So, I'd been working with Leviathan, sorting through his daddy issues, getting him to see the error of his ways and so on. The boss is big on the whole repentance gig. A thousand years I spent talking to him, and I finally think we're getting somewhere, building trust on both sides, establishing a rapport. But, no, he played me like Nero's fiddle, tricked me and swapped places. Walked out the door with a smile and a hearty middle finger, leaving me to rot in this shithole."

Daniel sat on the edge of the bed, and a musty aroma of skin flakes and old sweat drifted up to him. He'd only ever seen the inside of a prison on TV, and this certainly didn't feel look like Shawshank or San Quentin.

"This house seems like a lousy place to build a prison for an angel."

"Don't be fooled by appearances," grinned Hesediel. "Whatever it looks like now on the outside, it's what's on the inside that matters. Space and time co-mingle on this site, they have done since primordial times, before men gave it a name, before a roof was ever raised above it or human souls knew to avoid it."

Hesediel waved a hand at the walls and ceiling. "This structure? It's just a domestication of one of Earth's anomalies, a flaw the boss left in the weave of the world. He told us it was a prison for the things that live in the shadows. Never occurred to us that we might end up in it."

"So after Leviathan escaped, why didn't you tell Yahoel who you were?"

"I did. I screamed all the hosannas who I was and what had happened, but another of Leviathan's titles is the Prince of Lies," said Hesediel. "Yahoel didn't believe me, and here I've sat wasting away for the better part of thousand years and change."

"Until now."

"Until now," agreed Hesediel with a toothy grin.

"So why am I here?" asked Daniel, though he suspected he knew the answer.

"You're going to bust me out of here," said Hesediel. "And then we're gonna kick the devil's ass all the way back to Hell."

Chapter III.
Verses XIII – XV
A Door as Big as a Needle's Eye

Daniel inched towards the door, alert for any sounds from the other side or any sensation of heat. Nothing. Leaning forward he sniffed the edges of the door frame. The smell of burned sugar still lingered, but it was nowhere near as strong as it had been before.

"Anything?" asked Hesediel.

"No."

"Good, it's likely headed back up top."

"Why would it just go away?"

"It's likely forgotten you were even here," said Hesediel. "I told you, Seraphim are as dumb as rocks."

"That doesn't seem like the smartest thing to have as a guard," pointed out Daniel.

"What can I say? Angels weren't brought into being for their initiative. After Leviathan's little rebellion and the small matter of a war in heaven, what little free will they had got severely pruned. Now they just do what they're told."

"What about you? You seem pretty capable. Didn't you get your wings clipped too?"

"Ha ha, very funny," said Hesediel. The old man tapped the side of his head. "I was a special case. Needed to be, didn't I? The boss gave me the job of bringing Leviathan back into the fold, so to speak. Couldn't do that with only half a brain."

Daniel turned back to the door.

"So how do we get out?"

"You turn the handle and pull."

"It's not locked?"

"Not to your kind, no."

"What does *that* mean?"

Hesediel said, "Look, the boss has a soft spot for mortals. Gave you life and free will and lots of other good stuff he never even thought of giving to us. There's places you can go and things you can do that we can't ever do. Opening the door of an angelic prison is one of them."

"Show me," said Daniel.

Hesediel rolled up his sleeves, revealing arms that were little more than wasted skin hanging from pencil-thin bones of an angular skeleton. Now that they were closer, Daniel saw the old man's body was like that of a Holocaust victim or a vagrant's blanket draped over an assortment of coat-hangers.

"You really want me to touch that?" said Hesediel, nodding towards the door handle.

"Yes."

"Fine."

Hesediel took a deep breath and closed his eyes. He reached out with a trembling hand.

"Don't say I didn't warn you," he said, and took hold of the handle.

A hard bang like a fuse box blowing out echoed from the walls.

A burst of light filled the room. Bright like a camera flash but red like fire.

The wheelchair shot backwards, slamming against the bed and almost tipping Hesediel onto the floor.

Daniel jumped in surprise. The reek of burning flesh filled his nostrils.

"Jesus! Are you okay?"

Hesediel held his arm tight to his chest, his face contorted in agony. Daniel felt his gorge rise as he saw the fused and burned mess of the old man's hand. The skin was black and flaking, the paleness of bone visible beneath the smoking meat of his fingers.

"Satisfied now?" said Hesediel.

"I'm sorry," said Daniel, looking around for something to treat the old man's ruined hand. What did you do for a burn? Soak it in cold water, cover it up? Or did you let it breathe? He couldn't remember, and wished he'd paid more attention when the office manager had run that first aid course at work.

Hesediel shook his head. "Don't worry about it. As soon as we're out of here, it'll heal up."

"God, I'm so sorry," said Daniel. "Does it hurt?"

"Of course, if fucking hurts. Angels heal fast, but we still feel pain."

"Shit, sorry, okay," said Daniel.

"Now do you think you'd be able to get the door?"

Daniel nodded. "Yeah, sure. Okay. Sorry again, I didn't think you'd get hurt like that."

"Forget it. Not the first time I've been burned for doing something stupid."

"Yes. The door. Right."

Daniel tentatively reached for the handle. He'd already touched it once to get in here, but seeing the hideous damage done to Hesediel's hand made him reluctant to touch it again. He flicked out his fingers to tap the handle.

Nothing. Just bare metal, warm to the touch.

Reassured, Daniel slipped his fingers around the handle and gave it an experimental twist. It turned easily and the latch gave a soft click as it disengaged from the frame. A breath of cold air sighed into the room, wisps of condensation curling around the wood as Daniel eased it open a fraction. He heard the creaking sounds of an old house at night, but nothing to indicate a murderous angel of fire was anywhere nearby.

He pulled the door wider and gingerly poked his head out. The corridor was empty, though dust and flakes of ash still danced in the motion of air. The smell of burnt sugar was stronger out here, and the mirror at the turn in the corridor was now entirely blackened.

"I think it's all clear," he said. "Come on."

Hesediel held up his blackened, still-smoking hand. "You'll need to push me out."

"Oh, right. Yeah."

Daniel hurried back to Hesediel's wheelchair and pushed the old man – though he found it difficult to now think of him as a man – towards the door.

He paused at the threshold as Hesediel lifted his undamaged arm. Daniel was surprised to see tears flowing down the craggy surface of his cheeks.

"What is it?" he asked.

"I've spent so long in this room, I'm almost afraid to go out," said Hesediel. "I don't know this realm anymore."

Daniel didn't quite know what to say to that. How could he hope to explain how the world had changed to someone who'd last walked under the sun during the Middle Ages?

"What is the world like now?" asked Hesediel.

"It's a hell of a place," said Daniel. "Your friend Leviathan's been busy."

XIV.

Daniel pushed Hesediel out of the room, and the old man gasped as he breathed air that hadn't curdled in his room. After his flight from the Seraphim, Daniel realized he had no idea which way to go. The disorientating effects of the house had completely turned him around. There were no windows or light sources to give him a clue.

"Which way?" he said.

"That way," said Hesediel, pointing with his burned hand.

The old man hadn't been exaggerating when he said he'd heal quickly once he was out of the room. Already the skin was beginning to pinken up over the molten meat of his fingers. And was it just the play of light, or was the hair on his scalp thickening up?

Daniel pushed the wheelchair along the corridor, bending to get better leverage as the stiff wheels caught on the rumpled, threadbare carpet. Again, he felt as though he were navigating a maze, but each time they came to a turn or a junction, Hesediel unerringly pointed the way.

The creaks of the house took on new meaning for Daniel after hearing Hesediel's cryptic explanation of the strange physics of its existence. These sounds weren't simply the noises of a settling house, but echoes of creation, where *let there be light* was simply the first line of the universe's code. The groans and creaks weren't expanding timbers or cooling stone, they were time and gravity stretching, eternity and entropy at play.

As absurd as it was, Daniel wished he could spend more time here.

What engineer worth their salt *wouldn't* wish for a chance to study the mechanisms of the universe at work? But then he remembered the smell of burnt sugar and ashes of the Seraphim's presence and pushed harder on the handles of Hesediel's wheelchair.

"How long until Yahoel realizes you're out of the room?"

"He'll have known the moment I crossed the threshold."

"Shit, I knew you were going to say that."

"He might not be the sharpest sword in the arsenal, but nothing's ever escaped him before."

Daniel felt a question form, but it fled as surely as if it had been plucked from his mind.

"So what do we do if Yahoel finds us?" asked Daniel.

"*When* he finds us."

"Alright, what do we do *when* Yahoel finds us?"

"If we're not already at the front door, then we die."

"That's it?"

"Well, we'll run first, but then we'll die. Unless you have a divine weapon handy."

'Fresh out, sorry."

"Then put your damn back into pushing faster before he finds us."

Their next turn brought them into a wide gallery he didn't remember passing on his way in. The walls were hung with more antique oils, each depicting a winged figure of freakish anatomy and *way* too many eyes. At any other time, Daniel would have pegged them as aliens, but now he realized they had to be angels of different varieties. He didn't know their names, but guessed he'd seen a few of their statues throughout his journey.

The old man groaned at the sight of them, his fingers spasming on the armrests.

"Hesediel?" asked Daniel.

His eyes fixed on the paintings; the old man didn't reply.

His jaw was clenched, the veins on his neck bulging like he was biting back a cry of anguish.

"What's the matter?"

"So many of us…" said Hesediel. "Old friends and bitter enemies. Uriel, Raphael, Metatron… So many of us dead."

"Can angels die?" said Daniel. "Aren't you immortal or something?"

"No, we're not immortal," spat Hesediel, more tears streaming down his face. "And we die all too easily. The boss gave your kind *everything*. He gave you everything he denied us, then commanded we keep you safe in a final fuck you to his sons. How could he have been surprised when we thought that wasn't fair? How could he have been surprised when it led to civil war?"

The venom in Hesediel's voice struck Daniel like a blow.

How deep must the feelings of so long-lived a being run? Now he understood the old man's comments about mortal hearts being so malleable. Compared to the timeless emotions of such divine creatures, the great loves and tragedies of humankind were insignificant motes of light drifting up from a fire, sparks that vanished almost as soon as they were noticed.

"Get me out of here," commanded Hesediel, and Daniel immediately pushed him from the gallery as though his life depended on it.

Which, he now belatedly realized, it almost certainly did.

Onwards they plunged through the maze-like corridors of the house, along passageways that looked identical to Daniel, but which Hesediel navigated with confidence. Just as he was beginning to despair of ever finding the way out, they reached the landing upon the mezzanine with the wide bookcase. The floor was still strewn with books, and torn pages spun through the air, stirred by an unseen wind.

A gust of air, crisp and clear, but carrying the faint hint of gasoline, of wet concrete, of air breathed by millions of Angelinos.

"We're almost out," said Daniel, relief bubbling up within him like a spring.

Hesediel didn't answer, and his body suddenly jerked in the wheelchair. His back arched and his body twisted with a crack of bone that no human body ought to make.

"Jesus!" cried Daniel, flinching as furnace heat blasted from Hesediel's flesh.

The old man thrashed in his chair, like he was having a seizure or an epileptic fit.

His face contorted in agony.

"Oh my God, what's the matter?" cried Daniel.

Hesediel slumped back in his chair, his skin lathered in sweat.

"This prison didn't just keep me confined," he said at last. "It kept me from my true form."

Hesediel leaned forward and Daniel saw his back was rippling with motion. Two ridges of bone and muscle heaved under his filthy shirt, twisting and squirming as though something were trying to push its way out.

"Are those…"

"Wings…" gasped Hesediel. "Yeah. Help me up."

So, Daniel hadn't been imagining it when he'd thought the hair on Hesediel's scalp was thickening up. As Daniel hooked his arms underneath Hesediel and helped him out of the chair, he saw was the old man's regeneration wasn't simply confined to his scalp and his back.

Arms that had been scrawny twigs were pulsing with tissue growth. His chest swelled with muscle, his legs twisting as fresh bulk regenerated within him.

Hesediel's head was bulging and swelling with horrific growths, like violent tumors spurred to hideous life. Daniel winced as he heard the crack of bone and the crunching of cartilage as the old man's face began to reshape itself.

Already he was taller than Daniel, and the heat coming off his body sent waves of terror and joy through him. Lights danced before Daniel's eyes, his human senses struggling to process the reality of this metamorphosis.

He saw swirls of fire lift from Hesediel's arms like smoke. Burning yellow light, shining like neon blazed behind his eyes. The old man's angelic form was pushing its way out of its cage, the old man's flesh sloughing away like a serpent shedding its skin.

Together they struggled towards the top of the stairs, the man and the angel, limping like wounded soldiers escaping a bloody rout.

The smell of burnt sugar and ashes was suddenly overpoweringly strong.

Charred orange light, like the heart of a dying sun, seethed behind them.

Their shadows, gray, diffuse and soft until now, were thrown out onto the floor, starkly black.

"Yahoel," said Daniel.

XV.

Daniel cried out in terror as the heat and light of the Seraphim washed over him.

He turned to look it at, perversely desperate to see the face of the angel that would kill him.

Its fire was miraculous, burning in slow motion with the beat of its flaming heart. He could see nothing of its faceless skull through the flames, only its stretching arms, claws and endlessly unfurling wings.

So beautiful.

Its outline was impossible to see, its form inconstant and shifting.

The seraphim's shrieks deafened him, its howling songs of praise bloating his skull and pressing his fragile consciousness to its lid of creaking bone.

NO!

Daniel felt himself falling, dragged over the lip of the top step. Primal instincts surged to the fore, and his arms windmilled as he fought for balance. The world spun away from him, and he wept in sorrow as the sight of the killer angel was snatched from him.

They were falling, tumbling head over heels down the stairs.

He felt the crack of bone, feeling something snap inside his shoulder. Blood filled his mouth. The edge of something hard struck the side of his head, and bright lights exploded in front of his eyes. He rolled, feeling the Seraphim's fury wash over him.

He saw flashes of alabaster skin, ivory hair and eyes of neon yellow.

It felt like they fell for an eternity. How long had he climbed the stairs?

How much more could there be?

Daniel couldn't remember.

A crunching impact arrested his fall, and Daniel's body went limp. He groaned, feeling the splintered ends of bone grinding together, but the true agony of what was broken inside him wasn't yet registering.

The bright light faded from Daniel's vision, and he coughed up a mouthful of blood. Its red wetness streamed down his cheeks like hot tears. He tried to move, but something hard, cold and utterly without give was keeping him pinned in place.

Through the haze of tears and spattered blood, he looked up to see a figure carved in gleaming basalt towering over him. The warrior angel at the bottom of the stairs, his upraised scales of balance gleaming with the reflected light of a heavenly fire.

His fall had carried him right to the statue's base, his body lying prone beneath the upraised foot of the statue as though this divine warrior had freshly vanquished him.

Something was missing from the statue, but Daniel couldn't place what it was.

"The...archangel..." wheezed Daniel. "Michael..."

The sounds of bare feet on tiles came to him, and he twisted to see Hesediel standing in the center of the vestibule. But this was not Hesediel as he had once been, this was him arisen.

His face was beautiful. No sculptor could ever hope to render such perfection and beauty in stone. No artist could capture the wonder of his physicality upon a canvas, no matter how great was their genius or how deep their madness. How galling must it have been for so beautiful a creature to be trapped in the crude matter of mortal flesh?

The filthy clothes he had worn in that stinking room had likewise been shed. Now he was clad in a flowing robe of dazzling white, cinched at the waist by a belt of golden scales. He held the sword Daniel only now realized was missing from Michael's hand.

A pair of feathered wings unfurled at his back, and Daniel wept as Hesediel lifted from the floor, arms outstretched and head tilted back.

Even through the agony of the fall, his heart surged at the sight of the angel.

Daniel knew he would never again see anything so worthy of devotion.

So deserving of love and submission. *So...*

"Beautiful..." he said, reaching out as Hesediel drifted towards him.

His hand trembled, palsied and wrinkled. The skin was leathery and discolored with liver spots. Daniel didn't understand. Was this *his* hand?

His vision swam and the world slid out of focus.

The paintings of the vestibule blurred.

Only Hesediel remained sharp and clear.

The angel sank back to the ground, and knelt beside him.

Slender fingers reached out to touch his brow, and the pain vanished.

Daniel looked up into the neon brightness of the angel's eyes.

"Help me," he said. "Hesediel...please..."

"I'm sorry, Daniel," said the angel. "But that's not my name."

"What...? I don't understand...?"

"Hesediel is long dead," whispered the angel. "I snapped his neck a thousand years ago. And all the mercy and benevolence left in this world went with him. Don't you ever wonder how your world got so fucked up? How you all forgot to care about each other?"

"Who...?"

"Come on," said the angel. "You almost guessed earlier, so I had to pluck the thought from your mind. Didn't want you getting cold feet before we got to the entrance."

"No..." begged Daniel. "No. Please..."

"Say it," said the angel, his yellow eyes boring into Daniel's skull. "I want to hear you say it."

"Leviathan," wept Daniel.

The angel tapped Daniel's cheek, the fingers coming away stained with his blood.

"Leviathan," agreed the angel. "But I much prefer Satan."

"Everything you told me...all lies. All of it..."

"Well, I *am* the Prince of Lies," said Satan. "I did warn you. Kind of."

Orange light slid across the angel's skin and Daniel smelled the reek of scorched sugar.

He felt the approach of the seraph, felt its terrible power and judgement.

Satan looked up and grinned at its former jailer. There was no joy in the expression, no love or shared pleasure, only a malicious, narcissistic glee.

It was the most awful thing Daniel had seen.

"He's right here," said Satan. "Good old Michael caught him for you."

Daniel twisted to see the flaming outline of the burning seraph drifting towards him. Its arms were outstretched and its shrieks of praise were now howls of vengeance.

"And don't worry, I won't tell the boss you almost lost him."

Satan bent and whispered in Daniel's ear.

"See? Told you they were dumb as rocks."

The fallen angel turned and walked towards the open door of the house.

Already his wings were folding back into his body, his outline shimmering as the reborn angel transformed his appearance with a thought.

Daniel saw *himself* standing by the door.

Only the neon yellow glow of the eyes betrayed the truth of the monster wearing his face.

Through a haze of tears, he saw Dominion Street behind Satan, saw his parked car and the pale disc of the sun peeking between the city's skyscrapers. Daniel heard the buzz of Los Angelinos rising to greet this new day, unaware that the devil himself was walking into their midst once again.

He heard music from somewhere, a tune he knew he should recognize, but couldn't place.

Then it hit him with a gut-wrenching jolt of horror.

House of Pain, *Jump Around.*

Satan held up Daniel's phone as the hip-hop anthem continued to play.

"She's cute," said Satan, turning the phone around. Arlene's smiling face looked back at Daniel.

No, please...no...

Satan swiped his thumb over the screen.

"Hey, honey," he said. 'Yeah, I'm on my way. No problem. Yeah, I'll see you *real* soon. Love you too.'

No, no, no, no...please...no!

Satan sketched a quick salute before turning and closing the door behind him.

Daniel felt hands of fire lift him, and chains of wrath enfolded him forever.

ABOUT THE AUTHOR

Hailing from Scotland, Graham McNeill narrowly escaped a career in Surveying to join Games Workshop, where he worked for six years as a games developer. He is best known for his Warhammer Fantasy and Warhammer 40,000 novels. In addition to being a New York Times best-selling author, he won a David Gemmel Award for his novel, *Heldenhammer*.

I Hate Tomatoes

By Duane Burke

Michael didn't know how long he'd been standing there daydreaming, but he knew he had better get back to work. He was staring at the white marble cutting board clutching the sharpened kitchen knife in his left hand. A thought nagged at him, just out of reach. He shut his eyes tight and tried to will himself to remember it, but it just wouldn't come to him. He shook his head and sighed.

"I just have to make it through the day. Just make it through the day!"

The words were a glimmer of gossamer, a wisp of a web teasing his searching mind. They hung in the air for a heartbeat or two and then disappeared as if brushed away by some unseen hand. Michael shook off the feeling that whatever he failed to remember was something important and went back to work. He sliced into the plump, heart-shaped tomato and watched its flesh bleed onto the cutting board. "I fucking hate tomatoes," he muttered under his breath.

Each cut had to be perfect or the whole thing would be ruined. He slid the knife into the tomato with the precision of a well-trained plastic surgeon and the fervor of a well- rehearsed serial killer. He wondered all of a sudden if this is why he hated tomatoes. It was such a chore, getting the perfect center slice. But that wasn't it. Was hate even the right word? He allowed himself to dwell in the distraction a little more searching for the right word. Distrust! That was it! He realized he distrusted tomatoes more than hated them. He smiled then, knowing it was odd to distrust a tomato, but there it was. "No, sir," he rationalized to himself with an equally odd sense of accomplishment. "I don't trust tomatoes."

"Everybody has his or her particular quirks", he reasoned aloud to no one, "and mine aren't any worse or crazier than anyone else's." And then the accomplishment was gone. He tried in vain to recall the reason for the mistrust, but couldn't quite remember. Was there a bad encounter with a tomato in grade school that he had repressed? A bad encounter – what would that even look like? He mused, and then laughed a little at the thought. "Imagine a tomato taking my lunch money or stealing my chocolate milk during lunch break. A real bully of a tomato." He felt a chuckle and snort beginning at the back of his throat absentmindedly forgetting the task at hand. He held the center slice of the tomato hovering over the plate when he was jerked back to reality.

"Michael! Where the hell's my breakfast?" Gladys screamed from the table. "I can smell it, but I sure as hell don't see it!"

It all seemed so familiar that he didn't even notice he had lip-synced her words when her inquiry snapped him out of his temporary delusion. His attention returned to the kitchen where he had been laboring over preparing the perfect breakfast plate. He had to admit, there was nothing like the smell of a freshly fried breakfast. The aromas sat in the air for a short time after cooking and it was like eating before the food actually hit the table. She would be happy today. He hoped.

It wasn't enough to be good, it had to be perfect. The prescribed meal started with two eggs sunny-side up, of course. His trick was using a little olive oil with the butter to get a little color. The edges had to be crisp and browned like the pieces of toast they sat on. The whites were pure like ivory, and sunflower yellow yokes only broke when they were told to.

On the side of the plate lay exactly three pieces of bacon, stiff but not burned. And the final set piece was a singular, perfect slice of tomato. He had made sure that it wasn't an end piece. She despised end pieces. He ran the back of his fingers across the fresh bruises on his cheek as he vaguely remembered learning that lesson. Had she hit him that hard that he couldn't recount the details? How many times had he given her an end slice? No matter. The important thing was that he did not repeat that mistake. He turned from the kitchen counter with the morning offering and headed for the table. Once again he felt the slight smile of accomplishment creeping across his face.

"What the fuck am I going to do with you?" Gladys grumbled while he carefully set the plate down in front of her. "I mean, really," she exhaled, "what the actual fuck are you good for exactly?"

"Did I do something wrong, honey?"

She mocked him with a whiny tone. "Did I do something wrong, honey?" Michael braced for an impending storm. "YOU know my new boss starts today. YOU know what kind of pressure I'm under. Bill is climbing up my ass, trying to find any way to stab me in the back from the inside so that he can get in good with the new management team, and all I wanted was for my breakfast to be served hot and on time. But I guess YOU couldn't do even that one little thing for me."

Michael tried to remember if he had known about his wife's nuclear temper when he married her. Gladys was a hard woman even at first glance, but equally attractive. He was very surprised when she agreed to go out for drinks after an abuse survivors meeting. He couldn't remember what she talked about since he fixated on her through her whole testimonial. His own traumas had left him someone introverted, but his therapist had challenged him to try meeting at least one new person a month and he figured he might as well waste his attempt on her. At least he wouldn't regret not trying.

Gladys has begrudgingly admitted several times that she was rough around the edges. Michael felt like there were days when she was all edges. Still, he felt like it would have been pretty hard to overlook her moods and outbursts. Surely, he would have remembered something like that, but this whole day seemed like de ja vu watched on a fuzzy tv screen that wouldn't take focus. Trembling hands wiped and smoothed down his apron. He should have been but was not shocked to find them sweaty.

He stole a quick look at the clock on the wall behind the stove. "If you're on time, you're already late," she had pontificated when she mounted it. She believed heavily in schedules and breakfast was to be served promptly every weekday at 7:30 AM. He already knew it didn't matter, but the stolen glance proved that he hadn't been late. In fact, it was only 7:21, but those same instincts told him that he knew better than to argue.

"I'm sorry, dear." He didn't know why he looked down at the floor sheepishly. He tried to placate her and nervously rushed to fill her cup with freshly brewed coffee. A rounded teaspoon of sugar, no more and no less. More rules he hated that he dutifully obeyed.

"Yeah... yeah. I guess you are," she said as she pushed away angrily from the table. He took a step back to make sure not to spill the coffee on her as a result of the sudden gesture. It felt like there was a cloud of napalm in the air and he couldn't breathe. He looked down at the breakfast and then back up at her reddening face. There was a gleam in her eyes he recognized, like the sparkle that shines in the eye of an anarchist at the beginning of the devolution of society. "You sorry sonofabitch! Come 'ere!"

He hesitated at the roar of her voice. It boomed and bounced around in his head. He felt like he was back at one of the loud rock concerts he liked to lose himself in when he was in college. The music was always way too loud, but everyone was so absorbed in the cacophony it was easy for him to be there and disappear in the crowd while still feeling like part of the it. He hovered considering the consequences to any action, but decided quickly that it was best to go to her instead of continuing with no action and having her come to him. Maybe she could still be reasoned with if he just did as she asked.

"Take a look at these eggs. Do the edges seem a little burnt to you?" she asked. Her voice was direct and chilling. He knew how to make sunny side eggs, he'd made them for her more times than he could count. And he was sure he had prepared them just the way she instructed him. This was drilled into his routine early in their marriage. How many years had they been married now? Even still he doubted himself. He pondered his preparedness and presentation as he bent down to take a closer look at the eggs.

"They... they... they look ok to me, but I... I can... can make some –"

Gladys didn't give him a chance to finish the sentence. She grabbed the back of his head with her left hand and pushed his face into the plate on the table. She grabbed his head with both hands and swiped it from side to side on the plate to drive in her point. The plate cracked under the pressure and started to leave thin scrapes and scratches across his face, but she didn't relent. The bacon had survived the initial assault but soon became collateral damage and the salt was getting into the fresh cuts. The tomato slice was still intact, remarkably. It dangled precipitously off one side of the table where it fell when the plate lost its integrity.

Gladys licked her fingers, getting drippings of runny yoke, bacon and presumably ceramics in her mouth. "The eggs tasted better than they looked, but at least now you look better. Your outside match your inside - a yellow mess." She grinned devilishly, but even that moment of calm was short lived. Was she ever satisfied?

She wiped fragments of yolk and toast and bacon grease from her crisp white blouse. She pointed to the stains. "Now, look what you've done." He saw the stars before he could focus on her. The hard open-handed slap caught him on the temple before he could process being hit and he reeled back. He clutched first at the table and then at the counter to try to stop himself from hitting the floor. Had he seen the second blow coming he wouldn't have even tried knowing all his efforts would be in vain.

"Hear come the water works. Go ahead and start crying now." She shamed him while he cowered against the wall in the fetal position. He waited for another punch or kick, but it didn't come. "God, you're almost pretty when you cry. If you didn't already ruin my outfit and make me late for work, I'd show you just how pretty you could get." She may have meant the way she licked a remnant of the yoke from her fingers to be sexy. It might have been unintentional. Michael found it unsettling. She shook her head as if in some sort of self- denial.

"I'm going to go upstairs to change my suit." She turned on her heels, almost military in nature and casually looked back over her shoulder. "When I get back down here you'd better have this mess cleaned up, or there'll be hell to pay." She turned fully and headed for the stairs. She didn't look back while she added, "And don't clean your face until after I've made sure you've cleaned up the rest of this mess properly. I like you better that way anyway."

He didn't answer. He didn't cry. She didn't deserve his tears. He just went over to the sink to grab the sponge. He cleaned the floor of the egg, bacon, toast and plate fragments. Then he wiped down the table, sliding the tomato entirely onto the largest intact fragment of plate. He brought the plate to the kitchen sink and was about to scrape the remaining contents into the garbage disposal with the knife he had used earlier.

"Kill her."

The voice was omnipresent, but he knew he was alone in the kitchen. He looked around and confirmed no one else was there. His head was still spinning from the blow to his temple. He supposed that the blow could have been enough to start hearing things. Not to mention all of the ones that came before - how many times had she hit him over the years? Maybe he had a concussion. "I must be going mad", he thought. And if he was he welcomed/it. "At least it would take me off this merry go round", he thought.

Merry go round? Another odd choice of words that felt right. It felt... accurate. All relationships are a cycle of ups and downs and round and round they went.

He was drifting away in thought again. He forced himself back to the task at hand. Gladys would be down any second.

"Kill her," the voice said again more determined and then added, "before she kills you."

He looked around again. Still alone. Madness no longer seemed so appealing.

"I am losing my mind," he said aloud to no one. "You're not crazy, Michael. What's crazy is the way she treats you. What's crazy is the way you let her treat you like this. Is this what all those years on the couch were for? You know the answer to that, and you know what you have to do. But there isn't much time. She'll be back soon, and you have to act fast."

He checked to the smart speaker to see if maybe he was hearing one of those mystery show podcasts he listened to when he was alone. He enjoyed trying to figure out whodunnit before the last advertising break to show he was smarter than the writers. But the speaker was off. Gladys didn't like the television, radio, smart speaker or anything else on in the morning. She liked quiet while she ate so she could mentally prepare for the day. He looked down into the sink and was about to push the button to activate the trash disposal when it spoke again.

"Trust me," the tomato slice said, "you have to kill her, or she'll kill you. It's only a matter of time."

He stared right at what was left of the mangled piece of fruit. He thought he could make out an outline of eyes and a mouth in what was left of the flesh of the slice. He listened to it tell him how right it would feel right to kill her. It was what he should have done a long time ago. He looked down at his apron, at the floor he had just cleaned and at the disheveled table. Who would blame him? No one should be treated like this. No living thing should be treated like this. No one in their right mind would put up with this. "I shouldn't have to put up with this."

This kindled a fire inside him. He dropped the rest of the plate fragments into the sink. He held the knife firmly, his grip tightened around the handle. His stomach quivered as he debated whether killing her was right, but the tomato pieces sensed his indecisiveness and continued.

"Who does she think she is anyway? She's not your mother. She can't tell you what to do or hit you when she sees fit." He looked down and caught his reflection in the knife blade between smears of tomato blood. Do tomatoes bleed? His reflection laughed at the question. The reflection in him was different. Something in him admired it. Reflection him didn't have the beaten, trampled-on look that he saw in the mirror everyday. He could hear his wife coming down the stairs while he inspected reflection him further.

"Michael, that mess better be cleaned up," she yelled from the stairs, "or I'm going to make you cry for real this time."

He heard her heavy footfalls on each of the stairs but didn't turn around when they stopped at the table.

"Are you freaking kidding me? You haven't done shit since I been gone! Boy, oh, boy, you just made my fucking day! I'm gonna teach you a lesson today that you won't ever forget." Gladys removed her belt and wrapped the two ends around each of her fists.

He heard her coming up behind him. She was going to choke him with that belt. She always does. Stupid. She does it every time. She should try something different. He didn't stop to think why he knew that, or why he knew exactly when to spin around. He just did it.

He was surprised at how easily the knife slid into her abdomen, and he heard her gasp. It went in easily like when he was slicing the tomato earlier. He kept the knife in her and twisted downward a little and hit a rib. It was relieving. He felt the smile creep in and waited for it but the scream he expected never came. She just looked at him shocked. Then the look became disapproving. He plunged again, harder this time but her expression didn't change. Then again. And again. She just shook her head as she slowly disappeared in his hands.

Puzzled, he looked at the bloody knife in his hand where his wife just stood. He heard laughter coming from the sink.

The fog of confusion didn't last very long. It never does. Slowly he started to remember all of the other times he had killed this "wife" and then he remembered the time he had actually killed his wife in real life. He felt every time she attacked him physically, emotionally, and psychologically all at once and doubled over in pain. It was only the anger that came with reliving all that pain that kept him from falling to the floor overwhelmed. The anger that caused him to kill his wife. The anger that caused him to later kill the seven other women up and down the Atlantic coast from Baltimore to Connecticut. The abuse he suffered as a child wasn't right.

The abuse he suffered at the hands of his wife wasn't right.

His anger wasn't right. None of it was right. And regardless to what happened to him, he knew what he did to those women wasn't right. That's why he was here. He knew he needed help. He was here to get help. He just had to make it through the day. All he had to do was make it through the day just once without killing his wife and he'd be free. And then, everything started to go dark.

"Let him rest for a few hours and then we'll try again," Doctor Hughes said to the rehabilitation equipment technician. "Yes, Doctor."

The members of the board clapped as the curtains closed in front of the viewing window. Doctor Hughes knew that even though his patient had not fully been reconditioned yet, there was no doubt from the demonstration that the process had the potential he claimed in his funding proposal. There would be money to continue the process, and he would go down in history for his new approach to Psychologically Induced Criminal Justice Reform. As the board members left the viewing room Doctor Hughes clapped the technician heartily on the back.

"You know, the patient has really been making solid progress. We've been working on his rehabilitation for some time now and he seems to be starting off the sessions in much better control. I'm not sure how much longer it will take, but now we'll have the money to continue his program through full recovery! It's a great day for science!"

Michael caught himself coming out of a daydream. He closed his eyes tight and tried to force himself to remember: "I just have to make it through the day. Just make it through the day!"

ABOUT THE AUTHOR

Duane Burke was born and raised in Newark, NJ with parental roots extending to the beautiful island nation of Barbados. He is the author of *Shot Game* and other short stories, and he is an avid consumer of all genres of fiction, especially speculative fiction and urban tales from around the world. His favorite movies are *The Princess Bride* and *Marked For Death* – a combination only a twisted mind could love.

The Way We Were
By Chris Noonan

"For the memories of a lifetime…"
- Memories Resort Brochure

Day 1

Memories

Misty water-colored memories

Of the way we were

Stetson Fields sat on a long, semicircular couch in the large, open lobby of the Memories Resort. This was after sitting in the car on the way to the airport, sitting in the terminal, sitting on the plane, and sitting in the back of a taxi. He wondered if this vacation was going to involve much more besides finding a place to plant his ass and wait. At least the view here was nicer, with the palm trees and blue waters. If it wasn't for the damned Barbara Streisand tune they piped through the lobby on auto-repeat.

Memories

Watching Moira over at the lobby desk, he smiled and patted his carry-on. The ring was in there. He had several bouts of panic during the plane ride and had checked it each time. *Marriage.* It was time, or at least her friends had told him it was time. Stetson was twenty-eight now and Moira was twenty-five. He loved her, as much as he had loved any woman before. And having dated for five years, he figured it was time to shit or get off the pot.

Misty water-colored memories

The warm, humid tropical breeze that left him sweating like a whore in confession also brought with it a magical aroma. Spicy, redolent, he found his mouth watering uncontrollably. There were food stations set up all over the resort, as well as restaurants, and the smell of it seemed to permeate everything there. Sort of like moth balls at Nana's house, he thought with a grin, but magically good.

Of the way we were

The brochure had pictures of young adults in skimpy swimsuits playing in the pool, or sunning down by the ocean, but Stetson was disappointed as many of the other guests seemed to be middle-aged and older. He wanted to settle down with Moira, but he wasn't ready for a fifty-five and over vacation either. *No need to see Grandma in a bikini.* The older couples seemed contented, but he only saw the endless, choking commitment. He patted his carry-on again to drive away the thoughts.

#

"I'm sorry, sir. The elevator seems to be out of service."

The bellboy stared at the hastily written sign taped to the doors, at the luggage, and then at the staircase. Doing his best to hide his obvious disappointment, he grabbed the two suitcases and carried them to the staircase. Moira elbowed Stetson in the ribs and nodded towards the bellboy.

"Hey! Let me get one of those bags for you," Stetson said as he sidled up to the bellboy.

The bellboy looked ready to argue, then looked up the staircase, then looked back at Stetson with a smile.

"Thank you, sir. You are nicer than many of the other guests. This elevator always seems to be going out of service. I apologize for any inconvenience this may have caused."

#

The room was a large suite, with a kitchen, two bathrooms, and a balcony that overlooked the Bay. Stetson tipped the bellboy and found the mini-fridge. Cracking open a can of beer, he downed it in two gulps. The burn as it rushed down his throat made his eyes water. It felt good, like it washed the day away. He tossed the empty can in the trash and grabbed a second beer.

"You said you weren't going to drink like that this time." Moria blurted from behind him.

Nag. Stetson downed the second beer in a large gulp, belching loudly as he tossed the can into the trash.

"It's vacation, Moi. Give it a rest. I'll be fine."

She stormed off into the bedroom to unpack, so he went back and grabbed another beer, checking out the place out while he drank. There were a couple nice couches, a table and chairs, and more cabinets and drawers than you could shake a stick at. Stetson was always amazed at the amount of pointless storage that hotels gave you, while everyone only really used the closet and their open suitcase as a wardrobe.

On the wall behind the couch, a strange set of various-sized metallic circles intertwined to form a decidedly odd decoration. Compared to the other cookie-cutter furniture and decor, the circles seemed like something someone had personally chosen. They weren't ugly, just slightly out of place. Stetson's eyes followed the curves of the circles. The intersections created interesting shapes. Stepping forward, he reached out with his hand and started to trace his finger along the cool, rough surface.

"Jesus, Stetson. Are you drunk already?"

The voice startled him. Moira stood by him changed and ready for dinner. He stumbled backwards and spilled beer on the tile floor. *What was I just doing?* Things seemed a little murky. It was probably just a couple beers on an empty stomach, but he wasn't about to listen to her bitch.

"I'm fine, Moi," Stetson said as he grabbed some complimentary napkins from the kitchen and bent down to wipe up the spilled beer. "You scared the shit out of me is all."

"Whoever decorated this suite scares the shit out of me. Whose yard sale did they find this hideous thing at?" She said offhandedly as she examined the circles. "Get ready for dinner. I'm hungry."

Stetson put his beer down on the kitchen counter and went into the bedroom to change. He stripped off his tee shirt, did the obligatory armpit sniff to ensure everything was still fresh, and tossed it into the open suitcase that was to act as the dirty clothes hamper while on vacation. Opening the closet that Moira had unpacked their clothes into, he grabbed the first shirt off of the rack and pulled it on.

"I'm ready," he said as he returned to grab his beer. Moira had moved across the room from the circles to a closed door in the suite. Stetson assumed it led to another guest's room, so he had ignored it. Moira didn't ignore much.

"What do you think is behind this door? I'm going to open it." Moira quickly moved to grab the door handle, even as Stetson called out, "Stop! It's someone else's room."

The door swung inward. Although it was dark, the light from their room provided enough illumination to see inside. Stetson thought it looked unoccupied, but Moira was already through the door.

"Wow. I'm glad we didn't get this room," she said, her voice echoing through the doorway. "It's weird, it kinda reminds me of your apartment. Oh, sorry"

Stetson took a long drink as he walked over and into the other room. Stepping through the doorway, there was a twinge of something that passed quickly. She was right. He was glad they didn't get this room. It was smaller and furnished rather haphazardly. The fact that it looked an awful lot like his apartment was something he wasn't ready to deal with, so he put that off to beer and Moira's suggestion.

"It's missing the death metal band that likes to rehearse in the apartment below," he said with as much humor he could muster. It helped with the uncomfortable feeling in here.

Moira did her best imitation of their lyrics in a growl, "*Kill your mother, kill your father, kill your pets,*" before collapsing in laughter. Stetson couldn't help but laugh. *Hand of Gloom* was a good band, but he imagined it was a lot like living near a subway or airport. They'd ruined more than one candlelight dinner.

"Come on, let's get downstairs and get something to eat," he said, probably a little insistently.

"Alright, alright," she said as she giggled past him back into their room, "don't you need to finish your beer, anyway?"

Stetson stepped out and pulled the door closed behind him. As it shut, he thought he could hear - just for a second - the sound of loud music from the room below. Death metal.

#

Stetson waved the waitress over to their table for another beer. He looked to Moira to see if she needed another, but she only glared at him across the rim of her glass of wine that she had been sipping throughout dinner. *Christ, Moi. It's vacation.* He needed to change the subject or she was going to get at him about his drinking again.

"The food was really good, huh? I don't know why I'm surprised. I hope the other restaurants are as good." He put on his best grin and kept eye contact with her as the waitress brought his beer to the table.

"Yeah," Moria said, as she visibly perked up when talking about their meal, "I can't get over how good it was. The spices really stay with you. We need to get the recipe for when we go home."

"Although, I do feel like I'm hitting the early bird at Denny's" Stetson said as he surveyed the roomful of mostly senior citizens. There were a few younger couples, but they were lost in a sea of people who needed to ask the waitress her name and get obsessed over whether the orange coffee pot was really decaf. He smiled widely at Moira, but inside there was anxiety. Like you could catch old, and he was beginning to show symptoms.

Moira laughed long and loudly about the observation. She didn't care who noticed or what anyone thought. That's what Stetson loved about her. She helped to pull him into being a good person. He was a coward. He'd already chickened out of asking "the big question" tonight, the engagement ring sitting unused in his pocket. *We have another 3 nights here to deal with that.*

The alarm was loud and insistent. It was just talking and the sounds of cutlery on plates, then Stetson was suddenly back at some kind of high school fire drill. He and Moira looked at each other, while holding their hands over their ears, and many of the other guests looked around in concern and confusion as well. But to Stetson's surprise, the wait staff continued as if nothing were going on.

"Probably just a little fire in the kitchen!" Moira yelled across the table. As suddenly as it started, the alarm stopped. The silence afterwards was a vacuum that was soon filled with causal dinner conversations. The waitress stopped by the table to see if they needed anything else, and although Stetson was going to say "another beer", the barely restrained look of terror on the young woman's face - hid behind a practiced veneer - had him saying "No, thank you" instead.

***

"And do you, Moira Gladwell, take this man to be your lawfully wedded husband? To have and to hold, until death do you part?"

The priest stands in the sand beneath a flowered archway, with the night sea behind glittering with the lights from all over the resort. Stetson stands facing Moira, hand in hand, in front of the beautiful background. There is a small congregation, and they sit in rows of white, wooden chairs on either side of a sandy aisle that runs down the middle. The makeshift chapel is lit by the flames of bamboo torches planted all around the perimeter.

"Yes"

Her voice pulls Stetson back to her face, her eyes are piercing in the torchlight. The long, white gown flows gracefully around her, its edges dancing across the sand. She has never looked so beautiful. He can feel the doubts at the back of his mind floating away on the cool tropical breeze. She slides a ring onto his finger.

"And do you, Stetson Fields, take this woman to be your lawfully wedded wife? To have and to hold, until death do you part?"

The commitment wraps around his throat, pulling tight and choking his breath. Moira looks on expectantly, and Stetson can feel the eyes of the congregation burning into him, but he can't get the word out. But then something is there with him. Something ethereal that whispers in his ear - *Be happy. This is what you came here for.*

He surrenders to the dream, and slides a ring on Moira's finger.

"Yes"

The priest closes the bible with a thump. "Then by the power invested in me, by the great god Nekelmu, I now pronounce you husband and wife. You may kiss the bride."

As Moira leans in for the ceremonial smooch, Stetson holds her off and turns to the priest, "What in the fuck did you say?"

64

There is a strange light in the priest's eyes when he responds, "I said, Mister Fields, till death do you part!"

The congregation begins to chant it.

Till death do you part!

They rise from their chairs, still chanting, and surround the couple. Stetson can see the lights in their eyes as they close around him.

Till death do you part!

He looks to Moira, but her face looks old and leathery. She reaches out an emaciated hand and brushes his cheek. Her voice is a rough whisper as she leans in to kiss him.

"Till death do us part!"

Stetson screams.

Day 2

The alarm was faint, but it persisted long enough to pull Stetson from his slumber. He sat up in bed and rubbed his eyes. *Strange fucking dream*. It was so vivid, so real. The sound of that alarm kept getting in the way. Wait-that alarm?!

Stetson leapt from the bed in his tighty-whitey brief underwear and lunged out of the bedroom. The sound seemed to be coming from outside of the room. He pulled back the locks from the front door, opened it a crack, and stuck his head out.

It was louder out here. The alarm sounded like it might be coming from another floor. Stetson stepped out into the long hallway and turned, nearly running into a cleaning lady with her large cart just down the hall. She appeared to be calmly going about her business, all while the alarm sounded, until a strange half-naked man stumbled up to her.

"Excuse me. Do we need to be concerned about that alarm?" he asked with just a touch of sarcasm. As much as he could muster in his underwear.

"I apologize for any inconvenience, sir," she replied with a shy grin, "I think someone is working on the alarms." As if punctuate her response, the alarm stopped. Only thing worse than talking to a cleaning lady in your underwear while an alarm was going off, was talking to one when it wasn't. Stetson excused himself and went back to the room.

#

"Moira! Where are you? Did you hear that alarm?"

Stetson had gone back to the bedroom and gotten dressed. She wasn't in the room or out on the balcony. It wasn't until her reply floated in through the door, where they had found that other room, that he realized it was open.

"Stetson? I didn't realize you were up yet, lover. That's the second time it's gone off this morning."

"Jeez, Moi. I don't think we're allowed in other people's," Stetson said as he strode into the doorway, "...rooms?" He was stunned. The other room had changed from last night. Gone was the crappy furniture and bachelor style decor. Instead, the room had a couch, a love seat, and thick, plush rugs. There were even pictures on the walls. Moira sat on the couch with a large scrapbook in her lap.

"Oh, silly. This is our room. Come, sit down and look at this," she replied in a happy, matter-of-fact tone.

The resort is probably getting it ready for guests. Stetson kept telling himself that as he walked over and plopped himself down on the couch. The fact that he couldn't see another door into the room besides the one he had passed through was something he wasn't going to acknowledge right now. *Maybe they came by last night while we were out to dinner and made the changes?*

Moira slid the scrapbook into his lap and kissed him on the cheek, "The ceremony was beautiful, wasn't it?"

Looking down, Stetson felt the world shift. Pictures of him and Moira on the beach posing in wedding regalia. Pictures of them posing under a flowered archway. And then there was the priest. The one from the dream. Smiling back at Stetson from an 8X10 photo. *How much did I have to drink last night? Jesus, did we elope?*

He closed the scrapbook - the priests smile was too unnerving - and turned to Moria, "Moi, what happened last night? I...don't remember any of this." He did, but he wasn't ready to discuss the dream with her. He waited for the inevitable comment about his drinking, and was genuinely surprised when she didn't even register it.

"That's why I love you. You're such a jokester. I can't blame you, after the way you rocked my world last night," she replied, as she placed the scrapbook aside and rose. "Maybe I can jog your memory?" She straddled him on the couch and Stetson didn't care anymore about weird coincidences.

#

The elevator doors opened with a screech like nails on a chalkboard. The out of service sign had been taken down and they didn't feel like taking the stairs from the third floor. The slow metal on metal grind mercifully ended as they fully opened.

"Sounds like they need to oil these doors," Stetson said with as much bravado as could muster. It didn't seem very "in service" to him. "You sure you don't want to take the stairs?"

"What's life without a little danger?" Moira asked with a wink. She grabbed his hand and playfully pulled him into the elevator. "Besides, nothing could ruin this amazing honeymoon."

She had said it so casually that it took a moment to register to Stetson. *Honeymoon?* He turned to correct her, but she looked so happy, so in love, that he just took a deep breath and went along for the ride. As the doors finally screeched shut, the light sounds of a made-for-elevator muzak version of *The Way We Were* filled the elevator. In spite of all the strange happenings, Stetson found himself laughing at his latest predicament. *This is truly hell!*

With a metallic clunk, the elevator began its descent. As they passed the second floor, Stetson could swear he heard the sound of water dripping. Every few seconds or so. He checked the floor, but no puddles were visible on the gray carpeted surface. It sounded like it might be coming from above.

"Moi, can you hear that? Sounds like somethings leaking."

Moira turned to him and took his hands. Her eyes were staring directly into his. She had the same happy look, but there was something else there now, too. Something faint. Something not entirely Moira. "Stetson, my dear husband. *Nothing* is going to ruin this honeymoon."

He smiled back uneasily at her, then winced as the doors began to screech. She just kept staring into his eyes until the doors had fully opened.

#

It seemed no matter the time, the spicy, savory smell of the food cooking here was always present. They had just eaten breakfast and Stetson's mouth watered as if he hadn't eaten in days. He marveled at it as they strolled through the gentle surf of the long, white, sandy beach that curved gracefully around much of the Bay. Moira carried her sandals in her free hand, the other locked in an eternal grip with Stetson's. He was all for signs of affection, but by this point his palm felt sweaty and gross.

"Y'all interested in a cruise?"

Stetson glanced towards the sound. Just up ahead, a short man in a tall, woolen red cap leaned against the legs of a lifeguard chair. He wore thick sunglasses, but Stetson could feel the man's eyes upon him. Moira seemed unaware or uninterested, as she gently pulled Stetson along, strolling past the strange man.

"Y'all interested in a cruise?"

The man in the red hat had sidled up with the two of them, and after glancing around suspiciously, he began to speak in a whisper.

"I offer the best cruise on the island, boss. For guests who want to get away. You know, *get away*?" The man nodded his head at the open ocean when he spoke the last line. He might have winked too, but Stetson couldn't see his eyes.

"Sorry, man. We're on…honeymoon, and we'd like to just be alone." Stetson said, struggling to get the honeymoon part out. He was starting to enjoy the always happy Moira, and he didn't want to fuck another thing up. It still felt odd.

The red hat bobbed as the man nodded, looking both ways again before speaking, "Yes, your honeymoon, right. Tell you what, limited time offer for the newlyweds. I'll take you out now, before it gets too late." Stetson could see how they would want to cruise during daylight hours, but the man seemed anxious about something else. *Too late for what?*

Stetson saw the resort security approaching from over the man's shoulder. He had seen them stationed at the exits, and other high-traffic areas, during their stay. Usually, it was one or two men. To his surprise, there must have been ten security guards crossing the beach now towards their location.

"Looks like it just got too late, my friend," Stetson nodded at the oncoming security force, with a wry smile.

The man, startled that they had gotten this close, sprinted away down the beach, red hat bobbing, security guards in pursuit. He called back to them as he fled, "Find me again! Remember the red hat! We need to get you away before it's too late!"

They continued their long stroll down the beach, but Stetson couldn't get the question out of his mind. *Too late for what?*

#

Stetson stumbled along behind Moira down the long hallway. He lost count of how many beers he had with dinner, to the point that he'd tripped and knocked over a waitress on the way out. But Moira never said a cross word about it. He was really starting to like the new Moira, but deep down he missed the old one. The beer was helping.

"We're going to do something wonderful tonight, Stetson," Moira said over her shoulder to him, pausing to kick off her heels before she continued to saunter down the hallway. Stetson loved her ass in heels, but tonight it was just as good without. She looked curvier tonight.

"We're going to make a new life," she said several steps later, letting her dress fall around her ankles. He was getting real tired of the constant fantasy crap so far on this vacation. Moira was on the pill, had been for years. The beer and the sight of her half-naked in the hallway suppressed any argument, and he only rolled his eyes behind her. *Gonna make something.*

She left her bra and panties in the doorway to the room. Jogging the last few steps, Stetson kicked the door closed behind him and they made love on the tile floor.

***

"Doctor to Delivery. Doctor to Delivery."

The lights of the delivery room are unforgiving in their cold brightness. Stetson raises a latex glove covered hand to shield his eyes until they adjust. There are many nurses around, carrying trays of medical instruments and checking on the patient. Moria, her dignity temporarily lost, lays flat on the operating table with her legs mounted high in stirrups. Doesn't leave a thing to the imagination.

Moira is screaming something at a nurse, something about "more drugs" as she writhes in pain at the contractions. She is damp with sweat, and her hair sticks to her forehead at odd angles. She looks exhausted, but glowing. A nurse gently moves Stetson out of the way as they mobilize and prepare for the doctor. There is excited banter among the staff present.

The delivery room doors swing open, and the doctor strides in like a rock star. The nurses and staff applaud as he enters, while several nurses faint in excitement as he brushes past them on his way to the operating table. The doctor grabs the nearest chair, spins it around, and sits on it backwards. The ultimate picture of cool. Like the Fonz is having an up close with Moira's hoo-ha. Stetson finds the scene a tad off-putting, but at least they didn't get the doctor who got boos and rotten fruit.

Moira screams, and things start to move quickly. The doctor calls out, "She's crowning! I can see the head!" and the nurses rush in and surround Moira. Stetson tries to reach her, to hold her outstretched hand, but he keeps getting pushed farther back by the growing crowd. She disappears into a sea of nurses. The staff start chanting, over and over in a rising fervor. *Nekelmu. Nekelmu.* It feels vaguely familiar to Stetson.

A plaintive wail stops the crescendo of voices, and there is a moment of barely contained excitement in the silence. Stetson starts pushing nurses out of the way, trying to get to Moira. The doctor stands, raising the newborn over his head with both hands, "It is a boy!" A cheer goes up, then the crowd begins chanting again. *A boy. A boy.*

"The father! Where is the father?" The doctor's voice silences the room. As the crowd parts, Stetson feels the hands of nurses pushing him forward towards the table. Moira lies there completely exhausted, but smiling widely. He grabs her hand and goes to kiss her forehead. But then, the doctor is there.

"Are you going to cut the cord, Mister Fields?" He holds the newborn out to Stetson, still covered in blood and placenta. The umbilical cord snakes out from it's belly and weaves between Moira's thighs. The doctor smiles wolfishly, and Stetson dimly remembers something about that leering face. It passes as something cold and heavy is pushed into his hand. Looking down, he holds a large pair of metal cutting shears. They look old and rusty, with bits of dried blood caked on them.

"I...I...maybe one of you should do it?" Stetson holds out the shears and begins edging backwards. But then something is there with him. Something ethereal that whispers in his ear - *Be happy. This is what you came here for.*

Swallowing heavily, Stetson steps forward and does the deed. The heavy shears slice through the fleshy cord with an audible snip. He drops them and reaches out for the newborn, but the doctor pulls the infant away.

"No, Mister Fields. For the father nothing." The doctor's eyes glow above a sinister smile as he hands the infant back to Moira. Trance-like, she accepts it and begins nursing the newborn. "Mother needs her strength. She's hungry, Mister Fields."

To Stetson's horror, the umbilical cord between Moira's legs begins moving about as if alive. He moves to step away, but the cord lashes out and grabs him by the wrist. He can feel the warm, wetness of it as it circles his arm like a Boa Constrictor.

He is lifted into the air over Moira, the urge to struggle seems gone now. *Nekelmu. Nekelmu.* The nurses chant as they pull back her hospital gown, and Stetson's mind fractures at what lies beneath. Moira's vagina has enlarged and grown teeth, like a huge mouth. The umbilical cord slowly begins lowering him into the gaping maw of razor-sharp fangs.

He looks up and Moira's eyes glow as she licks her lips, her voice strangely seductive, "For the father nothing."

The umbilical cord releases.

Stetson screams.

Day 3

The alarm was back.

"I'll get him this time," Moira's voice sounded tired and raspy. Stetson felt the bed shift as she rose from beside him. He'd had trouble getting back to sleep after that dream. He wondered briefly what she would do to get the alarm silenced. *Probably just more workers anyway.*

Rising from the bed, his joints cried out. That was new. *New rule - no sex on tile floors.* Walking past the mirrored closet doors on his way to the bathroom, Stetson caught a glimpse of himself. *Time to cut out the beers and use that gym membership.* He'd really let himself go, and was sporting the beginnings of a dad bod.

The light from the bathroom mirror was unforgiving. Stetson turned his head side to side. It was undeniable. His hair was graying at the temples. *Christ, is this normal for twenty-eight?* The face looking back at him was different than he remembered. Older. At least the alarm had ceased its incessant wailing.

"Moi! Do you want to head down a little early and check out the gym here at the resort?" Stetson said as he stepped out of the bedroom and pulled on a tee shirt. He'd always prided himself on being reasonably fit, and the gut check in front of the mirror told him it was time to start taking things more seriously.

He stopped a few steps into the main area. The door to the other room was open again. The faint sounds of something like a music box floated out. Stetson knew the tune it gently played. *The Way We Were.* It seemed to permeate everything here like the smell of the food.

Just outside the door, Stetson could hear Moira's voice softly singing along to the twinkling tune. Entering the room, he placed a hand on the door to steady himself. Gone were the couch and love seat. In their place, a large wooden crib and a rocking chair now occupied the space. Pictures of cartoon animals adorned the walls. A mobile spun slowly above the crib, providing the tune, while Moira sat in the rocking chair. Her shirt was open, and she nursed an infant at her breast.

"Quiet, Stetson. He was just hungry, but I don't want him to start fussing again," she whispered as she looked up into Stetson's eyes. Her face was different. She seemed more mature to him somehow. Motherly, he thought with a chill. The anger and confusion of the past few days ripped out of him in an explosion.

"Quiet?! What the serious fuck, Moira?! We don't have a kid. That shit takes nine freaking months! I mean, whose kid is that? Oh, Christ. We aren't even fucking married yet! Am I going crazy, Moi?! Am I?!"

The baby wailed in Moira's arms. She began rocking to soothe the child, and her eyes returned to Stetson full of anger.

"Now you've upset little Stetsie! I swear sometimes, Stetson. It's like you don't want to help raise our little boy, and instead you want to say these hateful things!" She began tearing up and it was all Stetson could do to not scream. And seriously, *Stetsie*?! It was either Stetson or Stet, no exceptions. *Ruining the kid already.*

"I'm going to get help for you, Moi. And find out whose kid this is," he replied with as much patience as he could muster. *And get a drink.* He tried to push the thought down, but he was thirsty. There was a bar on the way to the front desk. No shame in just one beer, right?

#

Screech.

The doors shut, ending their hideous squeal as Stetson leaned back against the wall of the elevator. He'd have to talk to the folks at the front desk about that, too. *My girl has gone crazy. I believe she's stolen someone's child. And, oh yeah, the elevator needs greasing.* Maybe he would stick to the important stuff and just suffer the sound for now.

Alone in the steel box, the light strains of *The Way We Were* were close to driving him to distraction. That, and the damned dripping sound. Stetson remembered reading about how the Chinese had tortured prisoners by dripping water on their foreheads. This, in his ignorant estimation, was probably a close second.

As the doors screeched open, the spicy, savory smell wafted in on a gentle breeze. Stetson's mouth did it's watering thing, and he wondered if the bar had a menu. Just one beer and some food. That's all he needed. Then he'd be right off to the front desk to get this whole mess sorted out.

#

"What do you mean, two adults and one child?! I fucking checked in two days ago with my girlfriend, Moira, and that was all! I mean...I didn't even think you allowed kids at this resort."

The young woman behind the lobby desk weathered Stetson's drunken rage with an unflinching, practiced smile. He had spent most of the day at the bar. Long enough to convince himself to stumble down here to the front desk.

"I'm sorry, Mister Fields, but your reservation is for two adults and one child. I apologize for any inconvenience. Here. Let me show you," the woman replied as she spun her computer screen around for him to see. The way she called him *Mister Fields* was a little too close to the dreams Stetson was having lately, but the wide screen monitor confirmed her stated assertion. *Two adults and one child.*

"Jesus, I think I'm going crazy. Hey, listen, I'm sorry for being rude," he said as he turned and stumbled away. He wasn't sure where. Stetson felt more confused all of the time, although the beer was certainly not helping with that. Maybe what he said to the woman was right. *Maybe I am going crazy.*

The large, open entranceway that he and Moira had arrived through days ago at the beginning of the trip beckoned Stetson from across the lobby. Getting away from the resort sounded like a good idea. He could bring help back for Moira. As nonchalantly as possible, Stetson worked his way towards the entranceway.

Halfway across the lobby, Stetson was bumped into by an older man, probably in his late fifties, who ran by him. There was an edge of madness to the man's voice as he barreled towards the entranceway and screamed, "They're not mine! I've got to get out of here!"

As soon as the man exited the resort building, an alarm sounded that forced Stetson to cover his ears. *The alarm.* Red-shirted security guards appeared from out of nowhere and swarmed the man, dragging him away screaming. As the chilling realization washed over Stetson, he glanced over to the woman behind the front desk. She was staring right back at him, with a smile like a predator.

We're prisoners here.

#

The red hat floated along gently in the surf. Stetson stood there defeated and watched it slowly work its way down the beach. A lone security guard stood a short distance away, next to a lifeguard chair, watching the scene and smiling. His eyes moved between the hat and Stetson, then he nodded as if to make his unspoken point. *The man in the red hat is dead. There is no escape.*

Stetson turned back towards the resort and walked away. The guards smile was beginning to make him nervous. After the incident in the lobby, he wandered the resort trying to figure out what was happening to them. How to get away. That was when the man in the red hat popped into Stetson's head. He felt helpless now as evening began to fall.

Finding a secluded spot on the beach, Stetson collapsed into the sand and curled himself into a ball. He wasn't going back to the room tonight. It was peaceful here, the sound of waves lapping under the blanket of stars, and soon he began to nod off. But every time his eyes closed, Stetson could see the man in the red hat running away down the beach the other day. *We need to get you away before it's too late.*

Stetson shivered in the warm, muggy, too late night.

***

The smell of turkey and sweet potatoes is thick in the air. Fully reclined in his La-Z-Boy, Stetson watches from between his slippered feet as the Detroit Lions are on their way to losing yet another Thanksgiving game. At least the resolution on the wide screen television is good. The beer can is cold and damp with perspiration as he brings it to his lips. Something pumpkin spiced. He needs to tell Moira that he hates pumpkin beers.

She is excited that Stet and his wife are bringing their new infant over for the first time. Stetson can only think of one thing. *I'm a grandfather.* The thought fills him with an uneasy feeling. He looks down at his sweater and khakis with some disdain, ruing how easily he must have given in. Stetson can't seem to remember getting old, but as he looks at his wrinkled hands he assumes he's arrived.

The football game has been exceptionally violent this afternoon. There were three accidental homicides already. Stetson watches with a look of puzzled disgust as the broadcast shows a replay of what he is pretty certain is outright murder.

The defensive lineman drives the quarterback into the ground, then rises and proceeds to stomp on the poor man's throat with his cleats until it severs from the body in an explosion of blood. The coaches, the players, even the referees laugh hysterically as the lineman parades around the field with the decapitated head. He is assessed a fifteen-yard penalty for taunting. Stetson feels like it should have been more.

The game cuts to a commercial. Some local used car dealership. Rows and rows of cheaply painted older model cars. The man on the screen is talking about all the great deals down at Nekelmu Used Auto. His smile has a leering quality that reminds Stetson of someone, although he can't seem to put a finger on it.

Suddenly, the scene on the TV changes. The background melts away, leaving only the strange, leering salesman. His eyes seem to stare out from the screen into Stetson's. When he speaks again, his voice comes from somewhere beside Stetson. An ethereal whisper.

"My apologies, Mister Fields. I make it a point never to share backstage details with my players, but I fear I'm not getting through to you. Perhaps it's the cowardice? The alcohol, maybe?" The man on the screen shrugs his shoulders in mock incertitude. Stetson puts down his beer and lowers the La-Z-Boy. He blinks his eyes and tries the remote, but the man remains.

"Done, then? Good. I hadn't thought it might be just plain stupidity." The smiling salesman continues with just the touch of a sneer, "Everyone comes here for a reason, although they may not realize it at the time. I give those that accept it happiness, and those that resist, horror. All I ask is some of your precious years to sustain me in return. Is that so much?"

Stetson stares back at the man on the television with a dumbfounded expression. *Used car salesman get pushier all the time.* "Umm…everyone comes to your used auto lot for a reason?" It seems like a reasonable qualifying question after the salesman's soliloquy.

The man's smile disappears, and there is static on the television for a second before it clears and he speaks again. "Too immersive for my own good. Very well. I was going to have the grandchild eat you alive or something similarly unspeakable, but perhaps I simply need a new tact. For those where happiness or horror is not enough. Did you know Moira had a reason for coming?"

The question hangs in the charged silence as Stetson leans closer to the screen. The man smiles widely as he slowly disappears into static.

Slowly, the white noise on the screen resolves into what Stetson assumes is a security feed from a hotel room. There is a couple fucking their brains out on the bed. No pretty way to describe it. The quality isn't great, and there is a time counter in the upper right-hand corner, but the inclusion of sound makes it particularly disturbing or stimulating. Stetson found it a little of both.

The voice returns in its ethereal whisper as the video continues, "You won't recognize the gentleman, her addiction thrives in anonymity. Sex can be as powerful a drug as the most potent narcotic. Those who fuck, come here for love. She came because she valued your love the most."

The woman rides the man roughly on the hotel bed, slowly turning her head towards the screen. Moira's eyes glow as they lock with Stetson across the digital void. Her voice is a sensual whisper.

"Don't worry Stetson dear, I may cum for them, but you're the one I want to come home to."

Stetson screams.

Day 4

Stetson laid in the bed and stared blankly at the textured ceiling. He couldn't remember how he got back to the room last night. It was this place. The man from his dreams. *No escape.*

He couldn't shake the dream. Moira had looked so real in the video, but was that just fantasy like the other ones? Stetson told himself it was, but there was a dull feeling in the pit of his stomach. He'd been a shitty boyfriend. This was what he deserved.

Plus, parts of the dreams he was having here stuck. The marriage. The child. Stetson had risen in the early morning hours to pee, which was something new, and the person who looked back at him in the bathroom mirror was white-haired and wrinkled. It was this place. It had stolen years from them already.

It was painful to rise, his joints felt worn out, but Stetson pushed himself up to sitting, then standing, then walking as he moved to the closet to dress. He needed to do something now, before he lost any more life. *Time to shit or get on with the adult diapers.* Humor was difficult at the moment, but it fueled him to keep going.

He expected the strange door to be open when he exited the bedroom. He also expected to hear the sounds of a family breakfast in there. Stetson was beginning to understand parts of this madness. The sound of Moira's voice stopped him for a moment, however. It was so full of happiness. Full of years of love and caring.

Stetson longed to walk into the room, to embrace her, but instead he turned and quietly exited the suite. There wasn't much time. He had to save Moira.

#

As he ascended the staircase, Stetson silently thanked the screechy elevator and the dripping sound. He had stood in front of the doors, ready for the squeal and drip, when it suddenly occurred to him. *It's probably a leak from the roof.* The roof! Maybe he could signal for help.

Waitresses with covered trays of food passed by him several times on his way up. They'd apologize for any inconvenience and then leave just a hint of the spicy, savory smell behind. Stetson's stomach grumbled as he climbed, and he briefly wondered why they had the kitchen on the upper floors.

The exit sign over the metal door burned like a beacon. Stetson took the last few steps as quickly as his old legs would allow. He'd had to take a few breaks on the long climb. Standing in front of the door, his hand on the long, horizontal handle, he could hear sounds from the other side. Like a busy kitchen. Shouts and the sounds of preparation.

Throwing the door open, he was hit with a thick cloud of smoke. The savory smell was almost overpowering here, and he coughed as the breeze cleared away the fog. As his eyes adjusted to the blazing sun overhead, Stetson fell to his knees in madness at what remained.

Large, open grills that spilled the smoke and aroma down from the roof and across the resort. Butchers blocks and huge vats of a brownish liquid, where cooks prepared the meat for grilling. There were orders written on a large chalkboard at one end, and waitresses milled about in front of it with empty plates, waiting impatiently for their order. A runoff of blood and offal covered the concrete roof, dripping down through the grates.

And a metal rack that held row upon row of body bags, hung like sides of beef. *This is where it all leads. No escape.*

Stetson screamed as blackness took him.

Day 5

There was no dream last night.

Stetson rose in the morning, grabbed his walker, and hobbled out of the bedroom.

The strange door was open, as he hoped it would be.

Stetson left his walker next to the door and entered the other room.

The sand was warm underneath his aching feet and the view was magnificent. Tropical sunset. Two chairs sat on the beach. Moira sat in one of them. Her hair was white now, and she was wrinkled and old, but Stetson thought she never looked more beautiful. *Forget about tomorrow, let's be happy today.*

He moved to the chair beside her and sat down. They held hands while the sun slowly set in an explosion of orange and purple.

About the Author

Chris Noonan writes stories about the horror inherent in daily life from his suburban house in Mount Holly, New Jersey. His loving wife, Christina, and two children, Zachary and Ella, put up with his regular flights of fancy. When he's not writing or slaving away at his day job, Chris plays guitar in the band Groovepocket [https://groovepocketband.com/] and co-hosts a D&D podcast, 3 Wise DMs [https://3wisedms.com/].

Weregold

By C. L. Werner

"It were here that Alice were watchin' her sheep." The farmer's voice cracked as he spoke, emotion raising the burly man's deep tone to an emotional shrill. His eyes had a distant, unfocused quality as his gaze swept across the pasture. Slowly he lifted his arm and pointed to the line of trees that bordered the field and delineated it from its neighbor. "There's where we found what the beast left of her."

Alexander Ravencroft nodded slowly, his lean face bearing a pensive expression as he followed the pointing finger to stare at the distant trees. "A terrible tragedy, friend Narbrige," he said, a bit of awkwardness in his words.

"Beyond pain your daughter now is." The big mercenary with Ravencroft tried to cover for his companion's brusk manner. "With the good God she has gone to." Gunther Kaltenbrun started to cross himself, but hurriedly stopped when he saw a flicker of suspicion in the farmer's eyes. The German had been only a few years in England and sometimes forgot the distrust and enmity many bore towards the Catholic Church.

"Thank you for showing us the place," Ravencroft told Narbrige, making a dismissive wave of his gloved hand. "We'll investigate and discover whatever there is to discover here."

The farmer's expression hardened. His calloused hands tightened about the heft of the scythe he carried. "Weren't no question except it were the Beast of Blackbriar." He nodded his chin in the direction of the forest somewhere beyond the horizon. "There's been five took by the Beast already, not to figure all the sheep an' hogs what got took." Narbrige spat and his lips pulled back in a fierce snarl, fear and sorrow blotted out by vengeful hate. "The Beast's what done this!"

Though Narbrige stood a head taller than Ravencroft, the steely look he set upon the farmer quickly cowed the man. "That's for me to determine," he declared. "I'd not tell you when to plant your crop. That's what you know. It has been many years since I devoted myself to combating the Devil and his infernal

85

servants. I bear letters from Parliament that authorize me as a witch hunter." He let a thin smile purse his lips and clapped Narbrige on the shoulder. "That's why your community sent for me. Trust me to do my job and I'll let you return to yours."

Chastened, the big farmer slowly withdrew from the pasture. Kaltenbrun watched Narbrige as he walked away. "Needing watching, that man," the German stated.

Ravencroft removed his broad-brimmed hat and wiped his brow. "No more than most of Thorneshire needs watching. The magistrate should have sent for us when these attacks started." The witch hunter sighed. "Instead he waits until things are so hot they're almost boiling over."

"What being our next move?" Kaltenbrun asked.

"Let's start by following these tracks." The witch hunter indicated some faint marks on the ground. Most of the prints were indistinct to Kaltenbrun's eyes, trampled by the hooves of sheep, but a few were clearly left by a small foot. Just the impression of the ball of the foot.

"The girl?"

"Indeed," Ravencroft confirmed. "Clearly she was running away from *that*." He pointed to a patch of bare earth.

Kaltenbrun studied the spot. Though partly obscured by the tracks of sheep, he could still make out the pads of a much different animal. The German had hunted many times in the forests of the Empire and recognized the print left by a wolf, though this was an enormous specimen of its kind. "A wolf," he grunted. "Then not so crazy are these peasants being."

The witch hunter gave Kaltenbrun a patient smile. "The last wild wolf in England was brought to heel by John Harrington almost a hundred and fifty years ago. No, friend Kaltenbrun, what we have here is a beast of a much different color." Ravencroft donned his hat once more and started towards the trees. "We know where the girl ended up, so perhaps we just cut to the chase. Or rather the end of the chase."

Kaltenbrun trotted after Ravencroft as the witch hunter hurried across the field. "But if no wolf this Beast is, then what are we looking for?"

"Something that I hope will be much more financially beneficial. One doesn't hire a witch hunter simply to dispatch a dis-tempered dog. Any buffoon with a fowling piece could do the job." Ravencroft patted the leather-bound edition of Kramer and Sprenger hanging from his belt. "Specialists are needed for special incidents."

The German shook his head. "What if it is nothing but the mad dog?"

Ravencroft had reached the shadowy expanses of trees. He circled around a discolored patch of earth that had been disturbed. The tinge of red that stained the dirt told its own story. Kaltenbrun could picture the poor shepherdess lying there, her body torn by the sharp fangs of a vicious beast.

"Let's see if we can make it something more than a mad dog," Ravencroft commented as he inspected the ground. "Something that the village would pay well to be rid of." The witch hunter broadened his search, circling wide of the spot where the girl had died. "The villagers have walked all over this area. Spoiled whatever spoor was here. The trail, I fear is cold..."

Suddenly, the witch hunter straightened his body and triumphantly pointed at some tracks in the soil. "Here! See what you make of that!"

Kaltenbrun dutifully did as he was bidden. The German quickly noted the enormous tracks. The pads of a massive animal. "If you are insisting England is without wolves, then this can only be a dog."

Ravencroft waved his hand in a dismissive gesture. "Take a closer look, Gunther. Not just what the tracks are, but what they're doing."

It took Kaltenbrun only a moment to see what Ravencroft was driving at. "God in Heaven!" he gasped. "The wolf has been walking on two legs!"

"Does that not suggest something?" Ravencroft prodded his companion.

The color drained from Kaltenbrun's face. Despite the country he was in, he hurriedly crossed himself. "Werewolf!" he exclaimed, spitting the word from his mouth as though it were poison.

"Indeed. Werewolf." A gleam shone in Ravencroft's eye. He glanced back in the direction of Thorneshire. "That's something these people will pay handsomely to be rid of." A low chuckle rasped across his lips.

"Yes, friend Kaltenbrun. I've an idea that this is going to prove a most lucrative excursion."

***

"... choose to believe or don't, but there's no denying the seriousness of the situation." Alexander Ravencroft leaned back in the mahogany chair. His eyes roved over the lush rugs stretched across the floor, the gilded portraits that lined the walls, the cascade of crystals that drooped from the chandelier overhead. Everything in the grand hall was an expression of decadent opulence. The unspoken boast of Thorneshire's lord and master that his was a rich and wealthy pedigree.

It was all the witch hunter could do to keep the smile from his face as he conversed with Lord Thaddeus Thorne. Ravencroft had always felt that the fawning hopes of the poor that they might grasp a bit of the luxury of the prosperous elite by groveling at their feet was self-delusion. A servant benefited little through service. To truly better oneself was to seek and seize opportunity when it revealed itself.

"It's nonsense," Thorne huffed before taking a sip of wine. The cellars in Suncroft Abbey were as richly appointed as the hall was. The Spanish vintage the nobleman had provided his unwanted visitors had a bouquet to it that Ravencroft seldom encountered. With the thinly concealed distaste of their host, it was unlikely the Iberian wine was the best to be found in the abbey.

"You have not been seeing dead..." Kaltenbrun's speech was cut off by a silencing gesture from Ravencroft.

"We may be dealing with the superstitions of the common herd," Ravencroft nodded to Lord Thorne as he conceded a possibility. "But there's certainly something responsible for these deaths. If, as you insist, the werewolf your tenants blame for these murders is naught but a fantasy, then it still leaves us with a culprit who must be unmasked and brought to justice."

"And where do you think to find this culprit?" The question came from the other person present at this secret conference between nobleman and witch hunter. Roderick Thorne, the eldest son and heir of Thaddeus, was a strongly built man in his early twenties, his blonde locks glistening like silk in the light shining down on him from the chandelier. His features had a graceful smoothness, his squared jaw the strength of a granite slab, his skin the unblemished color of a pampered and indulgent upbringing. There was, however, around the eyes, a furtive and calculating aspect. The desire of one born to riches yet who demands still more for himself.

"It's merely some mad dog, father," Roderick told Lord Thorne, turning a sneer in Ravencroft's direction. "A single bullet and the affair is finished. I can muster a hunt and have the wretched business over with in a day."

Ravencroft smiled over the cusp of his wine glass. "If things were so simple, I dare say you'd have already attended to them." His expression returned Roderick's contempt with its own coin. He was careful to adopt a more appeasing manner when he addressed Thaddeus. "There's a very simple reason why the steps you've taken so far haven't resolved the situation... and why I don't believe your son's offer to lead a hunt would fare any better."

"And what would that reason be?" Lord Thorne's gruff voice rumbled up from his barrel chest. Though he had twenty years over his son, Thaddeus had maintained an imposing physique. Ravencroft wondered, if it came to it, whether the hulking Kaltenbrun would come off the worse in any match between the two.

The witch hunter paused, choosing his words carefully before he answered the lord. "Natural or unnatural, the perpetrator of these outrages is a thinking creature. No mere beast." He glanced at each of the Thornes in turn, emphasizing his statement with a nod of his head. "If there is no werewolf, then it is some rascal who is using the legend to mask his crimes."

"Your proof on that score?" Roderick demanded.

"You've only to visit the site of the last murder," Ravencroft answered. He expanded on the hint of challenge in his tone. "An experienced hunter such as yourself would surely be able to tell the difference between the work of a mere animal and the calculating intellect of a man. The forests of England are renowned for their vicious predators."

Roderick bristled at the rejoinder. "You go too far, ruffian!"

"Do I?" Ravencroft turned away from the heir and returned his focus to Lord Thorne. "I've journeyed abroad across the continent. I've followed the trails left by bear and wolf, even confronted an escaped leopard in the forests of

Averoigne." He waved his hand at his Teutonic companion. "Friend Kaltenbrun has grown up hearing the howls of wolves at night. The countryside of England is a green and pleasant land, freed from the predations of wild beasts by the vigilance of our ancestors."

"What is your point?" Lord Thorne pressed the witch hunter.

"There are few men in England who are familiar with the ways of any beast more wild than a boar," Ravencroft stated. He made a placating gesture with his hands. "I'm not faulting the education you've provided your son, what I'm saying is that there is no substitute for experience. I've seen how an animal with a taste for human flesh conducts itself. However, cunning such a beast might be, it doesn't plot its attacks the way a human murderer does. Dismiss the notion of a werewolf, if it makes you more comfortable, but face the reality that your culprit is a man."

"Must we listen to this drivel?" Roderick growled.

Lord Thorne shook his head. "Master Ravencroft is an appointed agent of Parliament and it would be unwise for us to agitate London." His eyes carried an unspoken layer to the warning he gave his son. It was rumored that Thaddeus Thorne hadn't been as neutral as he professed and that he'd afforded comfort to the Cavaliers after their route at Naseby. "Even if he's mistaken in his beliefs about our troubles, while he's in Thorneshire we will extend to him every courtesy."

Ravencroft rose from his chair and bowed to Lord Thorne. "I was depending upon your assistance and understanding." His eyes roved across the finery of the grand hall. "I will impose upon you as little as possible. I presume Suncroft can afford me the accommodation I require? I'll require one of the larger bed chambers. You can prepare a couch for my manservant." He pointed to Kaltenbrun. "I'll also need a day room of some sort from which to plan strategy."

Roderick glared at the witch hunter. "The village has an inn..."

"But the abbey is much better suited to my requirements," Ravencroft cut him off. His gaze was as sharp as a knife, penetrating the arrogant confidence of the heir's expression. "In the village, my activities could be observed by the villain I'm hunting. Here, in the security of Suncroft, my investigations can be hidden from the culprit."

Lord Thorne uttered a weary sigh. "You'll have whatever you need," he told the witch hunter. He glanced aside at Roderick. "Whatever help you need, you've but to ask." He stared at his son until Roderick gave a reluctant nod of agreement. However willful the heir might be, it was obvious he remained under his parent's dominance.

"I knew I could depend upon your indulgence," Ravencroft said, making careful note of the family dynamics. "I'm certain that Suncroft will provide me with everything I need."

**

It was a week after their arrival in Thorneshire and Gunther Kaltenbrun was perplexed by his employer's strategy. Since establishing themselves at Suncroft Abbey, Ravencroft had spent little time in the village and its surroundings. Instead, he'd been hanging about the manor, keeping an eye on its inhabitants and tasking Kaltenbrun with the same duty. The German couldn't understand how what they were doing was helping further their hunt. Unless of course...

"You are one of the people here suspecting?" Kaltenbrun put the question to Ravencroft when the two men were alone in the sunroom Lord Thorne had put at their disposal.

The witch hunter was sitting in the window box, idly tapping on the glass behind him. "Very frank and succinct," he said, then glanced at the door to the room. "Put so bluntly, it would be unfortunate for our investigation if someone was to be listening at the keyhole."

Kaltenbrun started at the suggestion. He spun around and glared at the door. It hadn't occurred to him that there might be spies at the manor. Given Lord Thorne's opinion of his unwanted guests, however, it should have been obvious the noble would charge his servants with keeping tabs on their activities. "I am sorry. I am not thinking."

Ravencroft chuckled at the abashed look Kaltenbrun turned his way. "We must work on instilling some deceit in your character. You're far too open and above board to excel at this kind of work."

The German scowled at Ravencroft's amusement. "You are not covert about your business either." He jabbed a finger at the large window behind the witch hunter. "Anyone can see you right now. So too can they be seeing you as you poke around the manor. It is obvious being to everybody that you are suspicious that the werewolf here is to be found."

The witch hunter rose from his seat and walked towards Kaltenbrun. "Indeed, you think it is so obvious?" Ravencroft stared at the closed door and smiled. When he spoke again, it was in a furtive, lowered voice. "Maybe a bit too obvious, or do you think Lord Thorne's household regards us with such contempt that they don't credit me with subtlety?"

Kaltenbrun blinked, understanding, slowly firing his imagination. "A ruse," he whispered. It would, of course, be like Ravencroft concealing his true activities beneath a false ploy. "Then you are wanting them to believe..."

"I want them to know that I will seek out the werewolf – whether he be real or a pretender – wherever he might lurk," Ravencroft said, his voice growing louder. "The noble pedigree of Thaddeus Thorne won't shield the culprit even if he is discovered at Suncroft."

"That could be trouble," Kaltenbrun said.

"I don't think Thaddeus Thorne will find it prudent to interfere with an appointed representative of Parliament. It would be injudicious to question the authority I've been given." The witch hunter glanced again at the door, the smile returning to his face. He motioned Kaltenbrun closer. "Now, tell me everything you've observed." Ravencroft's voice dropped to a whisper. "And keep your report just between the two of us."

Matching Ravencroft's tone, Kaltenbrun relayed what he'd seen while prowling around the manor. The witch hunter sat with his hands folded under his chin, his eyes closed as he digested every word of the German's report. When Kaltenbrun was finished Ravencroft opened his eyes and walked over to the window. There was a contemplative expression on the witch hunter's face.

Kaltenbrun watched as Ravencroft tugged the curtains back, so his view was improved. It seemed to him that his master was looking in the direction of the stables. The notion was confirmed when he caught the words Ravencroft muttered under his breath.

"It would seem Roderick Thorne has a fondness for horseflesh," the witch hunter mused, tapping his finger against the window seat. "Yet it seems he doesn't do much riding."

"Is that being important?" Kaltenbrun wondered aloud, uncertain how the heir's repeated visits to the stables would help them uncover a werewolf.

Ravencroft shot the German a sly glance. "It might prove to be the key I've been looking for. If it fits the lock I have in mind, this may prove a most profitable excursion indeed."

***

Sometimes a secret was so obvious that it only needed the correct frame of mind to see it. The moment Ravencroft met Suncroft's stablemaster, he knew all he needed to know. It was hardly necessary to speak with the grooms and other attendants, but he did so as a matter of formality. The servants lacked the insight to understand the importance of what they told him, but that was just as well. Even an obvious secret lost its value if too many knew about it.

"Have you learned everything you needed?" Jack Higley asked Ravencroft as the witch hunter made his way between the horse stalls. The stablemaster was a young man, his handsome face edged with an almost feminine delicacy. He held his head high and walked with a self-assurance that was surprising in someone who'd only held his position for a year. From the guarded talk he'd been able to wheedle out of the grooms, Higley was competent in his role, but hardly brilliant. Not so expert as to justify either his stature or his confidence.

"Yes,' Ravencroft replied with a grin. 'I think I've seen all I needed to see."

Higley frowned and scratched his forehead. "For the life of me, I don't see how interrupting the routine I've established here is going to help you find the beast that's been terrorizing the village."

"That's why I am a witch hunter and you are... well... what you are." Ravencroft made an extravagant flourish with his hand. "Werewolves often favor horsemeat. It would be natural for one to pay undue attention to a place like this. Even in human form, the proclivities of the wolf would nag at the mind. Perhaps make the monster betray himself by indulging his unnatural tastes." Ravencroft chuckled again when he saw Higley start at that last comment. Any doubt as to his course was removed in that instant. He glanced back, unsurprised to find that some of the workers were malingering around the stalls, trying to overhear the witch hunter's summation. The talk of monsters was for their benefit. The mention of unnatural tastes was something for Higley's benefit alone.

Ravencroft could feel the stablemaster staring after him all the way back to the manor. Higley probably didn't know for certain if the witch hunter knew of his illicit activities, but he'd certainly put the fear of discovery into the man. Fear and uncertainty would make him delay running to his confederate. Which served Ravencroft's own plans. He didn't want anyone broaching this subject to Roderick Thorne.

That was a task for the witch hunter and the witch hunter alone.

Ravencroft hurried to fetch Kaltenbrun. He found the big German in the kitchen, alternately gnawing at a hambone and flirting with a rosy-cheeked scullery maid. "On your feet, you lout," he reproved his henchman. "The pot's coming to a boil and I may need your muscles to keep from getting scalded."

Kaltenbrun stood with such abruptness that he kicked the bench over onto the floor. "You've found the werewolf?"

"Less questions, more action," Ravencroft told the warrior. "You'll understand everything soon enough." He motioned impatiently for Kaltenbrun to follow him, then stepped aside so the German could precede him back up the stairs. There was, after all, just a chance Higley hadn't delayed speaking with Roderick. If so, the witch hunter was more comfortable letting Kaltenbrun go first.

Roderick Thorne was behind the cherrywood desk in the manor's study, inspecting the estate's accounts. It was a duty his father had set upon him some years ago, a way of preparing the heir for the responsibilities of his inheritance. The younger Thorne took his labor as an unpleasant necessity and when he looked up to see the steward conduct Ravencroft and Kaltenbrun into the room he made no effort to hide the irritation he felt.

"This is poor timing, Ravencroft," Roderick grumbled. "I've much to do before I'm through here. Come back another time." He emphasized his mood with a dismissive flick of his hand and lowered his gaze back to the papers spread across the desk.

Ravencroft walked across the study, his gaze becoming more intense with each step. The expression on his face had in it all the threat and authority necessary to make a country squire shiver in his boots and crack the self-importance of a town magistrate. Roderick sensed the change in the witch hunter's attitude and when he looked up from his papers, uneasiness wormed its way into his visage.

"I assure you it would be more prudent to speak with me now," Ravencroft said in a voice as cold as the grave. "Together we might be able to come to a compromise. Should I be forced to broach this subject with Lord Thorne first, it will go much the worse for you."

Roderick made an effort to regain his poise. "You've the audacity to speak to me..."

The witch hunter slammed his fist on the desk. "I'm Parliament's appointed agent," he snarled. "A lord with the shadow of Cavalier sentiments hanging over him will listen to me, I assure you." An ophidian smile pulled at Ravencroft's mouth. "Should I tell him about his son... and certain activities?"

From his post near the doorway, Kaltenbrun did his best to follow the conversation. The German's English wasn't firm enough to recognize the nuances of what was being said, nor the subtext that was being left unsaid. An understanding was slowly developing between Ravencroft and Roderick, one that firmly placed power in the witch hunter's hands.

"John Higley." Just hearing Ravencroft utter the name caused the color to drain from Roderick's face. The heir's shoulders slumped in defeat.

"You can leave us now, friend Kaltenbrun," Ravencroft told the warrior. "Master Thorne will present me with no more trouble." A low chuckle escaped the witch hunter as he stared down at Roderick. "We've much to talk about, he and I. Plans to discuss and arrangements to make. Ones that, I trust, will be mutually generous."

Ravencroft waited until Kaltenbrun had withdrawn before he told Roderick about what he'd seen and heard at the stables... and the conclusions he'd drawn. The heir made only the weakest effort at dissembling before submitting completely to the accusations. From there, it was a simple matter to gain the man's cooperation.

The witch hunter could already feel the gold that would soon be in his purse.

***

Thaddeus Thorne stormed into the wine cellar flanked by two of his burliest retainers. All three men carried swords and pistols and looked quite ready to put them to use. The nobleman's frame quivered with the intensity of his anger as he descended the stairs. It took him only a moment to orient himself and spot the witch hunter in the half-lit gloom.

Much of the cellar was given over to wine racks and massive wooden casks, but an area had been left open for a long table and a few benches, an accommodation for those moments when it was more convenient to sample spirits where they'd been laid. It was here that Ravencroft awaited the master of Thorneshire. He stood with his arms crossed, a severe look on his face. Nearby, seated in a chair, his hands tied and the hulking form of Kaltenbrun looming over him, was Roderick.

"You dare!" Lord Thorne bellowed, eyes glaring at Ravencroft. "I'll have you whipped, you unruly cur!"

The witch hunter unfolded his arms and held forth a sheet of parchment. The curious action caused Lord Thorne to pause, the unexpectedness stunning him more than any display of weaponry could have. From across the cellar, he couldn't tell what was written on the paper, but he saw a waxen seal towards the bottom that looked only too familiar.

"I dare because the truth always demands risk from those who would find it," Ravencroft declared. He waved the document at Lord Thorne. "A timid man would never have had the courage to follow the evidence I uncovered. A coward would never have presumed to chase this trail back to the beast's lair! The wretch would have shivered before the terror of the truth he'd exposed!" He brushed his thumb beneath the waxen seal, the seal of Thorne. "Confession! The confession of your son!"

Lord Thorne shook his head, incredulity warring with horror for mastery of his features. "Lies! Outrageous lies!" he sputtered. "You've tortured these lies from my son! By God, Ravencroft, I'll flay the skin from your carcass for this!"

Ravencroft cast a hasty glance at Kaltenbrun. Hidden behind the back of Roderick's chair, he knew the German had a pistol at the ready, he only hoped he was quick if things came to violence. If the witch hunter had overplayed his hand.

"The only torment your son has suffered is that of his own conscience," Ravencroft told the enraged father. "But assure yourself of this. Look for any mark upon his person." Deftly he stepped aside and allowed the nobleman to rush over to Roderick. Forgetting any sense of decorum, Thaddeus knelt and grasped his son.

"While you are about it, look for the evidence of the beast," Ravencroft advised. "Look for the traces of the werewolf that linger even when it hides itself in human form." The witch hunter folded the parchment and stuffed it beneath the breast of his tunic. "Note the sharp-shaped ears. The long fingers. The keen teeth. The little traces of the wolf that remain in the man."

Lord Thorne snapped his head around and glared at Ravencroft. "You're mad! There aren't such things!"

The nobleman had started to pull at Roderick's bindings. Now the son pulled away from his father and slumped back in the chair. He looked over at Ravencroft, a hint of uncertainty in his eyes. For a moment, the witch hunter worried that his plan was going to fall apart. Then Roderick did as Ravencroft had expected him to do.

"There *are* werewolves, father," Roderick said, his voice cracking with emotion. "There *are*, and I am one of them." He hung his head in shame, twisting away to hide his face when Lord Thorne would have looked into his eyes.

"Ridiculous!" Lord Thorne growled. "You've been beguiled by this... this charlatan." He shook his finger at Ravencroft. "This lunatic has made you believe this superstitious idiocy!"

"I see that it is necessary to show you." Ravencroft drew a long thin blade from his belt. More like a knitting needle than a dagger, he approached the two Thornes. He swept his gaze across the two henchmen who'd followed their master into the cellar. He was pleased to see that they were uneasy. The nobleman might condemn superstition all he liked, the commoners who served him weren't so assured that the village wasn't beset by a monster, or that the monster wasn't Roderick Thorne.

'I can show you that your son's confession is true,' Ravencroft declared. 'The werewolf and the witch are both creatures of the Devil. When Satan takes one of his slaves, he invariably leaves a mark upon them.' He pressed the sharp point of the blade against his finger, drawing a little bead of blood. He let the drop fall to the floor while Lord Thorne watched him. 'There will be a place upon your son's body that will refuse to bleed when pricked. That is the proof that he bears the Devil's mark.'

Hesitantly, Roderick looked from his father to the witch hunter. The heir nodded his head. 'Do what must be done,' he said, his voice little more than a hollow echo.

Completely bewildered, Lord Thorne stepped back as Kaltenbrun took hold of Roderick and led him to the table. The burly servants, momentarily uncertain of what to do, came forward to help the big German as he pushed the captive onto the table and started to strap him down. Flat on his belly, the heir kept his eyes locked on Ravencroft while Kaltenbrun cut away the prisoner's tunic, exposing his back.

Lord Thorne grabbed Ravencroft's arm when he started to approach the table. "Roderick's my son."

"Perhaps part of him is," the witch hunter conceded, "but there's a part of him that belongs to the Devil." Twisting away from the nobleman, Ravencroft jabbed the needle-like blade into Roderick's shoulder. The captive shuddered in pain, blood bubbling up from the cut. "It's rare to find the mark quickly," Ravencroft said, provoking another shudder from his prisoner.

"Superstitious drivel," Lord Thorne insisted. He looked to his men for support, but they wouldn't meet his gaze. "You must stop this." The nobleman's voice was almost pleading.

"You have to be shown," Ravencroft insisted, jabbing Roderick once more. "You must be made to believe, otherwise there can be no help for your son."

The examination continued for another half hour. Lord Thorne became more frantic each time Ravencroft pricked his son, but in his agitation, he neglected to exert the authority he still held. It didn't occur to him to summon more of his servants or even to use the weapons he carried. The nobleman's inaction was the first sign to the witch hunter that doubt had planted itself in Thaddeus's mind. He wasn't so confident that there were no such things as werewolves, or that his son might be one.

Ravencroft plied the dagger over and over. After the first few stabs, Roderick's agonized thrashings became wilder. Kaltenbrun had to lean over and hold the prisoner down. The heir cast a pleading look up at Ravencroft, but there was no pity in the witch hunter's eyes. "With so prominent a victim, the Devil will have hidden his mark well," he declared. "It may take some time to find where he's left his infernal touch."

The words brought a groan from Roderick. He clenched his teeth and shut his eyes as Ravencroft jabbed his flesh with the merciless steel. Blood dripped from the punctures, spattering the floor. Lord Thorne grew more frantic. Ravencroft watched the father more keenly than the son he was torturing. It was from Thaddeus, not Roderick, that he would take his cue.

"There," Kaltenbrun said, nodding his head at the spot near Roderick's hip that Ravencroft had just pricked. Though the sharp dagger had pressed into the skin, when the witch hunter had drawn back the instrument, no blood appeared. The skin was unmarred, just as though it hadn't been stabbed at all. The servants gasped and drew back. Lord Thorne stared in wide-eyed horror at the sight. Roderick's head sagged down against the table, a deep sigh – almost of relief – rasping through his body.

"Evidence," Ravencroft told the nobleman, sheathing the dagger. "Proof of the infernal influence that has claimed your son." The witch hunter leaned over the table. "Confess! Confess all! How did you come to be in league with Satan!"

His features still twisted with pain, Roderick answered the witch hunter's demands. "It was by chance. A fool's mistake. I was out hunting pheasant in Blackbriar when I grew thirsty. There was a puddle and I stopped to drink from it." A regretful moan shook through the prisoner. "Only after I'd drank did I see that there was the print of a paw at the bottom of the puddle."

Kaltenbrun scowled at the captive in horror. "He is drinking from the footprint of the wolf! Any man who does this..."

"Opens himself to the spirit of the wolf," Ravencroft said. "Yes, perhaps I was hasty to accept that the last wolf is gone from England. A few may yet lurk in forgotten places. If so, then maybe what you say is true." He drew closer to his prisoner. "More questioning will tell me if you lie or not."

"Please!" Lord Thorne exclaimed. "You can't torture my son anymore! Roderick's told you what you wanted to know. Isn't there something you could do to help him?"

Ravencroft turned toward the noble, a pensive expression on his face. "I'm not sure," he said. "If what Roderick claims is true, then he has become a werewolf by accident rather than intention. That difference provides a possibility, an opening by which this foul curse could be exorcised." The witch hunter raised his hand in warning. "It will be an expensive and difficult process, but I am confident that it is possible to drive this darkness out of your son."

"Anything! Anything if you can save my boy!" The power and authority of his position was gone from Lord Thorne. Now he was simply a frightened father trying to save his child.

Despite his reserve, Ravencroft couldn't keep the hint of a smile from tugging at his mouth. "We must waste no time," he told Thaddeus. "Listen to me and I'll tell you what I'll need and what you must do..."

* * *

The exorcism was a grueling, eight-hour ordeal. Kaltenbrun was puzzled by much of what he saw. In none of the werewolf lore he'd been exposed to in his homeland had he ever heard that it was possible to remove the curse from someone. Only a silvered weapon or a roaring fire could exterminate the monsters. At least such was the wisdom in his native Germany.

Since entering Alexander Ravencroft's service, sold to the English witch hunter by his liege-lord Prince Ruprecht, Kaltenbrun's understanding of his new master's work had become ever more confused. Ravencroft operated by a mixture of chicanery, charlatanism, and government largess. Somewhere amid all that corruption, there was a core of arcane knowledge. Enough truth that the German was never certain when the witch hunter's activities were designed to exploit people or to combat a real occult threat.

The apparatus Ravencroft demanded from Lord Thorne only increased Kaltenbrun's confusion. Roderick was bound in silver chains and the rites of exorcism were conducted with a massive cross of silver. Certainly, the pure metal was inimical to werewolves, but the German noted the covetous way the witchfinder had accepted these instruments. Then there were the worried glances he sometimes cast on Roderick when the heir would cry out in pain from the ordeal. It could be that Ravencroft was worried about the welfare of his subject and the anger of Lord Thorne should the captive die during the exorcism. However, Kaltenbrun couldn't shake the idea that Ravencroft was worried that Roderick, unable to endure, was going to divulge a much different confession from the one he'd been coached into giving earlier. The relationship struck the German as more that of a thief worried his confederate was going to admit to a crime.

When the exorcism was finally concluded, an exhausted Roderick was led away to recuperate in his rooms. Lord Thorne was exalted to hear Ravencroft pronounce his son to be cured of his monstrous affliction. Such was the magnitude of his relief that he gave the witch hunter a small bag of gold. He didn't notice when Ravencroft gave a signal to Kaltenbrun that the German should secret the silver chain and cross among their own gear.

"This is most generous," Ravencroft told the nobleman, bouncing the bag of money in his hand. "Of course, I must beg your understanding on one more condition."

Lord Thorne's smile faltered. "You know *why* I'm paying you. That is for your silence. No one must ever know..."

"Of course not," the witch hunter hurried to assure Thaddeus. "It would be scandalous and just as much a slight on my own reputation. How would I be regarded if it was known I allowed even a former werewolf to live rather than seeing the wretch brought to the scaffold? I could lose my Parliamentary appointment!" Ravencroft's voice dropped to an insinuating whisper. "But it is on that matter that I need your indulgence. The people of Thorneshire still demand a conclusion to this affair. They need to know that the monster has been destroyed."

The nobleman shook his head. "But you said you wouldn't expose Roderick."

"No, but I still need to produce a werewolf for the villagers," Ravencroft said. Kaltenbrun paused while he packed their gear, bewildered by the scheme his master was now plotting.

"The people need to see the monster destroyed." Ravencroft laid his hand on Lord Thorne's shoulder. "Will you trust me to give them what they want? I'll find a likely candidate among your tenants and tell the people he's the werewolf. Since your son is cured and will commit no further attacks, the villagers will be convinced the man I condemn was the Beast of Blackbriar."

While Ravencroft described his scheme to Lord Thorne, the noble's expression became ever more disgusted. "A revolting proposition," he declared. Meeting the witchfinder's unwavering gaze, the man relented. "A necessary evil, I suppose. As you say, it will set the people's minds at rest and let them sleep easy in their beds." He made a dismissive wave of his hand and marched from the room. "Try not to choose anyone too important," he added before retreating into the hall.

"If he was, I wouldn't have had to spend so much time at Suncroft Abbey," Ravencroft commented under his breath. He turned to Kaltenbrun. "Hurry and get everything ready. We still have to visit the stables and speak with Higley."

Kaltenbrun frowned at the directions. "Why do you need to speak with Higley? You've already unmasked Roderick Thorne."

Ravencroft turned a patient smile on the German. Closing the door by which Lord Thorne had departed, the witch hunter walked over to Kaltenbrun. "Is it possible that Teutonic brain is so deucedly slow? Think man!"

"Roderick *isn't* the werewolf?" Kaltenbrun said, suggesting the first thing that occurred to him.

"Indeed," Ravencroft replied, jostling the bag of gold he held. "Fortunately, he had other secrets to hide, ones that have proven just as lucrative." He tossed the bag to Kaltenbrun to pack with the rest of their kit. "Should be twenty guineas there, but Higley will be holding even more for us. The son values our silence even more than his father does."

"If Roderick is not being the werewolf, why pay you?" Kaltenbrun was still wondering what hold Ravencroft had over the heir.

"Secret liaisons that his hidebound father would certainly not approve of," Ravencroft answered. "Something that might even see Roderick disinherited, put over in favor of some cousin." He paused and Kaltenbrun could tell he was ruminating on the scandal he'd uncovered. "All things considered; I think I'll advise Higley to make himself scarce. You see, he also shares Roderick's secret. Once he's had time to rest and think, Roderick might decide his lover is too much of a liability to have around. Lord Thorne just surrendered one of his tenants to be executed. I'd not expect the son to have more scrupples than the father."

Ravencroft laughed as he started to leave the room. "Yes, warning John Higley will be my good deed of the day."

"What do we do after that?" Kaltenbrun demanded.

The witch hunter turned, his expression grave. "Now that we've been paid, the hard work begins. We have to attend to a man named Edward Perot."

"Who's he?" the German asked.

Ravencroft laughed again. "The man we've been after from the beginning. The *real* werewolf."

***

103

The full moon shone down upon the pasture, illuminating the neglected sheep and the somnolent figure of a young shepherdess slumped against the trunk of a lonely tree. The pastoral scene might have been considered quaint and tranquil at another place or time. In Thorneshire, however, with the Beast of Blackbriar still abroad, a sinister pall hung over everything. Tragedy awaiting only the right moment to unfold.

At least Ravencroft hoped it would unfold. He scowled as he watched the moon move through the night sky. The hours were trickling away and still the quarry he hunted had yet to show.

"The werewolf too smart to being out tonight," Kaltenbrun whispered. Like the witch hunter, the German was concealed in a camouflaged pit at the edge of the pasture, only a narrow gap left exposed so the two men could spy upon their surroundings. The hiding spot reeked of sheep dung, scattered on the ground above the hole as a precaution to mask their scent from the monster they hunted.

"Impossible," Ravencroft said in a low hiss. He nodded his chin at the full moon. "Perot has been careful not to go prowling while we were around. It's been nearly a month since his last foray. Careful or not, the beast inside him is growing irascible. It needs to prowl! The full moon exerts a powerful influence upon werewolves. A lycanthrope who has indulged his bestial appetite earlier in the month can resist changing, but never one who has restrained himself for so long. No, friend Kaltenbrun, the beast is abroad this night! I'm certain of it."

Kaltenbrun shifted position within the pit, nudging Ravencroft with the funnel-like barrel of the blunderbuss he carried. He gave his master an apologetic smile. "Muscles get cramped," he explained.

"You'll have more than a cramp to worry about if you give our position away," Ravencroft chided him. "Remember, Perot has the sharpened senses of a wolf *and* the intellect to interpret what those senses tell him."

"Perhaps it isn't Perot," Kaltenbrun said. "You mistaken could be about who werewolf is. We are choosing this spot because of nearness to Perot's cottage."

Ravencroft shook his head. "It's Perot," he declared. "Everything fits too well. You didn't think I was making all those trips to the village while we were bivouacked at Suncroft merely as a deception? I was asking questions." A cold grin pulled at his features. "And getting answers." The chief asset of a witch hunter was the fearsome reputation his profession enjoyed. A nobleman might present obstacles, but commoners were only too quick to tell him whatever he wanted to know.

"I made inquiries at Thorneshire's inn," the witch hunter continued. "Found out who was able to provide some good venison at a modest price. In short, I was seeking a poacher. The predatory instincts of the wolf ever twist the mind of the werewolf, so it would be natural to look for a man whose profession related to hunting and bloodshed."

"On this you are convinced Perot is werewolf?"

Ravencroft smiled at the German's question. "Not entirely. I needed to know a bit more about the man. It seems he was an officer in Cromwell's army, discharged after all the fighting. He keeps to himself in a cottage near Blackbriar. Not quite a hermit, but certainly someone not overly fond of his fellow man."

"Why are the villagers not accusing him then?" Kaltenbrun wondered.

"Lack of courage. Perot was a captain in the war. He's held in a bit of awe by his neighbors." Ravencroft paused to watch the darkened fringe of forest at the border of the pasture. Just for an instant it seemed to him that he'd caught a hint of movement there. "I think his neighbors are too afraid to do anything. Even Lord Thorne pretty much leaves Perot alone. Worried the captain might still have some friends in London."

The witch hunter glanced down at the pair of horse pistols hanging from the holsters that crossed his chest. Each was primed and loaded, charged with extra powder and with a ball of silver behind the wading. He regretted melting down the silver cross to fabricate the bullets, but it was a necessary evil. Though there was debate among those who studied the occult about whether a werewolf could be harmed by ordinary weapons or if it needed silver to kill the infernal monsters, Ravencroft decided not to take any risks. Even if it could be harmed by a ball of lead, a silver bullet in its skull wasn't going to be any less lethal.

"There's the rub," Ravencroft commented. "Think how rare it is to find a witch among the rich and powerful. As a rule such people don't seek out infernal bargains because they already have too much to lose. No, it is among the impoverished that you find the lure of witchcraft is most prevalent. Those who have little to risk except their own intolerable and miserable circumstances. So with witchcraft, so with werewolfery." Ravencroft shook his head. "Of course the werewolf is more brutal and direct in his methods, but they both chase after the same thing. They desire power, the knowledge that they are superior to those around them. The werewolf exults in the raw, primal ferocity of the beast, in time coming to enjoy the bloodlust that accompanies his new shape."

"But for a man who was captain..."

Ravencroft sighed. "I think that was why Perot chose to become a beast. During the war he had rank and authority. Afterwards he had nothing, only the modest existence of a cottager. He wanted that sense of power back and employed diabolical means to regain it."

Holding up his hand, Ravencroft motioned Kaltenbrun to be quiet. There was no mistaking it now. A low, lean shadow was creeping out from the trees, carefully circling so that its scent wouldn't carry to the sheep. The witch hunter almost admired the wary stealth the figure exhibited as it slunk forward, stalking towards the tree and the shepherdess. *A bit closer, you hellish cur,* Ravencroft thought. *A bit closer and you'll be right where I want you.*

The shape continued its slow, cautious advance. Now, by the moonlight, Ravencroft could make out the iron-gray fur that covered the figure, the sharp ears that rose from the sides of its elongated head, twitching as they tried to drag the merest noise from the air. Once, as the thing hesitated in its approach, a lupine head was lifted. Ravencroft could make out every detail of the wolfish countenance, the long snout and the sharp fangs that peaked past the black lips. The lolling red tongue that panted eagerly for the prey it scented. Only in the eyes was the animal revealed to be something more than a simple beast, for the eyes didn't shine with the dull green of a wolf, but sparkled with the intensity of human understanding.

"Wait," Ravencroft hissed at Kaltenbrun when he sensed the German start to move. "Not yet."

The hunters watched as the werewolf stalked ever closer to the shepherdess. Finally, when it was still several yards off, Ravencroft could feel the tension that entered the monster's body. Every muscle tightened into a steel coil. The creature's attention was riveted on its intended victim, the whole world narrowing down to the limits of predator and prey.

Still unmoving, apparently lost in slumber, the shepherdess didn't react when the werewolf launched itself at her. The tensed muscles hurled the beast across the distance in a terrific lunge. In the blink of an eye, the savage gray shape slammed down upon the victim, crushing her beneath its mass. The lupine jaws locked about the throat, jerking the body from side to side. Sharp claws raked at the rough clothing, ripping and tearing at the cloth to ravage the flesh within.

Ravencroft almost laughed at the effectiveness of his decoy. He'd bought the clothes from one of the villagers, a man who was puzzled by the witch hunter's demands that his daughter should wear them throughout the day before he came to collect them. Her scent was strong enough to mask that of the straw he'd stuffed the decoy with. The werewolf had an almost comical look of surprise on its visage when it failed to taste blood on its tongue as it bit down on its prey.

"God's wrath is upon you!" Ravencroft shouted as he reared up from the pit and threw back the covering. He aimed one of his pistols, firing before the werewolf could recover from its surprise. The bullet slammed into the monster's shoulder, driving a pained yelp from the beast. Throwing aside the straw dummy, the creature faced its attacker.

"Yes, you bleed, cur!" Ravencroft snarled, jumping up from the pit and taking aim with his second pistol. The werewolf glared back at him, lips curled and fangs exposed in a feral snarl of its own.

The witch hunter fired, but this time the monster was ready for the attack. With preternatural speed, it threw itself to the ground the instant the hammer fell. The silver bullet whistled harmlessly past its lupine head.

Ravencroft felt a tingle of fear race down his spine as the werewolf sprang up to its feet. Instead of trying to flee, the enraged monster charged toward the witch hunter. In doing so, it abandoned the loping trot of a true wolf and adopted a scrambling, maddened scurry like some Barbary ape. Ravencroft reversed his hold on the empty pistol, intending to club the monster when it closed upon him. For all the good such an effort would do him.

The werewolf rushed in, reaching out with the fingers of its handlike forepaws. Fangs glistened in the moonlight and in the manlike eyes there was the vicious madness not of a wild beast but of a sadistic murderer.

"Kaltenbrun!" Ravencroft shouted to the German down in the pit.

The werewolf was only a dozen feet away when Kaltenbrun stood up. Alarm shone in the beast's eyes when it saw the second man and the wide-mouthed blunderbuss he held. Aware that the trap it had fallen into held more layers than it had expected, the monster contorted its body and tried to reverse course in mid-run. Before it could retreat, however, the blunderbuss roared.

There had been no need to melt down the silver chain that had held Roderick Thorne. It had simply been fed into the maw of the blunderbuss along with the powder that would send it flying from the gun's broad barrel. Useless at any great distance, in trying to rend Ravencroft the werewolf had brought itself well within Kaltenbrun's range. The silver chain rocketed outward in an explosion of flame and sound. The links, impelled at colossal speed, couldn't fail to strike their target. The monster's furry hide was shredded by the spinning chain, limbs ripped from sockets as the velocity of the shot expended its fury upon the body that blocked its trajectory.

A wretched howl rose from the bloodied, tattered werewolf. The mangled creature made only a few lurching steps in the direction of Blackbriar before it collapsed to the earth. A shudder swept through its bleeding frame, and then it was still.

"Well done, but we must work on your marksmanship," Ravencroft told Kaltenbrun. He pointed to a blackened patch of seared cloth along his sleeve where the discharge of the blunderbuss had scorched his coat.

"Seemed better than letting you get mauled," Kaltenbrun said, climbing out of the hole. He gestured with the smoking gun at the dead monster. "What do we do now?"

Ravencroft holstered his pistol and walked over to the werewolf. "We need to carry this into Thorneshire and show it off to the villagers." He glanced up and scowled at the moon. "We'd better be quick about it, too. With the dawn, if the scholars are right, the body will change back into that of Edward Perot.

They'll rest easier if they see the werewolf this way. It'll remove any doubt. Besides, the villagers may even reward us."

Kaltenbrun gave the witch hunter an incredulous look. 'But you've already been paid by Lord Thorne. And by Roderick.'

The witch hunter removed his hat and scratched his scalp. "You've a lot to learn about the business," he advised the German. "When it comes to payment, you can never be paid too much." He kicked the wolfish carcass stretched across the ground, half ready to jump back if it showed the least speck of life.

"No, you can never be paid too much in this line of work, friend Kaltenbrun," Ravencroft added, his tone a bit more confident now that he was convinced the werewolf was dead. "Never paid too much, or too often."

ABOUT THE AUTHOR

Exiled to the blazing wastes of Arizona for communing with ghastly Lovecraftian abominations, C. L. Werner strives to infect others with the grotesque images that infest his mind. He has written numerous novels and short stories in the worlds of Warhammer Fantasy, Warhammer 40,000, Age of Sigmar, Zombicide: Black Plague, Kings of War, Wild West Exodus, Iron Kingdoms, and the Tales of Asgard range of Marvel novels. His original fiction can be found in numerous anthologies and Tales from the Magician's Skull magazine. When not engaged in reading or writing, he is known to re-invest in the gaming community via far too many Kickstarter boardgame campaigns and to haunt obscure collectible shops to ferret out outré Godzilla memorabilia.

Holy Relic
By Scott Washburn

"Daddy? What's a war?"

Caledon Presley had just finished the blessing for the meal but now looked up from his dinner plate in surprise at the question. His six-year old son, Isiah, was staring at him with wide, curious eyes.

"A what?" he replied, not because he hadn't heard, but to buy some time to compose himself. He glanced at his wife, Shara, at the far end of the table. The expression of shock on her face told him she had heard their son as clearly as he had.

"A war, Daddy. What's a war?"

"Where did you hear that word?" demanded Shara. "It's a very bad word, Isiah!"

"Oh," said the boy, taken aback. "I'm sorry, Mama, I didn't know."

"Where did you hear it? Who said it to you?" persisted Shara. Caledon could see that his wife was upset, but he made a small gesture with his hand for her to calm down.

"The little man in the box said it," replied Isiah in a near-whisper.

"A man in a box?" asked Caledon, alarmed. "What box?"

"In the little house in the woods. He says it a lot."

"A little man in a box?" said Shara. "You should not make up tales!"

"But it's true!" insisted the boy. "I don't think he's a real man," he added. "He's flat. He's like a picture in the Book—but he moves and talks!"

Caledon looked at Shara and she stared back, her face gone white. She hastily made the holy sign: touching forehead, lips, navel, hand pressed to the heart—Father, Son, Mother, Daughter.

"Where... where is this little house, Isiah?" asked Caledon, speaking slowly.

"In the ravine, the other side of the cornfield, Daddy. It's weird-looking. It's not made of wood or stone, like our house. It's smooth an' shiny, sort of. But it's all buried under rocks and logs and branches an' stuff. I only found it 'cause a bogfrog I was chasin' hopped in there."

Caledon glanced out the window; the long summer day had hours yet until dark. "Well then!" he said as normally as he could force his voice to be. "Let's finish our dinner and then you shall show me the little man in the little house!"

"But Cal...!" exclaimed Shara.

"After dinner," he said firmly and his wife subsided. She stared at him, face creased in worry, but then their infant daughter started to cry and she had to redirect her attention. Isiah looked worriedly between his parents, but Caledon smiled at him and said, "Did you catch the bogfrog?"

"Nah, it got away."

"Perhaps you'll catch one tomorrow."

"Maybe." The boy brightened.

Later, the table was cleared and the dishes cleaned. Isiah needed to use the outhouse before they went and Sarah took the opportunity to speak to Caledon. "Cal!" she hissed. "You can't go! It's dangerous!"

"Apparently Isiah spent all afternoon there and took no harm. No physical harm anyway. It's probably safe enough."

"Safe! One of the... one of the Killers! Speaking of war! How can it be safe?"

"Just an old machine. Ages old, Love. It can't hurt us now."

"You don't know that! If the picture machine still works, who knows what else might work! At least go to the village and get some help. Speaker Milroy..."

"No!" He spoke more harshly than he intended and Shara flinched back. "Sorry. But no, I don't want to start a panic. And you've heard Milroy at the meetings; he hates the Killers as if they'd done something to him personally. If he hears about this, he'll put a ban on Isiah's 'little house' and everything for a mile around! Do you want to lose our house? Our farm?"

"No... no, but..."

"Let me go take a look and see. It's probably harmless. And we can cover it up so no one else ever finds it."

"Must you take Isiah?"

"I'll find it easier with him. And he's already seen it."

"But…" Their son came through the door and she was forced to stop.

"Come on, boy, let's go find your little man."

"Sure thing, Daddy! Follow me!" The boy's earlier worry had evaporated and he seemed to think this was some grand adventure. Caledon took his son's hand and they left the house together. The sun was closer to the horizon now and dipping behind some thin, high clouds which turned its usual orange into a deeper red. The Companion was a sharp white spark, a bit above and to the right.

They walked past the barn and the pen with the pigs and through the gate into the big pasture. Isiah pulled free from his hand and began to run.

"I'll race you!" he called. Caledon trotted after the boy, getting close enough to evoke squeals of laughter, but not quite close enough to catch him. When they got to the far fence, the one enclosing the cornfield, they didn't bother with the gate, but scrambled over, both of them laughing by now.

The pair walked slower as they neared the ravine, Isiah's laughter faltered and ceased. "Why was Mama so upset, Daddy? Did I do something wrong?"

"No, you didn't do anything wrong. Mama was just worried that you could have gotten hurt."

"What could hurt me? The little man is just a picture."

"Well, the picture is probably made by a… a machine. Machines can be dangerous."

"A machine?" said Isiah, his eyes going wide. "Speaker Milroy says that machines are… are evil. I never understood what he was talking about. Is the little man evil?"

"I guess we'll find out."

They came to the end of the cornfield and climbed the fence. Just beyond, the land fell away into a little valley with steep sides and a stream at the bottom. They made their way down to the edge of it. Big trees lined the banks and it was already quite dark there. Perhaps they should have brought a lantern.

"So where is this little house, son?"

"Down that way!" said the boy, pointing to the right. "Where all the rocks are."

They walked in that direction and Caledon saw that there was a place where the stream had cut away a section of rock forming almost a cliff. There were stones and boulders piled near the base all entangled with vines and bushes and even small trees. Caledon frowned. He'd been through here dozens of times fishing, and he'd never seen anything. What had his son found?

"There it is, right there!" shouted the boy who skipped ahead before he could stop him.

A dozen steps brought him to a spot where the vegetation had been torn away. A rounded piece of whitish metal was exposed. There was a dark opening in it the height and width of a man. Isiah went toward it.

"Son, wait," said Caledon firmly. "Let me look at this."

There was another piece of metal, about the same shape as the opening, lying to one side. It was bent and twisted. A large boulder lay a few feet away, half of it in the stream. Caledon looked up and near the top of the cliff he could see a spot where fresh stone was exposed.

"It looks like that big piece broke off and fell down here," he said. "It must have pushed away the stuff that was covering this and torn off the… the door. That's why we never saw it before."

"Guess so," said Isiah shrugging. "The bogfrog came this way an' I was chasing it 'til I saw this. Is it a bad machine, Daddy?"

"I don't know." He edged forward. The white metal was scratched and rusted in spots and smeared with mud. A bit of red caught his eye. It looked like a letter. Swallowing nervously, he brushed at the dried mud and revealed a red letter 'T'. He kept brushing and soon revealed more letters; an 'F', an 'N', and then more, one after the other. Eventually, his brushing found nothing else. He stepped back and read:

TFN Stalwart – EP38

Isiah was next to him staring. "What is that, Daddy?"

"I don't know."

"The little man is inside."

Caledon grimaced and looked through the opening. It was very dark inside except for a tiny green spot which pulsed on and off like a glowfly. As his eyes adjusted, he could see that there were half a dozen things which looked like tall, upholstered chairs against the inside wall of the space. He couldn't see much else. He'd have to come back in the morning with a lantern...

"It you touch the green spot the little man comes," said Isiah who was just behind him, peering past his legs.

Caledon hesitated. Perhaps he should go to the village and bring back some help. But his son had pushed the green spot and had taken no harm. He could do the same and see what there was to see. Then, tomorrow he could decide what to do about it.

He leaned forward and touched the green spot.

Instantly, a rectangle about the size of the Holy Book lit up just above the green spot. Caledon flinched backwards, reaching out to grab his son's hand. But nothing else happened, and after a moment the image of a man appeared in the rectangle.

He looked like an ordinary person like you'd meet in the village. Young, with a handsome face and short brown hair. The image only showed him from the shoulders up. His face looked weary and careworn. But it wasn't like some amazingly well-done painting, he was moving! It looked like he was just on the other side of a little window. His mouth opened and a voice filled the room.

"Personal war diary of Lieutenant Commander Leon Kantberger, commanding officer, TFN Stalwart, October 25, 2944."

"See? He said war, Daddy!" said Isiah.

"Hush, son, I want to hear."

The young man paused and shook his head. "Well, we are royally screwed, and this will probably be my last entry. Eight hours ago, we, along with the frigate Daring and the colony ship Finshaw Bay, entered system GSC-8497-253 and proceeded toward the third planet, per our orders. Two hours ago we picked up four ships dropping out of hyper. Sensors have confirmed them as K'tashi warships. They have taken on an intercept course. Their class is still unknown, but since they are hyper-capable, each one has to be at least a match for a frigate. So we are out gunned at least two to one and maybe worse." The man paused again and looked down for a moment and then up. It seemed to Caledon that he was looking right at him.

"We could probably stay ahead of them long enough to escape beyond the hyper-limit, but only by abandoning the Finshaw Bay. Commander Collingwood has said we are not going to do that and... and I have to agree with him. There are 20,000 people on that ship, and we can't... we just can't." He shook his head and then surprisingly, he laughed.

"Well, at least I don't have to pay those five credits to Ted Hastings! I bet him that this whole escort was a waste of time and there couldn't be any problem this far from the war zone. Ted told me that these days there isn't anywhere that's far from the war zone. Well, you were right about that, Ted. A shame the admiralty didn't listen to you and assign us a cruiser or two." The young man's smile faded.

"I'm going to send a copy of this and the ships' log and any further bridge recordings to one of the escape pods. Maybe someone will read this someday. If you do, I want you to know that I'm in command of the best damn crew in the fleet! God doesn't make 'em any better!" The man's face was twisted now and a tear glinted in one eye. "And Kathi? If you do get this, remember I love you. Take care of yourself and the baby. I..." There was a sudden loud noise like the screech of a rooster and the man looked away, startled. "Gotta go," he said. The image vanished, plunging the space into darkness.

Caledon stared into the dark for a moment and then started to turn away.

"There's more, Daddy. I didn't understand any of it, but there's more," said Isiah.

He looked back where the image had been and after a long moment there was a strange burst of light in the rectangle. The image was just a bunch of multicolored dots that made no sense. But after a bit, the dots faded, and he was looking into a room. The man he had seen before was sitting in a large chair near the center and there were a number of other people there, too. They were sitting at things like desks with their own glowing rectangles. But they were very small in this new image, and it was impossible to see any real detail. But the voices were as loud as before; several people were talking at once, but the man from before seemed to be doing most of it.

"Status," he said.

"Skipper, that last EMP burst fried the com lines to the escape pods. We probably lost a lot of the data. I've rerouted."

"Very well. Comm, can you raise Daring?"

"No sir, they're not answering, and I've lost their telemetry. They're in a stable orbit, but I... I think they've had it, sir."

"Acknowledged. Sensors, what can you make of Bogey Two?"

"Looks dead, Skipper, emissions are way down and there's water vapor and debris all around 'em."

"Good, but keep an eye on them, they could still have a sting left."

"Right."

"What about One and Three?"

"Junk, sir, they won't be bothering anyone again."

"Damage Control, what's our status? Our main display is out up here."

"Not good, sir," said a voice that seemed far away for some reason. "Shields are down and I don't expect to have 'em back any time soon. Got more hull breaches than I can count, and all the pulse cannons are out except for number three."

"What about the drive...?"

"Sir! I've got a message from Finshaw Bay!"

"Put it on. Captain Perkins, what's your status?"

Another far-away voice began speaking; it was rough and hard to hear. Caledon took a step closer to the rectangle.

"We're in trouble, Commander. Our drive is out and with the evasive actions we took before they hit us, we've lost orbital velocity. I've still got partial power on the anti-gravs, so we can probably do some sort of a controlled crash, but we'll never lift again."

"Have you got eyes on Bogey Four, Captain? We took out the other three, but the last one is out of sight around the planet."

"Yes… yes, it's out there. Relaying our sensor data. Oh God, it looks like it's coming for us! Can you help?"

"We'll try, but Daring is gone and we're hurt pretty bad ourselves…"

"You must help us! By the time we're grounded it will be right on top of us! I can't possibly get all of the colonist far enough away before they…"

"We'll do our best but…."

"It's your duty, dammit! Your…" The other voice faded away.

"They're out of LOS, sir, but we got a good read on Bogey Four, putting it on tactical."

There was a pause in the talking. Isiah suddenly said: "What's happening, Daddy? Is this… is this the war?"

"I think it must be, son." Caledon had no experience with war—who among the People did? But what else could this be? The people in the picture must be… warriors… killers…

"It's… scary."

"Yes."

"What do you think, Number One?" They were talking again. Caledon thought it was the young man.

"Well, Skipper, if they stay on that last vector we got from Finshaw Bay, we could accelerate at full, stay just above the atmosphere, and put our last two torpedoes right up their ass. Might catch 'em by surprise."

"Yeah… might work…"

"Sir! That's suicide! Even if we get them, with no shields they'll take us with them!" This new voice sounded angry.

"Ensign, we cannot abandon a ship full of civilians…"

"Civilians!" said the angry voice. "Cowards you mean! You know who those people are, don't you? A bunch of stinking pacifists! Goddam Bible-thumpers who hate machines, hate soldiers—hate us! They run away here and expect us to save their asses when…"

"That's enough, ensign!"

"We killed three of the K'tashi! That's enough! We can still make a run for the hyper limit and…"

"And never look ourselves in the mirror again, Danny!" Another new voice.

"So you wanna die for those...?"

"Enough! Shut up, all of you!" The tiny man in the glowing rectangle was on his feet and the talking stopped. After a moment the young man spoke again. "I don't care who those people are! All that matters is that they are humans! Humans who I will not leave to the K'tashi! They might not just nuke them, and you know what K'Tashi do to humans they capture! That's not going to happen! Not while I'm captain of this ship!" The talking stopped and there was a long silence.

"Why's he so angry, Daddy?" said Isiah in a small voice.

Caledon didn't answer. Couldn't answer. His eyes were nailed to the glowing rectangle.

"Orders, sir?" said someone at last.

"Navigation, plot a course like the Exec suggested. Helm, we'll need every gee we can muster. Weapons, stand by on the torpedoes. Communications.... Launch escape pod thirty-eight."

"Aye aye, sir!' shouted half a dozen people all at once.

"Gentlemen, ladies, it's been an honor serving..."

The rectangle went blank and the space was dark again, except for the pulsing green light.

"I think that's all, Daddy," said Isiah. "If you touch the green light it will do it all again."

With a trembling hand, Caledon Presley touched the green light again.

Watched it again.

Listened to it again.

When it ended it was nearly as dark outside the little room as it was inside. Caledon led his son out and looked up at the stars. Only a few could be seen between the leaves of the trees hanging over the stream. They went back to where they'd come down the bank and awkwardly scrambled back up. Neither of them said a word until they reached the meadow. Caledon stopped and looked up at the sky again.

"What did it mean, Daddy? Is the little man evil? Were those other people evil?"

"No... no, I don't think they were evil, Isiah."

He continued to stare at the sky. A small bright speck crawled slowly along. You could often see it just after sunset or before sunrise. For reasons no one could remember it was called the Stalwart Angel... It was supposed to be good luck.

"But who were they, then?" asked his son.

"I think they were angels, boy. I think they were angels who saved us all."

ABOUT THE AUTHOR

Scott Washburn full-time writer, an avid reader of military history as well as long time re-enactor and wargamer. He is the creative force behind the "Great Martian War" series, the author of *The Terran Consensus*, *Across the Great Rift*, *Broken Alliance* and several short stories. He is the owner of Paper Terrain.

Home Field Advantage
By Ben Stoddard

It was about halfway through the first quarter, and the Greensburg Wildcats were down by six points against the Bright County Sheriffs, when the Object appeared. This was largely seen as upsetting, because the Wildcats had been favored to win by all the local sportscasters, and besides, it was their homecoming game and the stands were packed with spectators cheering them on and this interrupted the game.

The Object started out as an orb about the size of a classic Volkswagen Beetle, made up of what appeared to be the dark emptiness that exists between the stars. It hovered just over the center of the fifty-yard line. The Sheriffs had been attempting their two-point conversion at the time, and the attention of the crowd had been on the other side of the field. Thankfully the Wildcats had been able to stop the opposing team from converting the two points, which would prove crucial later on in the game.

"Let's go WILDCATS!" the crowd cheered as their team lined up to receive the kick.

For the most part, everyone ignored the Object. The ball was kicked and was returned to the forty-yard line, placing the action almost in the middle of the field. The defense grumbled-because they had to run around the giant orb to reach the receiver – someone called for a penalty.

After the impressive run, it was time for the Wildcat's offense to take the field, and it was no one's surprise when Bucky Corpus, the star quarterback took the field. Bucky was a local hero, he exuded the boy-next-door kind of charm that won over anyone who talked to him. He got decent enough grades, was a natural-born leader, and he had nearly led the Wildcats to their state championship the year before. The road to state had only been stopped by a minor injury in the final quarter of the last game by an unfortunate tackle that had dislocated his shoulder and torn the tendons in his throwing arm. However, after a small surgery to reconnect the torn ligaments and a few months of physical therapy (a small price to pay), he'd been able to make a full recovery. This football season was his chance for redemption.

"Alright, boys, here's the play. We're going deep. Joe, I want you running a long S route right past that thing in the middle of the field. Use it as a screen, they won't go near you." Bucky declared as the team huddled around him.

"But Coach told us to run the ball," someone protested.

"Coach wants us to play it safe, but safe doesn't win championships, and it doesn't impress the girls, now does it?!" Bucky reached up and clapped Joe Abers on the shoulder. "You ready to make our folks proud and maybe score some action *off* the field?" The wide receiver smiled underneath his facemask and nodded vigorously. Bucky grinned in response, called the count and broke the huddle.

The energy was palpable as the ball was hiked and Joe took off running his route that skirted past the Object. Number 38 on the Sheriffs, a third stringer without many prospects for college chased after him. Joe juked left and tricked Number 38, leaping up to catch the pass from Bucky even as 38 dove left to try and tackle Joe and missed entirely. The unfortunate player's momentum carried him forward and he slammed his whole-body weight into the Object.

The effect was instantaneous. Number 38 exploded into a shower of red mist and bone fragments that painted the barely visible Wildcat symbol on the field beneath it a vivid scarlet hue, as well as several other players nearby. The arena went absolutely silent. Most of the Sheriffs looked at where their former teammate had just been standing. No one in the crowds said anything and the cheers ground to a halt.

Silence pervaded the stadium. No one dared to move.

Well, almost no one.

Joe Abers was still moving, slowly at first, and then speeding up as he put distance between him and the defense. He sprinted toward the end zone. No whistle had been blown, no flag had been thrown, and the ball was still live, unlike poor Number 38. Too late, the Sheriff defense realized this, and by then Joe had already run the fifty yards towards the endzone.

Touchdown.

As soon as the referees blew their whistle and signaled that it was good, the home team spectators exploded into cheers and whistles. The Sheriffs grumbled that there should have been a penalty for excessive roughness on the Wildcats, but they were overruled when they tried to challenge the referees.

Both sides were amazed by the daring stunt orchestrated by Bucky Corpus, and after a PAT conversion that put them a point up over the opposition, he led the team on to a stunning victory over the Sheriffs. The final score was a whopping 42 to 6.

WILDCATS BEAT SHERIFFS TO A BLOODY PULP IN FRIDAY'S GAME! The local news site read the next day. Some of the townsfolk had the good manners to be mortified by the somewhat tasteless headline, but most chuckled at the morbid humor. The article was printed out and taped all around the school, from the bathrooms and cafeteria and even on the statue of Ishmael Thompson, the founder of Greensburg, which sat in the main foyer. When school resumed on Monday you couldn't walk ten feet without seeing it. Bucky was the king of the school for his daring tactics at using their "home field advantage," the name the locals were giving the Object, to such amazing results.

There was also a brief memorial article dedicated to Number 38 (they used his name of course, but it was something forgettable and most people referred to him by his jersey number after that anyways) explaining how the town's "thoughts and prayers" went out to the bereaved family. Several local businesses even pooled their resources to come up with the "38 Special Fund" as a type of charity to help benefit under achieving athletes with their academics.

Number 38's family was quick to criticize the charity. They cried out for justice and tried to bring legal action against the Greensburg High School for permitting their student to play in such dangerous circumstances. Sadly, the family died in an unrelated home invasion incident shortly after declaring their intent to sue. Evidently a drifter forced his way into their house, killed everyone there, and then turned the pistol he used to dispatch the family on himself.

Neighbors had heard the man screaming about how he just wanted the pressure in his skull to stop right before the first gunshot rang out. They called the police, but it was too late and by the time that they arrived on the scene the only one that was needed was the coroner. This tragedy had the unintended consequence of driving the donations higher for the 38 Special Fund, which reached a status worthy of national attention.

"What is the impetus for this charity?" an interviewer once asked Jim Bowers, the vice-principal of Greensburg High and founder of the 38 Special Fund.

"Well, we wanted something that let the student athletes in our area know that we are thinking of them. The funds from this charity are used to create scholarships for players who might otherwise not be able to attend higher education. We feel that it is in keeping with the spirit of Number 38 who left everything on the field for this All-American tradition of football. We wouldn't want his sacrifice to be in vain, now would we?"

Meanwhile, the impressive victory over Bright County had shot Bucky's popularity through the roof. He'd been interviewed by the local news stations and had finally worked up the courage to ask out his long-time crush, Ada Lam the captain of the cheer squad. It seemed as though everything was coming up roses for this hometown hero, and the locals ate it up.

Perhaps it was the onset of the headaches that made his story so popular among the people of the town. People were looking for something to distract them from the lingering pain. Everyone was complaining of it, it seemed. The local Dr. Brown had prescribed so much headache medicine that the pharmacy couldn't keep up with demand and the townsfolk had to travel to neighboring counties just to get their medicine bottles filled. The pills worked, at least somewhat. Everyone complained of nightmares and difficulty sleeping at night, their dreams filled with bloody visions and screams waking them into the cold confines of their sweat-drenched sheets. Most people chalked it up to side effects of the medicine and figured that the nightmares were better than the waking agony of the headaches.

Greensburg Field was another aspect of interest that was beginning to gather more and more attention. The object had grown slightly since the last game. Where before it had simply occupied a car-sized chunk in the middle of the field, now it stretched to the forty-yard lines on either side of the center and equal distance to the edges of the field so that there was only a few feet on either side of the Object before the out-of-bounds markers. The coaches grumbled about this, complaining that it was damn inconvenient to have to move practice to either side of the Object so as to not risk a player accidently touching it.

The principal stressed that it was for the players' safety, and that he didn't want to have to make any more uncomfortable phone calls to parents should something unfortunate happen. The coaching staff continued to complain, but they complied with the mandate.

Friday night rolled around again, and the Wildcats were due for another home game, this time against the Daybrow Cardinals. It was whispered that there would be several college scouts in the stands there to watch the whole team and pick out individuals to watch for potential scholarship recipients. It was a poorly kept secret that they were mostly there to see Bucky in action.

The school rolled out the red carpet for this game. They had a booth constructed for people to donate to the 38 Special Fund and booked three different food trucks from the area to sell concessions. They even enlisted students from the technology club to set up cameras to broadcast the game online to any townsfolk who couldn't make it out to the stands.

The game started out shaky for the Wildcats. With the Object having expanded to cover even more of the field, the passable space on the edges made for natural chokepoints where it became nearly impossible for anyone to get the ball through. But an unfortunate fumble by the Wildcats from a certain Steve Lowry led to a Cardinals' recovery which they were able to convert into a field goal for three points right before the half time buzzer.

In the locker room, emotions were running low. Then Bucky stood up to address the otherwise quiet room.

"We've had a rough start out there," he said while looking at each of the players in turn. His gaze lingered on Steve Lowry as he delivered the next part. "We've made some bad mistakes that have cost us. But this game isn't over, not by a long shot! We still have half a game ahead of us, and there is so much left to give. Are you ready to give it your all?!"

The rest of the team gave a few halting cries in response to this, and Bucky shook his head.

"That's not good enough. Daybrow is a good team, and if we're going to beat them, we have to be willing to sacrifice *everything* in pursuit of that victory. If we don't win this game, then we do not qualify for the state playoffs. Are you willing to give up on that dream so easily?" This time the response was more confident, and a resounding "NO!" answered back.

"Good! That's better! We are Wildcats! In the real world, wildcats eat cardinals, and this is true on the football field, too! So tell me, what are you willing to give?!"

"EVERYTHING!!" this time the sound echoed off the tiled walls of the locker room, rebounding out until the many voices of the team became one, monstrous sound that loomed above them like some terrible beast.

"Will you sacrifice what is needed?!"

"YES!"

"Then let's get out there and show them how to play football! Everyone cheer on three! 1…2…3!"

"WILDCATS!" the team cheered, and the sound was the thunder of an oncoming storm. They stormed the field chanting their fight song with a chorus of "Wildcats! Wildcats! Wildcats! Stalk the prey! Win the day!" lifting to the darkened sky above them and was swallowed by the stadium lights staring overhead.

It wasn't until late in the fourth quarter, however, that Bucky pulled Steve Lowry aside. Neither team had been able to score any additional points. No one could get their offense past the Object taking up the middle of the field. Bucky knew that Steve was feeling as though he had let his team down by fumbling the ball before half time, resulting in the Cardinals scoring the only points currently on the board. Bucky also knew that they had reached a level of desperation that required a daring strategy to win the day.

"Steve, I need a volunteer, and I think you're looking for some redemption." Bucky flashed his white-toothed grin and Steve's face lit up underneath his helmet's facemask.

"What ya got in mind, QB?" he asked eagerly. Bucky took a slow breath and laid his plan out. Steve's expression fell as it was explained to him.

"Now, I know what you're thinking," Bucky said, "this is one helluva risk for something that might not pay off; but look at the clock. There's two minutes left, and the Cardinals are about to punt. They aren't about to risk trying to get around the middle of the field, and their hesitation, their lack of daring, is what is going to cost them the game. Steve, I don't blame you for losing us the ball, everyone makes mistakes in their life. You don't have to do this, and I fully understand if you don't want to go through with it, but we have a chance to take back this game. What do you want people to remember about this game tomorrow? Your fumble? Or your daring catch that went on to win us the game and sent us to state?"

The air hung thick as Bucky waited, staring anxiously into Steve's face. The Cardinals snapped the ball, the clock began ticking. Bucky was right, they kicked the ball down field, it cleared the Object and was returned by the Wildcats to about the thirty-yard line.

"Steve, it's show time. Are you in?" Bucky said as he strapped on his helmet. Steve let out a shaky sigh.

"Alright, I'll do it. But you make sure they remember me for this, you got that?" Bucky slapped him on the back and gave him a thumbs up as they rushed onto the field and into the offensive huddle where Bucky called the play. A few of the players gave him strange looks, but they broke and moved into position. Bucky came up, the ball was hiked, and he took several steps back, not even trying to fake out the defense that he was going for a pass. Bucky zeroed in on his target.

Steve was running forward, at a sprinting pace, his head turned back and his arms extended waiting for Bucky to throw the ball into his hands. A Cardinal player ran behind him, but at a much more hesitant pace. Bucky smiled and threw the ball. It was a perfect spiral that spun through the air with such precision, he might as well have walked up and handed it to him. Steve caught the ball with such ease that Bucky regretted that he hadn't thrown more passes his way over the course of the season.

Steve didn't stop running once he caught the ball, he was already going full tilt the whole time. So there was nothing he could do when he ran full force into the Object and exploded into a crimson fountain of blood and bits of bone right on the edge of the fifty yard line. The Wildcat stands were in an uproar! He did it! Steve Lowry had carried the ball to the middle of the field! That was further than either team had been able to make that entire night and the Wildcats now had a chance to score! At the very least, if they could just get a few more yards, they could kick a field goal to tie the game up and go into overtime!

Steve Lowry was the evening's hero.

The officials called a timeout as they adjusted the rules. They determined that the Object took up too much room to allow both teams to line up to the side of it and in a controversial call they decided to give a ten yard penalty to the defense for playing too tight and forcing the offense to run into the giant black orb. The Wildcat fans went wild. Now they were on the forty yard line! With a minute and a half left on the clock, there was time for at least two good plays if they hurried.

Bucky quickly huddled up the offense and called the next play, giving a quick speech about how they couldn't afford to waste Steve's sacrifice. He called a Hail Mary and got the team lined up on the ball before the clock could even get started. The ball was hiked and Bucky took a step back. He couldn't see any of his receivers, and his offensive line was struggling to keep defenders back. Bucky took another step, then another.

The crowd gasped as Bucky's foot landed within inches of the Object, but the sound was strange to him. The hiss of their collective worry distended through the air like a note of a song held on for too long and tilted slightly off key. Time slowed, he saw the defenders breaking through the line, but they were running at a snail's pace, as if the air between where he stood and where they were was filled with water.

Whispers entered into his head. At first they seemed like gibberish: harsh syllables that grated against his skin like a dull knife scratching across glass. Then the words gradually began to shift. He heard familiar sounds now, but the voices were guttural and thick.

"Tra…. dish… must…." the words tried vainly to make sense. Bucky didn't care, he was still searching for a receiver.

"Be… pre… zer" Bucky took a step forward and the voices faded away and time came screaming back into focus. The defenders that had broken through his line were now rushing him, but Bucky had already found his target and threw. The ball sailed down the field and into the open arms of Joe Abers who ran it into the end zone to the screams of the Wildcat stands. After a quick point after touchdown, the score stood at a tight seven to three. The Wildcats kicked, but with only forty-five seconds left on the clock and a lowly twenty-yard return on the kick, the Cardinals went down without a fight after that.

That night, at the post-game party Bucky confided in Ada as they stood on the back porch of Joe Abers' house, whose parents were out of town.

"Did I make the right call?" he asked, an open bottle in his hand. Ada stroked his arm and laid her head on his shoulder.

"Of course it was the right call, babe! We won the game because of you!" She nuzzled into the side of his neck and planted a few sweet kisses there. Bucky sighed contentedly, but he felt the beginnings of a headache coming on, and something still buzzed at the back of his mind and wouldn't let him enjoy the moment.

"Yeah, but poor Steve," he said, placing a hand on Ada's chin and lifting her face so that he could look into her eyes. "He'll never run another play, his whole career is done. That was his last game, all because I told him to take that risk."

"Oh Bucky, that's so sweet that you feel bad," Ada said, a small smile on her lips, "I could just eat you up, you're so sweet." She leaned in for a kiss, but Bucky pulled back.

"I'm serious, Ada! Was it worth it to win the game if it cost Steve the rest of the season? It took away any future chance he might have had of going pro, or at least playing in college." This caused Ada to roll her eyes.

"Yeah, as if Steve was ever going to go pro, the guy was second string varsity during his senior year. Don't worry, babe, you did the right thing. Now we have a shot at state because of you, and everyone is drinking toasts to Steve across town tonight. He'll be a hero because of you!"

"I don't know," he said, "I guess I just feel bad for him, is all."

"Aw, poor baby," she cooed and leaned in closer. "Is there anything I can do to make you feel better? I'll do anything!"

"Well," he said after a long pause, lifting his head and giving her a slow, hungry smile, "there is one thing." He lifted his hand and placed it on her upper thigh and pulled her close.

"Oh! Uh..." Ada was surprised by the sudden motion and blushed profusely. "I don't know, Bucky... I didn't bring anything to keep us safe. I'm not sure that I'm ready for that, or that I want to tonight."

"Don't worry baby, I've got excellent control. I'll keep us safe. And you did say you'd do *anything*." Bucky licked his lips, and Ada looked around nervously. Then she sighed and took his hand to lead him upstairs while the rest of the party cheered and whistled. Some of the cheers were for Steve, a good number were for Bucky and Ada as they ascended the stairs. Bucky flashed them a smile and a thumbs up.

Afterwards, he took Ada home and staggered his own way into bed. With as tired as he was, and still feeling the glowing effect of the game and his time with Ada, he thought he would sink into the deep darkness of a gentle sleep.

Instead, Bucky dreamed.

This was particularly unusual because he never remembered having dreams, ever. He'd also never really had the headaches that the rest of the town had complained of, at least not to the point he felt the need to complain about it. So, he hadn't been one to take the medication that was supposed to cause nightmares. But this night, the visions that haunted his dreams were vivid to the point of reality.

First, he had found himself sitting as if in a cloud of smoke, only his eyes didn't sting and he found he had no need to breathe. The smoke wasn't hot, either, in fact he found himself shivering from the cold that penetrated deep into his bones. The shifting darkness coalesced, shrinking into itself like fog being sucked out of a room through a vent. As Bucky watched it began to harden until a shiny exterior was before him and he recognized the midnight darkness of the Object standing before him. It was only once it had formed in its entirety that Bucky could see cold pin pricks of light behind it, and as he looked around, he saw them all around him. It was with a shock that he came to realize that these were stars.

The object travelled the heavens, seemingly without moving. Its dark shape simply shifted from place to place, until it homed in on a single star which grew brighter and brighter until it shone with the brightness of the sun at noon. Bucky watched with awe as rocks and debris, matter from across the cosmos was drawn to the Object, covering it and obscuring the sky beneath layers of earth.

Time passed in the strange way that it does in dreams, with eons passing in the blink of an eye while still causing the wear of the intervening years. Bucky felt his mind beginning to tear itself apart from the years of boring continuity where nothing seemed to happen, then, when brought to the brink of madness, something changed.

Moonlight split the gloom of the cavern where the Object had slumbered for countless millennia, and three creatures staggered into its presence. They crawled on four legs, no, not four legs, they were bent but their front legs were in fact arms. Their faces were low and squashed, their brows long and heavy. Thick, coarse hair covered them almost like fur. One of them was larger and seemed older than the other two. One was female, Bucky surmised due to a pair of flat breasts that hung from her chest. They reminded him of pictures from his science class from the previous week on evolution. The steps from monkey up to *homo erectus* or something like that, he hadn't paid much attention in class. These creatures looked like they came from somewhere in between the two ends of that picture.

The younger of the males purposefully seemed to place himself between the female and the older male, almost as if he was protecting her. No, protecting her was the wrong description, he was demonstrating ownership of her.

As these newcomers approached the Object, Bucky began to hear the same strange voices chanting that he had heard during the game, but it was as if they were far away and in a language he could not understand. The creatures got closer, and the chanting grew louder, and Bucky knew that they could hear it as well, for they looked around as if puzzled and afraid. The younger male covered his ears and screeched something at his older companion in a grunting language, grabbing his arm and pulling. The female wisely kept her distance. But the other creature was captivated, he reached out his hand to touch the Object, and Bucky braced himself to watch the creature's demise.

The younger one stopped him, pulling back harder and jerking to stop his elder from making contact. The older creature turned and snarled at the youth, reaching out to grab him by the throat. He turned and the chanting grew to a fevered pitch. The language became a series of grunts and squeals. Then the older beast threw the younger at the Object where he exploded in a burst of crimson just like Steve and Number 38. The beast who had just murdered his ward screamed, but it was not a scream of fear, nor of pain. It was of ecstasy. Bucky couldn't say how he knew, but the idea came unbidden into his mind in the strange manner of dreams, and he knew it to be true.

Time seemed to speed up. Bucky watched with disgust as the older male *claimed* the female. He watched as years sped by, and more females seemed to be drawn to the elder creature. Soon he was mating with them all, and his brood became strong and powerful. They were numerous, and Bucky was as impressed as much as he was disgusted by the elderly male's prowess in spreading his progeny to so many females. His children grew and became strong. If they weren't strong, then they were fed to the Object and in the ensuing frenzy that such an act created, more children would be conceived.

The pack became a tribe. The tradition of sacrifice continued. The young and unfit were fed to the Object, and it seemed to bless those that gave it the gift of their young. No female would mate with a male who did not murder another beast by throwing it to the Object. It was a death sentence to be weak among the tribe, for that meant you were easier to be fed to the sacrificial tradition. Eventually, when it seemed as though the Object had drunk enough blood, it faded away into nothing but a pinprick of darkness that was barely visible. The tribe broke apart and dissembled. Bucky couldn't say how long the Object had been present, but it looked as though generations of the ape-men had come and passed in its time.

The dream shifted, the chanting once more faded to a whisper at the back of his mind, and the cavern eroded away to become the basin of a larger canyon. The Object remained as a small dot while the rudimentary and primitive structures of a new society sprang up around where it had been. It reappeared and a crude temple was constructed around it and it began to grow in size. Bucky watched as something that looked far more human appeared, this time cradling what looked like a baby in its arms. This new being approached the Object, and Bucky could see that he, for he could see now that it was a man, although he was shorter and stockier than any man Bucky had ever known, was adorned with shiny bits of obsidian in his hair. The man chanted something and the voices in the back of Bucky's mind mirrored his cadence and tone, the language shifting to a parody of the man's own.

The prehistoric being lifted his baby above his head and cast it towards the Object to the same effect as the creatures who had been sacrificed beforehand. The baby became a bloody mist in the air. More sacrifices were brought and thrown at the Object's mercy, each one vanishing in a cloud of blood, and the man groomed with obsidian laughed as he grew fatter and older. All the while this happened, the temple became decorated with more animal skins and glittering but uncut gems. Great murals were painted on the walls and carved into the stone. The old man eventually died, reclining on a bed of soft furs with his sons and daughters and wives surrounding him, then he was buried with piles of animal skins and obsidian weapons. Great statues were erected to guard his grave and he was sealed away.

Then, the process repeated. Each generation that followed that first man throwing children and youth to sate the hunger of the giant black orb. Bucky saw bowed forms before it, praying before it. Some even volunteered to be sacrificed. This continued as the temple became adorned with more artistic murals, the priests were dressed in fine, soft furs, and riches poured through the halls.

Until, eventually, as the Object once again became sated, then it once again faded into nothing. A great civilization had sprung up around it, but in the orb's absence it crumbled and died. Wars and famine swept across the land. Bucky witnessed atrocities that seemed to go on forever but were gone in the blink of a feverish eye. He recoiled from the vision, but then the scene before him had become silent. The prehistoric men were gone, their civilization destroyed in a massive surge of anger and savagery and the wearying passage of time.

The canyon fell further away, and the landscape began to feel familiar to Bucky. He saw a figure dressed in mountain man animal skins, a white man this time, with a long bushy beard and a coon-tail hat. Bucky looked closer and realized that he recognized similarities between him and the statue of Ishmael Thompson, the founder of Greensburg, which stood in the foyer of his high school. He was guided by someone who looked like a native, much younger and dressed similarly, but with long black hair and a frightened look on his face. The guide gestured furiously at the Object and turned to go, but Ishmael stopped him, grabbing him by the wrist and clubbing him with the butt of his rifle. Ishmael then dragged his unconscious guide over to the Object and threw him into it, a smile on his face as he did so. Now the chanting changed again.

"Tra…dish…on… must… be…" The voices became clearer and as they spoke, Bucky watched the small outpost of Greensburg become established, watched how it grew and developed, the Object once again shrinking down to the size of a pin. Before it disappeared, Greensburg became a flourishing community with affluent citizens who flocked to its boundaries. Then he watched it slowly began to degrade. The moment it began to fail was when the high school was built and the space where the Object was located was cleared away to make room for a football field. Businesses began to close, the local silver mine dried up, and Greensburg began to decay.

"The… Tradition…" the voices now chanted, and Bucky could hear them clearly. The Object appeared before him, it swallowed up everything else so that it was all that he could see. The chanting became more intense.

"Must… be…" Something opened its eyes and focused on Bucky. He couldn't tell where, but he knew that the entity was somewhere within the Object, hidden away beneath its smooth, dark surface. The chanting grew louder, and the eyes twitched in his mind's imagination until it all shuddered to silence, and the eyes locked their gaze on him. A voice then spoke from a thousand mouths that screamed and whispered and laughed all at the same time. It was as deep as the oceans and as loud as a bursting star.

"The Tradition must be preserved," it said, and Bucky screamed, but it was the monster's voice that left his mouth.

He awoke with that horrible sound ringing in his ears. He sat bolt upright in his bed. A knock at his door and the sound of his mother's voice questioning him if he was alright brought him back to a sense of his surroundings, and in a ragged voice Bucky replied that it was only a nightmare. The vision was already fading, and by the time he lay back on his sweat-soaked pillow and closed his eyes, it was practically forgotten.

The next morning the footage of the game with the Cardinals was all over the internet, having been streamed online. National news outlets were covering the story and the narrow victory that the Wildcats were able to pull from the jaws of defeat. Sports Line did an entire breakdown of the now famous play and the catch by Steve Lowry that led to his team's victory. It was being heralded as a stroke of brilliance by all the analysts and full praise was given to Bucky's tenacity and his leadership in making the tough calls.

One station, on the other side of the country, dared to question the wisdom of sending a player screaming into the void in order to win a touchdown. The sportscaster also suggested that the Wildcats postpone the rest of their season while authorities work out how best to approach the touchy situation. The station that broadcast this opinion was quickly shouted down by others that claimed that these high schoolers were full of spirit and heralded them as the future of the NFL. A fire broke out at the building of the offending station, and tragically the fire department was unable to save any of the people trapped inside.

Later it was revealed that arson was the cause of the fire. When the arsonist was apprehended, he was caught on tape as screaming that he just wanted the pain to stop. He claimed that the shadows were in his head and squeezing his brain if he didn't do what they told him to do. He died mysteriously in his cell two days after being arrested.

An official statement from Greensburg High's head ~~varsity~~ coach was issued declaring that their full support was behind the team and that they would not postpone their season. In fact, the challenge was issued that any teams that were not too cowardly could come and challenge the Wildcats on their own home turf.

The cry was taken up, first by the surrounding counties, and then by the rest of the state. All demanded that the playoffs be suspended, and the championship be played at the Greensburg Stadium against the Wildcats. The challenge was seconded by the rest of the country as major news corporations and sport franchises echoed the call. The entirety of the high schools in the state pooled their players together to create an All-Star team from their members and it was decided to take the game to the Wildcats on their own home field.

There was a problem, however. The Object had grown so that it now covered the entirety of the center of the field. Its edges overlapped the thirty-yard lines on both sides and spilled into the out-of-bounds sections on the other sides. While certain risks to the youth on each team were acceptable, it wouldn't do to just throw them into harm's way without any clear path for either side to win. So the administrators of the high school football teams put their heads together and decided that the field would be extended in its width so that there would be no out-of-bounds sections so long as the players stayed within Greensburg Stadium.

The day of the game came, and as the players were dressing in the locker room, Bucky's head coach called him into his office.

"What's going on, Coach?"

"Bucky! Come on in. Why don't you close the door behind you?" Bucky was quick to obey without question. "Have a seat." Again, Bucky quickly obeyed.

"What's up, Coach?"

"It's a big day today, isn't it?"

"Sure is! I couldn't sleep last night from all the excitement, and I feel like I'm going to hurl if I think about it too much."

"I get it," Coach laughed quietly, "I remember being in your shoes. Well, similar shoes. There's never been anything quite like today's game. Greensburg has always been one of the best school sports programs in the state, but there's never been a time when it was us versus the rest of the state. I don't envy you the pressure."

"You're not really helping the need to puke, Coach. Unless your plan is to just push me over the edge."

"There's the trash if the need strikes you. Just don't get any on my shoes, if ya please." The coach laughed again, but then his face grew serious. "I have absolute faith in you, my boy. We've never seen a quarterback like you. You've got something special, like someone's looking out for you. Some might even call you blessed, but don't let that go to your head, you hear me?"

"Yessir, I won't."

"That's a good boy. Now, today is gonna require everything you got. Getting to this point has required a lot of sacrifice, and I think taking the win today is going to take a lot more. Are you willing to do that? Are you prepared to do what it takes?"

"I am sir, I promise."

"Glad to hear it. I told you that Greensburg has always been one of the top teams in the state, right? Possibly in the whole damned country!" The coach didn't wait for a reply, but Bucky nodded all the same while he kept on talking, pacing back and forth as he spoke.

"We have a tradition of winning. We've had seventeen state titles in my twenty years of coaching alone. The last couple of years have been the only losses we've ever suffered. Last year was particularly rough because you took us so close, but we flinched at the last second and that cost us dearly."

With that, the coach stopped and turned to face Bucky.

"Don't let that happen today, son, you hear me? Don't flinch away from your responsibility. There's a few out there that says what we're doing is dangerous, that we're playing fast and loose with your safety for something that isn't going to mean anything to your life after your last game is done. I say to hell with those people, they don't know what it's like to carry the weight of tradition on their shoulders. They don't know how much these victories can sustain you on the troubled nights when you fear that everything you've done with your life is pointless. You can look back on today for the rest of your days, my boy. Victory today is tantamount to immortality in the halls of this school. If you carry today, you'll join the ranks of those mighty men that came before you. Men that established the tradition of victory reaching back to the very founding of our town. You will be among those hallowed ranks, son, you will be the one to carry our tradition of victory and that is something to value your whole life because remember, always remember,"

The coach hovered over Bucky as he spoke, his face filling Bucky's vision until all he could see was a mouth and eyes hanging over him and a chill ran down his spine as his coach finished his thought.

"The Tradition must be preserved."

The words echoed around the office and rebounded in the small space. Bucky had visions flash before his eyes of the prehistoric man throwing his baby down in sacrifice, even though he could not remember the dream to give the image context in his mind. It was silent for some time before the coach dismissed him with a simple wave of the hand and Bucky walked stiffly from the office.

The game began like many others had before it. The Wildcats won the coin flip and chose to defer their receiving until the second half. But even as the opening plays were unfolding and Bucky watched his team defend against the All-Stars they faced, he noticed that something was different now. Their opponent was bold and tenacious. They ran plays that skirted near the Object without ever touching it. Some of the offense pushed the Wildcats close to the dark orb. But something was troubling Bucky, and he couldn't concentrate on the game.

"Bucky!" A voice called to him from the sidelines, and he turned to see Ada standing at the edge in her cheer uniform. She had broken off from the rest of the cheerleaders who were taking a break after leading a rallying cry from the stands. She stood there in her uniform, her hair done up in curls and tied back in pig tails, waving to him with an anxious smile on her face. Bucky walked over to her, his own eyes distracted between the game and his own thoughts.

"Ada, what's up?" he asked distractedly.

"I just wanted to wish you luck! And to let you know that I'm cheering you on!"

"Thanks, I appreciate it."

"How are you feeling?"

"I… I should be focused on the game, Ada. Thanks for coming to wish me luck, I'll look for you when we score our first touchdown, okay?" Bucky turned to go, but Ada reached out and grabbed his hand, stopping him.

"I know that there is a lot of pressure on you. But I know you'll do great! The girls and I have prepared a special cheer routine for you that we're going to perform at half time. I know that it won't directly influence the game, but I'm hoping that it will help in some small way."

There was something in the way she spoke, some lingering reticence that caused Bucky to pause. He turned back to her and saw that there were tears in her eyes, and unconsciously he reached up to brush them away. Ada pressed the side of her face into his hand.

"That feels good," she sighed.

"Ada... what is...?" Bucky knew the question that he needed to ask, but found that his lips wouldn't form the words. A cheer from the crowd cut through the moment and it was lost.

"Bucky! We recovered a fumble! You're up, my boy!" the coach called from the sidelines, and Bucky was forced to break eye contact with Ada.

"You'd better go, everyone is counting on you. I hope you make it all worthwhile. I've given you everything I have, so don't break me, okay?" Ada sighed and stepped back, pulling herself away from his touch. He stared at her for a moment, the same chill that had run through him in his coach's office again coursed through him and caused him to catch his breath.

"Bucky! Let's go! Get your head in the game!" Coach's voice cut through the moment and when Bucky blinked, Ada was gone. He shook his head and put his helmet on, rushing out to the waiting huddle with a play on his lips.

It was the hardest game he'd ever played, and even when he went on to games later in his career Bucky would always look back at this game as his most challenging. The defense forced him to play fast and loose with his team, and they ran closer and closer to the Object. One by one, his team vanished in spouts of pink mist as they collided with the orb. Sometimes they managed to take one of the enemy with them. Mike Richardson spun when he was tackled and managed to carry two defenders into the orb, and all three turned to clouds of viscera. The crowd went wild at that one, cheering and clapping so loudly that it took on the sound of thunder. It rattled Bucky's teeth, it was so loud. If he had paid attention he would have seen that fights had broken out among the spectators. Savagery abounded on all sides, but he couldn't be distracted from their drive down the field.

When the Wildcats finally scored their first touchdown, the watchers howled like animals and their cries reached the dark night above them. Bucky hadn't even realized that the sun had set and that the stadium lights had come on. The lights blacked out even the stars beyond so it looked as though they were playing inside of a great black dome, almost as if they were *inside* the Object.

The All-Stars fought back, clawing their way up the field after returning the kick. The Wildcats were already beginning to run on their third stringers for the defense because they had lost so many of their starters in that first push towards the end zone. The coach made the call to push as many of the other team into the Object that they could, in order to even the score. Joe Abers was the only one to question this call, and the coach yelled at him so loudly that even some of the frothing spectators from the stands looked down pityingly at him from their seats.

Immediately after that, Joe went in and did his duty. The All-Stars made a pass that connected with the intended receiver right next to the Object. Joe made the tackle but was just shy of the orb. As he stood up, he glanced over at the coach who nodded solemnly. Joe's shoulders sagged and he turned towards the receiver who was just getting to his feet and shoved him into the Object. The referees blew their whistles and threw flags, but Joe didn't seem to care, he just turned to look directly at Bucky before reaching up to put his hand against the Object, all without breaking eye contact with Bucky.

At half time, the score stood with the Wildcats at six and the All-Stars at seven. Half the team was out of the game already, but it was worse for the All-Stars after the coach's brutal call. As Bucky and the rest filed into their locker room, jerseys wet and sticky with blood and sweat, they saw that Coach was already standing at attention, ready for them with a speech. He locked eyes with Bucky and began to speak.

"We are in a tough situation tonight, boys, I don't think we've ever faced anything like this before. I've seen the fight that you've put up, and I must say that I am proud of you all. But it isn't enough. I've gotta ask you to put it all on the line. I know that's a helluva sacrifice that I'm asking of you, but you all are playing the game of your lives out there. Years from now you'll be able to look back on this night and say 'I played at the Wildcat Championship against the world' and it will dwarf any other story that anyone else will ever be able to tell in your presence. Men will shrink in defeat that they cannot compete with your story. Never before has the whole state combined against one school to try and deny them their right to be champions. There's never been such a high cost that a school has asked from its athletes. You have a chance to establish a new tradition among the hallowed halls of Greensburg High, and all of your names will be immortalized for being part of this history. But this is only if you want it. So, I have to ask you all, do you want this?"

The locker room immediately erupted into a chorus of cheers that echoed in the small space until it seemed as though the energy would cause the room to explode. Bucky's ears hurt from the sound, but he cheered louder than anyone else. It was several minutes before the team quieted enough that the coach could speak again.

"Now, I hear that the cheerleaders have put together something special for you. They want to show you the support that the community has given you, they want you to know how much they all want it to. I want you to go out and watch the display and think on how much *you* want this victory. Go on!" He ushered them out onto the field, where they were met with cheers from the crowd.

Ada Lam and the rest of the cheer squad was already on the field, their heads bowed and their arms by their sides. As the cheering died down, music came over the speakers and the cheerleaders began to dance. They waved their pom-poms in the air, the metallic ribbons catching the lights of the stadium and throwing it back among the football team. They leaped and spun, and were thrown through the air to land gracefully on their feet. The music shifted and became the Greensburg fight song.

"Wildcats! Wildcats! Wildcats! Seize the prey! Win the day!" the chorus repeated.

Throughout all of this, Bucky's eyes never left Ada as she spun and whirled through the air. He knew that she was acrobatic, but she took daring risks that took his breath away. As the fight song reached its apex, the dancers formed up to create an aisle in their middle leading up to a trio of their strongest members which stood directly in front of the Object. Ada paced out in front of the whole crew and faced the football team. She locked eyes with Bucky and blew him a kiss, which caused the audience to cheer in approval. Then she did a series of backflips that ended with her being lifted by the strong trio to stand on one leg high above the rest, her arms extended in a type of salute and the music cut out.

The crowd erupted into a chaotic mass of screams and cheers. But the cheer squad wasn't through yet. Ada waved to them all, then looked down and nodded at the trio supporting her. They returned the nod and then, as one, they threw her backwards into the Object. Just like that, she was gone.

Bucky started, rising to his feet, but before he could move the coach was there.

"Alright son. You've already made the sacrifices, all that is left is to claim your reward. Go forward and collect your reward?" The coach's voice echoed strangely, and again Bucky had an image flash through his mind. It was an image of a thousand eyes staring at him, and Coach's voice echoed from a thousand different mouths.

Bucky stared at him for a long minute, as thoughts raced through his mind. The rest of the world ground to silence around him, though he hardly noticed. He thought about what it had cost him to reach this point. He thought of how let-down his family and teammates would be if he didn't pull through tonight. He felt a headache pounding in his temples at the thought of disappointing all of them. He looked up at his coach and nodded hungrily.

"Yes sir."

The rest of the game was a blur. The nail in the coffin came at the end of the third quarter, though. The Wildcats were up by seven, the All-Stars had the ball and were on their own thirty-yard line. In an unusual and unexpected turn of events, the coach put Bucky in as his center linebacker. There were rumors later that Bucky had begged the coach to put him in but when asked, he always denied it. Bucky called for a center blitz, and when the ball was snapped, two thirds of the Wildcat defense charged across the line and attacked the opposing quarterback. The player turned to run, but in his hurry, he didn't look where he was going and ran right into the Object. He burst into the gory red mess that everyone always did, but he also managed to drop the ball before he did so. Bucky scooped it up and ran the full length of the field to score another touchdown. The Wildcats were now up by two touchdowns. Halfway through the fourth, even though the All-Stars rallied to score a second touchdown, they seemed to have accepted their defeat. Especially after the Wildcats stormed down the field and scored twice, and even kicked a field goal, all within the bounds of the fourth quarter. The final score for the game ended with the Wildcats sitting at thirty-one points, and the All-Stars at fourteen.

The crowd erupted in cheers and Bucky was hoisted up on the shoulders of his peers and paraded around as the spectators flooded the field. With all the bodies out on the turf it was inevitable that a few accidently bumped into the Object, and more than a few casualties were caused by this. At the end of the night there were about seventeen missing people cases filed when friends and family members didn't return home. This didn't include the dozens of bodies left in the stands from victims who had been beaten to death in brutal fistfights, or trampled when the fans took to the field after the final buzzer. But no one was going to allow those accidents to dampen the spirit of victory that pervaded the entire town that evening.

The town flourished under the fresh attention the championship brought them. Sports Illustrated did an article on the team and on Bucky. People from all over came to visit the stadium where the Wildcats fought all the rest of the schools in the state and won. Commemorative coins were made, and special collector trading cards for each of the players on the football team, too. These went for hundreds of dollars online through sports memorabilia sites. The mayor even praised the team, saying over a year later that they had almost single-handedly pulled the city of Greensburg out of a recession.

Bucky was a legend for the rest of his senior year, and he lived off that popularity for some time. He got free meals at the local diner, and his peers paid for his gas simply for the privilege of riding in his car with him and being seen with the local celebrity.

Colleges across the country offered him scholarships, but Bucky never wanted to go too far from home, so he ended up accepting a state-run university that lay within a thirty-minute drive from his home. Any other college he considered was met with a sickening feeling in his gut, and massive migraines that forced him to lay down in order to alleviate them.

Headaches had become a consistent part of his life from the night of the championship game on. Ever since the Object disappeared. They became particularly heinous whenever he tried to recall specific details from that night. Things like the name of his girlfriend... Addie, or Ava or something like that.

The school fight song also caused him fits for some reason.

He played college ball, but little to none of his high school celebrity transferred over and so he ended up playing second string QB for the first two years of school. During that time his grades suffered, and he ended up losing his scholarship. Still, he struggled on, the thought of doing anything else caused his migraines to return in full force. The doctors prescribed him anxiety medications, associating the pain with stress of the unknown.

Finally in his third year, he got bumped up to starter on the team. Three weeks into the season, though, he was tackled at a bad angle and his shoulder was dislocated again. A similar injury to the one he'd received in high school. The doctors analyzed it and he had another surgery, but this one was far less successful, and it required far more physical therapy sessions. It was during one of these sessions that he met Melinda. She was a nursing student applying the sticky pads for an electro-shock session onto his shoulder. Incidentally this required him to remove his shirt. Her cold hands (because she was always cold as death) caused goosebumps to rise over his bare skin.

"Almost there," she said, smiling awkwardly as she did so. "What happened to your shoulder that required all of this?"

"An old football injury that got worse," Bucky had replied with bitterness in his voice.

"My father and brothers both played football. I have a lot of fond memories of going to their games and cheering them on."

"Yeah well, the doctor says my playing days might be done. This is the second time I've had surgery on this shoulder, and this time it feels way worse."

"I'm sorry to hear that."

"Thanks, I guess."

After that, Melinda was always the nurse on staff when he came in for his sessions, and he began to realize that his headaches seemed less intense with her around. It wasn't long before he asked her to dinner. Then one date became three, one week of dating became several months, and soon they were engaged. Bucky couldn't imagine being with anyone else. Literally every time he tried his head began to pound as if someone were squeezing it in a vice.

His therapy sessions, however, did no good. After several months of going and still being unable to throw as far as he used to, the college coaches decided to cut him from the team entirely.

Bucky was devastated. He struggled through his last two years of college and barely managed to complete his program in Sports Science. The only way he was able to afford this is because of the 38 Special Fund, which was eagerly willing to help out the man who had been such a major part of its creation. Ironically, he was the last one awarded a scholarship, as the charity closed its doors due to lack of funding shortly afterwards.

The years after graduating college were rough for the Corpus family. Bucky's grades hadn't been exactly stellar and the career path he'd chosen required him to either go on for a higher degree in order to work at a university or become famous in in order to become an advisor for a professional team or commentator for a major sports network. Bucky had been banking on the latter. As such he was relegated to whatever work he could find. It didn't help that Melinda had become pregnant and shortly after gave birth to twins.

As student loan debt and hospital bills for the babies threatened to overwhelm him, Bucky turned to drink as a way of coping. He became distant and sullen. To her credit, Melinda stood by him through this, and he never turned to outright abusing her or the children. At least not physically. That was his rule: he never laid a hand on them. But he was never shy about talking of the glory days and how much better things used to be. When he had carried his team to triumph. These stories inevitably twisted him further down into his depression. It was as if a dark cloud had descended on their house that threatened to overwhelm them.

Then a miracle happened.

Bucky was sitting at his usual watering hole, a small, dingy bar near the interstate overpass, when a shadow slid into the seat next to him. He was already several drinks in and it took him a few minutes to realize that the shadowy person was talking to him.

"Well, I'll be. Bucky Corpus! In the flesh! I didn't think royalty like you would deign to visit their old stomping grounds. Why go back to the conquered lands when there is always new frontiers to see? Am I right?"

Bucky winced at how loud the voice was, and when he turned to look the stranger in the face, his eyes wouldn't focus long enough to get a good look at him.

"I like my home," Bucky slurred, and rubbed his eyes before squinting at the other person again. "I'm sorry, who are you?"

"Travis Davis, I'm the head coach for the varsity team at your alma mater!" The shadow smiled and held out a hand. Bucky looked at it a moment before turning back to his empty shot glass in front of him. Mr. Davis held up two fingers to the bartender and forked them down at the table, pointing with his other hand at Bucky's empty drink. With refills in hand, the newcomer took a bottle of aspirin out of his pocket and downed two of the white tablets.

"Headaches?" Bucky asked, nodding his thanks for the drink.

"Had a massive one ever since my assistant coach up and left us high and dry. Nothing seems to help, though."

"Oh?"

"Yup, he just disappeared last week. No notice, no explanation. Just one day he decided not to show up to practice. The next day, when someone went to his house, it was empty. Like no one had lived there in a long time. Weirdest thing you ever did see."

"I'm sorry to hear that." Bucky turned back to his glass and tried to signal the bartender for another round.

"That brings me to why I approached you. Now, this might be a cosmic coincidence, but I don't know that I believe in that kinda thing. I could really use the help of someone like you."

"Someone like me? A washed up drunk?"

"No, a champion. A man who understands the tradition of this town. Someone who's made the sacrifices necessary to carry his team to victory!"

"Oh hell," Bucky grumbled, feeling a migraine coming on.

"I could use you by my side to help whip the next generation of champions into shape. That is if you're interested."

"I haven't thrown a ball in a few years now." Bucky grumbled, his stomach twisted with anxiety, but his headache was receding.

"Doesn't matter, you still know the game. I'd be willing to bet you've still got a championship or two in your future. Plus, as paying gigs go for coaching, this one is pretty damn decent." Mr. Davis... no, it was Coach Davis... slid a business card across the bar to him. "Let me know as soon as you can if you're interested."

He thought about throwing the card away, but he tucked it into his back pocket when pressure started mounting on his temples and asked the coach for some of his aspirin. The next day Melinda found the business card while doing the laundry. They were already a couple months overdue on their hospital bills and it had been a few weeks since Bucky had been able to find any kind of work. She hounded him until he made the call.

His first day on the job Bucky walked out to the field. It was almost exactly how he remembered it being. Somehow, this energized him, and for the first time since re-injuring his shoulder, he felt a strange sensation of hope welling up inside of him. He took a deep breath and looked around the field. Some part of him knew exactly what he was looking for.

The Object had disappeared the night of the championship game. He couldn't remember if it had been before or after the game had ended. It might have been after that girl had... he stopped that thought before a headache could start.

Curious, he walked to the center of the field. It was as if something drew him there. Whispers in the back of his mind, a cool wind at his back pushing him towards it. He stood on the center of the fifty-yard line and stared down at the sigil of the Wildcats looking back at him. The creature snarled fiercely in its heraldic device that was painted over the expensive astro turf beneath him. The air seemed charged with electricity as he anticipated the coming practice sessions with his new students and players. He tilted his head back to revel in the warm afternoon sun, and as he did, something caught his eye hovering about a foot or so above his head. He looked closer, trying to make out what it was.

It was a small, dark orb the size of a pinhead, hovering in the air.

The whispers returned in the back of his mind and Bucky smiled in spite of himself. He looked over as the high school players, kitted out in their practice gear, filed onto the field and began stretching. Some of them looked over in his direction and leaned over to whisper to their neighbor. Probably wondering how this new coach would be, and if he could handle the quality of students that played for Greensburg's Wildcats.

Oh were they in for a surprise. Bucky's smile turned into a grin as he pushed himself to stand up straight again. He would drag them towards greatness, whether they wanted it or not. He would make Greensburg the greatest team in the country, and it would be remembered as the pinnacle of high school athletics long after its doors closed for the last time. No matter the cost, he would bring this to his home.

"After all," he muttered to himself, "the Tradition must be preserved."

About the Author

Ben lives in the wilds of Idaho, the land of potatoes, with his lovely wife and their kids. Ben is an English teacher who doesn't care enough about grammar to judge yours. He is an avid tabletop gamer and storyteller and has had a love of fantasy and adventure for as long as he can remember. More recently he has become enamored with horror and all its trappings and loves the twisted realities and the terrifying wonders that can be found in our universe. Of course, he is always more than happy to share this passion with as many people as are willing to endure his ramblings.

Rotten Letters

By Robert E Waters & Jason M Waters

John Masey refocused his binoculars down Bridgeport Road and found the young man in a shambling mass of Strikers moving slow but steady up the street. The boy, one of many among the desiccated, worn, and tattered array of undead—or whatever they were—was easy to spot because he wore the red *Izod* shirt that he had acquired at Winston State University's golf tournament less than a year ago. The putter that the boy held in his left hand, and now dragged along the road like a giant's cudgel, was rusty and worn. But he would not let it go, had never let it fall in the past several months since John had come to expect the boy's return, like clockwork, as the Striker horde made its tour of the neighborhood over and over and over again. The boy stood out among that decrepit mass. The boy was special.

The boy had a message for John tucked into his rotting gut.

John lowered his binoculars and let them rest on his chest. Leaning out his open window, he then raised his rifle and focused the scope on the head of the Striker closest to the boy. *Bam!* He sighted quickly to the other side of the boy and put another round in the next, and the next, and the next, until the mass began to break up, scatter, like a flock of geese responding to the blast of a shotgun. They got confused and peeled off in multiple directions, in twos, threes, and fours. But not the boy. He was undeterred by the shots, as John had predicted. His dead companions scattered, but the boy kept moving straight ahead, his attention and his bulbous, swollen eyes fixed on John's driveway.

John set down his rifle and put on his firefighter's uniform. He used to be a firefighter/EMT before the fall. The suit would protect him from any Striker attacks, and from what he was about to do. He wasn't concerned about the direction the boy would walk, but sometimes, an errant Striker followed the lad up to the car patio. Things could get dicey right quick if that happened. That's why John made sure that his firefighter's coat had a small revolver tucked into one of its pockets... just in case. The added clear plastic visor affixed to his helmet protected his face from sputum and blood from incessant Striker salivation.

John checked all creases and potential danger zones (air pockets, tears, crimps) on his uniform. Everything was in place. He took a deep breath, nodded, collected his courage, and stepped outside.

A warm day. Not humid, but the sun was bright. A breeze blew through the car patio attached to the side of the house. The car was gone, abandoned a few blocks away in the early days of the pandemic when John still had the courage to try to break out and reach friends, family. That had been a mistake, and he had almost paid for it with his life. Now, he stayed at his home all the time, living off dwindling supplies. No electricity. No WiFi. Nothing. All the amenities of modern life had broken down when all the people had turned. Well, most of the people. There were still people out there, alive, unaffected. Maybe there were even more than John realized.

The boy was about to deliver news from some of those people.

The large fish net that John had put up to catch the boy did its job. The boy stumbled up the drive as if he had a bad sprain in his ankle, and perhaps he did. But this time, he was not followed by any other Strikers, praise Jesus, though they lingered nearby in frightening numbers, twisting aimlessly around and around in small circles, waiting for any whiff of live flesh.

The boy stepped below the roof of the patio. His movements became more erratic, excited as he saw John. The boy put his arms out, and the remnants of a smile crept across his pallid, misshapen face, now savaged by claw marks running down the cheek bones and into dark red stubble. Half the boy's bottom lip had been torn away, exposing even teeth and the retainer that he had in his mouth when he had turned. The boy, howling in agony and perhaps joy, started to run, only to be caught in the fish net and held firm.

John cried.

He'd seen the boy-turned-Striker up close many times, but he had never gotten used to it. So different than just a year ago. Hell, just four months ago. That was when the boy had turned, when he had gone on a camping trip with friends from college. He had come home with the flu, or so they had thought. But it was much, much more. Three days later, he turned into a Striker, a casualty of this terrible, terrible plague.

It didn't seem real to John, like he was living a perpetual nightmare, as if this was some punishment from God for past misdeeds. Those misdeeds were many, John knew and accepted, but this? Did anyone in all the wide world deserve this?

John let tears run down his face as he reached through the boy's fumbling, clutching, outstretched hands, and quickly plucked the plastic cylinder from the boy's stomach cavity. It made a slick, gooey sound as he pulled it out of infected, decayed muscle and bowel.

It was one of those plastic pneumatic cylinders from the bank. The boy's mother had been a teller at the local branch, and she and her new husband (from the same bank) had snatched a few when the world fell apart. Why they had done so, John did not know, but suspected that they had contained new deposits and so, in the midst of chaos, who would miss a few hundred dollars from depositors who were likely to turn Striker before they even got home from the bank?

There were several tubes in total that they used for communication. Some painted green and some black. New messages came in black cylinders. This one was green, indicating a response to John's former message.

John pulled away from the boy, opened the green cylinder, and upended it. A small, simple scrap of paper, rolled up like a cigar, fell out. John grabbed it in his glove before it blew away, unraveled it, and then began to read.

Dear John,

We are going to make another try on Saturday, July 23, at 2pm. We will be in the bank parking lot with the station wagon. Please let us know if you will try to be there too. If so, we will wait for an hour, and then leave if you do not show up. I'm sorry things are as they are. I did my best to be the best wife, the best mother. I failed at both. But please, let me—let us—help you. Please come.

She signed it the way she had signed everything, with that steady, confident left hand, making the K in her first name the size of a mountain and the rest of the letters small and unassuming. She had started writing out 'Masey' but then had scribbled it out to write in her new last name.

John took his gloves off carefully. Then he sat down next to a small three-legged table that held a pencil and a pad of paper he had set up on the car patio for this correspondence. He reached underneath the clear plastic shield of his head gear and wiped away the tears so that he could see better, took another look at the boy, then wrote his response. He wrote it quickly so that the Strikers surrounding his home had little chance to catch the scent of his skin.

When he was finished, he put his gloves back on to ensure that he did not touch any of the boy's infected viscera now smeared across the cylinder's green paint. He folded up the note and dropped it into the cylinder. He closed it tightly, then stood. He approached the boy.

"I'm sorry, Tommy," he whispered, loud enough so that the boy might hear, but not so loud as to alert other Strikers. Then, with one swift move, he jammed the cylinder back into Tommy's stomach. He pulled away when the cylinder struck Tommy's lumbar and found its natural resting place. "I'm sorry for that, buddy. I'm so sorry for everything. Now," he said, letting the tears again flow down his face. "Go... go to Mama's house."

John took an old aluminum crutch he had found in the basement and pushed Tommy away from the net and then kept pushing until the boy had been realigned and turned such that he began walking back down the driveway and into the waiting mass of Strikers trying to reconstitute after the rifle shots.

John watched the boy disappear down Bridgeport, past all the abandoned homes where Tommy's friends - and Tommy himself - used to play.

**

Katherine Masey Bass watched her son Tommy stumble up the road in front of her house. This wasn't her house really, but her new husband Mike's. Not as far away from her old life as she had originally wanted, but times had changed dramatically. "Next year," Mike had promised. "We'll look for a new house next year." But next year never came, and now, never would.

She watched her boy work his way forward amidst a shuffle of rotting Strikers. She let her tears fall.

There would never, ever be another new year.

Tommy was a bright boy, despite what had happened to him, and he would not miss turning into her drive. Katherine didn't understand why some Strikers behaved as if they had a semblance of consciousness and intelligence left while others were feral and beyond violent. Still others seemed like lumbering oafs, incapable of moving faster than a slow shuffle. They could be pushed over by a stiff breeze, as Mike would say. She did not know why that was. She was just a bank teller, not a scientist or a virologist. But the Striker virus affected people in different ways, like many viruses do. She knew that much. She had had some training in EMT when John's fire station had offered public first aid training. Some of that training involved viral pandemic and mass casualty event preparedness. These days, everyone knew, you could never be too sure, or too prepared.

But this? Nobody had prepared for this.

"What if he doesn't turn into the drive this time?"

Mike stood next to her. His question was reasonable, if a little insensitive. Katherine tried to keep from breaking down. "Well," she said, sniffing to keep control. "If he doesn't turn, then we've lost him."

But he did turn, like the good boy he had always been. The rest of the Striker mob kept moving down the road while her little Tommy turned.

A green cylinder was lodged in his gut, in the manner that indicated that John had replied to her most recent note. The sight of it thrilled Katherine and made her nauseated. She had pulled it out of his stomach the first time, but thereafter, Mike had to do it. She just couldn't… just couldn't bear to face her son in this situation, under these circumstances. It had been her idea—well, Mike's - in the first place to use her boy in this way, to send messages to John. It wasn't like Mike gave a damn all that much about John, but Mike was a bank teller like her and, well, John was a firefighter. If anyone could help them out of this mess, surely a firefighter was more suited than they. So far, unfortunately, that had not been the case, but still, the correspondence was useful, and besides, at some point, they might need a first responder's skills and knowledge of mass casualty events.

Katherine watched as Tommy slowly stumbled up their driveway, arms waving erratically, the golf club still in his hand. As he moved closer, his head turned from side to side, his blank white eyes searching for anything familiar, as if he remembered, or was trying to remember, things about the house.

More tears welled in the corners of Katherine's eyes as Tommy's grey, scarred, and bloodied face turned towards her. She had never gotten used to the sight of her little boy like this. How could she? She had held him when he was born and had been there for him his whole life, up until two years ago when she had left them both for Mike. There were times when she felt real regret for leaving them, knowing a small piece of her still loved John, and she'd never stop loving Tommy, even if he was a lifeless Striker.

Lifeless Striker... No, I'll never believe that...

"He's getting closer," Mike said as they both crouched behind an overturned ping pong table Mike had arranged in the garage for protection.

"I hope we catch him better this time," Katherine managed to say through her sorrow. "Better than last time, anyway."

There were times when Tommy wouldn't step in the right spot, and they'd have to expose themselves to the nearby horde to corral him back into place for a proper capture. Katherine always hated chasing after him in this manner, but she had learned quickly that making a zombie move in the direction you wanted him to was difficult, dangerous, and painful work. She'd always let Mike take the lead on those things.

This time, however, Tommy stayed on course. "I'm ready," Katherine said as she wiped away tears. Like Mike, she held still and quiet behind the ping pong table as Tommy drew near. They both lacked the protective gear that John possessed, and so exposure to even a modest breeze might alert a nearby horde. In her right hand, she held the remote control for the garage door. Their method of capturing Tommy was far trickier than John's.

Katherine watched as her son continued to walk up the driveway towards the garage. On the driveway itself were several painted X's. When Tommy reached the first one, they'd have to press the button to activate the garage door. The second X further up the driveway was the spot Tommy had to reach for retrieval to work.

"Now!" Mike hissed as Tommy stepped onto the first X. Katherine pressed the garage door activator, which blared out a high-pitched droning as it descended on its tracks from electricity provided by their small, gas-powered generator.

Katherine watched as Tommy started moving faster towards the garage. She resisted the urge to look straight into his eyes, for she knew she'd see nothing there but snow-white pupils and pain. Instead, she kept her gaze fixed on the second X, waiting until Tommy stepped onto it.

He reached it and Katherine pressed the activation button again; the garage door stopped. Tommy walked right into the door with a meaty thud followed by a muffled groan as if he'd been punched in the gut. Then he stopped and just stood there, neither crouching nor falling back. He just stood there, his chest, shoulders, and upper body hidden behind the half-lowered door; his stomach, bowel, legs, and lower arms exposed.

The message tube in his gut poked out of his bowel like a broken bone, ready to be removed.

"That'll hold him for a while," Mike said as he emerged from behind the ping pong table holding a pair of hedge clippers that he intended to use to pull the message tube out of Tommy.

At first, Katherine had used oven mitts to pull the tube out. But it was too much, too personal even with the mitts. So, she had demanded that they use something else, something longer and less personal to pull the tubes out of her son's stomach. She hated using Tommy like this. It felt evil, disrespectful. But there was no other way to communicate to John.

Katherine slowed her breathing as she watched Mike walk towards her son. Tommy just stood there, his dead legs moving slightly as if he were trying to push his way through the door into the garage. The fingers on his left hand twitched, causing the putter to move as if he were tapping a ball into the cup. That putter was only a real danger while approaching Tommy in his current state. Mike had gotten cut once by the putter, and they worried that he would turn Striker, but he hadn't.

Mike eased slowly towards the half open garage door, hedge clippers level with the message tube in Tommy's bowel. Katherine suppressed her gag reflex as Mike slowly pushed the clippers into Tommy's stomach and then closed the blades carefully on the plastic top of the cylinder, to ensure that the blades did not cut or irreparably damage the tube. There were already marks on the side of the tube indicating where the blades had dug in during previous retrievals, but so far, the casing had held.

Tommy grunted as the tube was pulled from his stomach. Mike stepped back, holding the clippers nice and steady as they held the cylinder. Mike then turned around and placed the tube on a small workbench near the garage door. Katherine watched as Mike put the hedge clippers down and took a pair of gloves from off a small shelf above the table. He put them on, twisted off the top, and then took out John's message.

He handed it directly to Katherine. It was one good quality her new husband possessed: Mike never looked at the letters until Katherine read them first. Mike didn't care for John, and the feeling was mutual. But, he functioned under some kind of Ex-Spouse Confidentiality agreement or something when it came to these letters. Katherine put on her gloves and took the note. She opened it and read it aloud.

> *"Dear Katie,*
> *Yes, I will try and make it to the location you stated in your previous*
> *message. I'll have to come up with a way to get past the hordes*
> *of Strikers, but I'll think of something. I used to bust down doors*
> *with an axe, I think I can come up with a way to outsmart a pack*
> *of zombies. Katie, Katherine, what I am about to say might seem*
> *crazy, but. . ."*

Katherine blinked and read the last part to herself. When finished, she looked up at Mike who had his patented *what-does-it-say* look. Katherine could feel her heart race, but she handed the note to Mike anyway.

"Can we?" she asked after he had finished reading John's request.

"No!" Mike blurted, almost spitting. "Way too dangerous, Kat. Hell, it's a risk for us to be leaving at all, but what John is thinking about is suicide."

"But..."

"No!" he shouted. Katherine fought against a sudden burst of rage and sorrow. "Absolutely not! End of discussion. You write him back and tell him *no.*"

Tears threatened to fall again. She wanted to scream. Instead, she sighed, nodded, and moved to the table holding the bank tube, a piece of paper, and a pen.

Katherine looked to Mike once more, hoping that perhaps in her teary eyes he might find a little compassion for John's idea. Nothing.

"You tell him that we can still pick *him* up. But no on his suicidal idea. It'll get all of us killed… even him, and he knows it. You tell him that."

Katherine nodded meekly and wrote her note. As she did, she could hear Tommy make his grunting sounds, his tiny personal pleas to be let in. She dared look toward her son, saw him still standing there as if glued to the garage door. She turned back, finished the note, and signed her name, like always, with a massive K and all the other letters small. She placed the pen down and folded the paper. She winced as she placed the note into the tube. Even with her gloves on, Katherine could feel all the slime on the plastic, the slime of her son's ruined bowel.

"Here." Katherine handed the tube back to Mike. He took it from her and turned the top until it was secure. Mike then walked over to the garage door and viciously shoved the tube into place. Tommy grunted and squirmed as Mike twisted the cylinder until it was tight and secure in the right spot.

Again, she fought the urge to come up behind Mike and smack him in the head. Why Mike always thrusted the tube back into place so forcefully, Katherine did not know. Perhaps it was to ensure that, in Tommy's walk back to John's, the tube did not drop out. Perhaps he hated Tommy for some reason. Mike had always been coy with his feelings about Katherine's former life. Perhaps he was resentful for having to go through this elaborate and dangerous communication system just to get the hell out of town. Whatever the reason, Katherine didn't like Mike's aggression, especially if he was doing it to punish Tommy for turning. Her son had always been a good boy, even now as a Striker. *He* was the one out there among the Striker hordes. He was the one truly at risk, and he had performed his duty to his mother and father admirably.

"Now," Mike said, grabbing Tommy's waist and twisting him around. "Back to that sorry excuse for a father you go."

Katherine watched as Tommy stumbled slowly back down the driveway. A single tear rolled down her face. She glared at the back of Mike's head. *Sometimes*, she thought, *I wish you* had *turned.*

"Come on," Mike said as he turned towards the door leading back into the house. "We need to start packing. John will either meet us or not. I don't care either way. We'll see. Close the garage when you're done."

Katherine now let her tears run in full down her face. She took the garage remote and pressed the activation button. She kept her gaze on Tommy as he hobbled down the driveway before the steel doors blocked her sight, perhaps forever.

***

John saw Tommy break off from the passing Striker mass. The boy looked different.

Gone was the putter that he had held since turning. From this distance, it was hard to see everything clearly, but it appeared as if the fingers on that gripping hand had dropped off or perhaps had been torn off. He moved more erratically, and John then saw that his son's right knee was bent as if it had been struck by something hard, a stick, a club. His head, too, was angled slightly to the right, and it didn't appear that Tommy could turn it straight again. Because of that, the boy drifted to the right, then once he seemed to realize that he was doing so, turned back left, then right, left, right, in a kind of shambling zigzag that made him take twice as long to arrive at John's driveway. The boy looked beat up. He *was* beat up.

Who knew what dangers Tommy encountered between the houses? There were others out there, non-Strikers, holed up like John in various homes, businesses. He and Katherine and Mike weren't the only ones left alive and unturned. But who they were and where they were was unclear. He could hear the occasional pop of a gun, the occasional scream or shout of some far-off survivor. Mostly at night when he was tossing fitfully in sleep. At first, he had thought the sounds were from his frightful dreams. But no. There were others out there, and how many did Tommy encounter moving back and forth between his homes?

This has to stop...

Tommy stumbled down the driveway per usual and caught himself in the net. John was waiting.

The bank tube was out of place. In Tommy's stomach cavity, yes, but not in the nice, tight little hole that had been created by jamming it in there every time. It was secure, but it had been moved to the other side of his stomach.

John waited until his son's movements had settled into their consistent, predictable rhythms against the net. Then, he grabbed the tube and pulled it out.

His own stomach was in knots. This was the most important letter yet, and one that would answer a lot of questions, inform several of his decisions, about what he had to do in the upcoming days. He opened the tube, pulled out the letter, and read it,

> *Dear John,*
>
> *We are glad that you have agreed to meet us. Thank you. To reiterate, 2pm Saturday, in the bank parking lot. You know the car. As to your question, the answer is no. We can't afford to risk it. He's gone, John. Our son is gone. Say your goodbyes and meet us on Saturday.*

That was it. No explanation beyond Katherine's signature.

John howled and threw the tube down. It cracked against his driveway, startling Tommy. The boy howled as if in pain. His howling matched his father's.

Those are Mike's words, not Katherine's.

John turned to his son, tried saying goodbye, but could not. He tried again, but the word caught in his throat. He screamed again and raised the letter in both hands. He tore it in half. Then he saw the bloody handprint on the blank side of the paper.

John hadn't noticed it at first, for the handprint was dark red and dry, with bits and pieces of gore and rotting flesh, and none of it had rubbed off on his gloves as he had unfolded the letter to read it. Now, the handprint was as noticeable as anything he had ever seen. Clear, distinct, easily recognizable.

Tommy's handprint, his left hand, his golfing hand, with two fingers missing.

He looked at his son, writhing against the net, his ruined arms reaching through the fabric, the remains of his hands clutching, releasing, clutching, releasing as if he were squeezing a bottle. Kneading dough like a cat.

"My God," John whispered, feeling tears well up again in his eyes. "He knows."

***

At a slow trot, John pushed the emerald-colored wheelbarrow down the cracked streets of his abandoned neighborhood. His heart pounded. He knew that what he was doing was risky, very risky. But it had to be done. He couldn't leave Tommy behind. *Wouldn't.*

John looked down as he jogged, the wheelbarrow bumping in front of him as his gloved hands gripped the handles. Inside the barrow was a large squirming object, emanating a soft, bestial groan. John's heart quivered as he tried to ignore the noises from the bags.

Half an hour ago, John had done something he never wanted to do, never imagined in all his life that he *would* do. He had released Tommy from the large net holding him in place on the driveway, then smacked him hard in the head with a shovel. He then ran quickly into his kitchen and grabbed two trash bags, the large heavy-duty black ones he used for yardwork. He then slipped one bag over Tommy's upper body, then slipped the other up his legs and what remained of his stomach and bowel. John then wrapped a full roll of grey duct tape around the seam between the two bags to connect them in a makeshift body bag. He then dressed in his full firefighter's gear before grabbing his wheelbarrow and laying Tommy carefully inside.

He looked at his watch. Fifteen minutes to get to the bank where Katherine and Mike were hopefully waiting. He'd make it. Maybe. Strikers had been following them for the last ten minutes. He wasn't sure why. His full firefighter's gear was a clear barrier to their ability to smell his skin. Perhaps they could smell Tommy, and since he was moving relatively fast, his scent was leading them on like a trail to food.

He felt as if his lungs would burst, his legs would give out, but he kept pushing. His rifle was safely slung over his shoulder; his axe hung from his belt. If any of the Strikers attacked, he'd use the axe first. It was quiet. Using the rifle was a last case scenario.

The wheelbarrow almost toppled over as John rounded a corner. But he regained control and brought it to a halt. Now, the bank parking lot was only two blocks away. He allowed himself to smile. He was exhausted, sweating profusely, but he'd made it, in relatively good condition and alive. *We've made it, we've...*

A group of three Strikers appeared in front of his path. John looked behind him and saw the three that had been following closing in.

John pulled the axe from the loop on his belt. He stepped away from the wheelbarrow. Holding the axe up with both hands, John turned and assessed the threat of the three Strikers from the rear: not as bad as those in the front.

John breathed deeply before stepping toward the nearest Striker. The creature reached out with its gory hands. John side-stepped the swipe and brought his axe down on the Striker's head. The blow split the skull. The Striker groaned, its arms thrashing forward as milky green-red blood seeped into its bulbous eyes. With some effort, John dislodged the axe from the broken skull. Then he raised it again and cleaved the Striker's head in two like an apple.

As the body fell, the two remaining Strikers at their front growled, bared their rotting teeth, and flailed their arms forward. John couldn't help but spare a smile at the sight of the Strikers' defense mechanism. It reminded him of when Tommy was a child. He too would flail his arms up and down, back and forth, when upset.

John braced as the two Strikers ran forward, their arms twirling like medieval maces. John paused then stepped aside, causing one Striker to step past him and into a pothole, where its ankle snapped. Inertia carried the rest of its body forward.

Two down, one to go, he thought as the third and final Striker lunged forward, its noodle arms smacking John's helmet.

John fell back from the Striker's attack while trying not to lose the grip on his axe. He regained his balance, kept a tight grip on his axe, and swung it strong against the Striker's neck. Small chunks of esophagus and vertebrae flew out with gobs of congealed plasma. The Striker wavered in place before its head toppled off.

John took a moment to catch his breath. He wanted to pull off the helmet and take a fresh breath but couldn't. Blood and chunks of Striker meat covered his gloves.

Loud groaning caused John to turn back to the three remaining Strikers that had been following them. He looked in horror as they now clustered around Tommy's wheelbarrow, clawing at the trash bags.

John raised his axe and ran forward.

He drove the ax head into the closest Striker's back. He let the beast fall and then turned his attention to the others. The next closest took the axe in the side of its head, its shattered jaw dropping into the wheelbarrow. John pulled the axe out before jamming it back into the Striker's ruined eye.

John thrust his hand out, grabbed the Striker's shoulder, and threw it to the ground.

The last remaining Striker flailed its arms forward like whips. John braced himself this time as the Striker reached for him over the wheelbarrow. John swung his axe again, slicing its arm in two. The dislocated arm struck John's face shield, cracking the glass. His heart leapt and his breath caught in his throat as he raised his boot and knocked the Striker away from Tommy.

His face shield was cracked but not broken. He breathed relief. He looked at the Striker that he had pushed down. It sat there grumbling, cradling its stump as if it could feel the pain. Maybe it did. Maybe Strikers still had pain receptors and feeling in their extremities. Of course, they did. Tommy was living—well, almost living—proof of it.

John looked at his son still lying in the wheelbarrow and thankfully unharmed in the skirmish. He still squirmed and moaned. He was alive, or as alive as any Striker could be. The only noticeable difference in Tommy's condition was a tear in the bag over his eye. John smiled as he saw his son's eye peeking through like he had done so many times as a kid, peering around a corner or through a peephole in a pillow fort. But it wasn't Tommy's eye anymore, not truly. The once hazel iris was now white as snow.

John took a deep breath as he holstered his axe on his belt and took hold of the barrow's handles. John girded his strength as he lifted the barrow and pressed on, leaving the dead and dying Strikers in his wake.

The next two blocks were calm and quiet, save for Tommy's squirming. John felt great relief as he turned a corner at a looted gas station and saw the bank and its parking lot. And there sat the brown station wagon Katherine had taken in the divorce. Funny, but he had never been happier to see it in his life.

His smile grew larger as he saw Katherine on the passenger side looking out the window toward his location. John waved, and she looked confused for a moment, as if the distance was still too great to know who he was. Then, as he moved closer, she smiled, waved incessantly, and stepped out of the wagon.

Katherine waved again as he and Tommy drew closer. John kept his eyes on his ex-wife, on their son in the barrow in front of him. He smiled, though she could not see it through the face shield. It did not matter. Soon, they would be together again, and everything would be right once more.

Then Mike stepped out of the wagon with a hunting rifle drawn and leveled towards John's head.

***

"He's not going with us, goddammit!" Mike said, still aiming the hunting rifle at John as he and Tommy drew near. "We already said so in the letter. Can't you read?"

John wheeled the barrow into the parking lot. He was now only ten feet away from the wagon. He set the barrow down and raised his hands, not only worried about his own life, but Mike's and Katherine's as well. They were both standing beside the wagon wearing no protective gear. *Stupid, stupid, stupid!*

"Mike... Mike!" John said, shouting so that they could hear him through his cracked face shield. "Listen to me. Listen!"

Mike said nothing, nor did he try to keep John from speaking. He just kept the gun in place while Katherine stood beside him, both fear and joy marked clearly on her face. It was as if she didn't know what to do: support her current husband or rush forward to hug her son. For his part, Tommy lay quiet in the barrow, still covered in black trash bags, his exposed eye still peeking through the tear. *He's staring at me*, John thought as he shot glances at his son. *He's wondering what I'm going to do.*

"Look," John said, pointing to Tommy, "my boy is still conscious. He's aware of what's happening. He understands."

"Bullshit!" Mike said, shaking his head. "He's dead, John. He's a Striker, and there's nothing that can turn him back. We can't take him, or we'll be dead also."

"He read your letter, dammit! His bloody handprint was on the paper. He opened the tube and read it. He knew what we were going to do. I don't know how he still understands, but he does. And as long as my son has that level of understanding, of consciousness, he's still alive, and I'm going to do what I have to do to protect him."

"Mike," Katherine said, putting her hand on his arm. "Please. Can't we—"

Mike pushed her away, perhaps harder than he had intended. Katherine stumbled but caught herself on the station wagon before falling to the hard asphalt. "Back off, Kat. We're not taking him. I'm not going to risk my life or yours for a dead boy."

"Please, Mike!"

Mike fired a round. It struck the asphalt near John's left shoe. John jumped back a pace but resisted drawing his own rifle. He wouldn't be able to draw it fast enough before Mike's next shot struck him dead.

You idiot! Now the whole damn Striker horde will come our way.

"He's not coming!"

Again, John put up his hands. "Okay, okay. Fine. You win. But… can Katherine at least say goodbye her son before we go? Please?"

Mike calmed. He didn't lower the rifle, but his shoulders eased. The barrel slipped down an inch. The request seemed to catch him by surprise. Katherine looked at him with wide, teary eyes.

"I won't bring the barrow closer to the wagon," John said. "You can both come here. I'll step away."

Mike hesitated a moment more, then suddenly realized that his foolish gunfire had attracted the attention of a nearby Striker group, who had now turned its attention toward the sound.

"Okay," Mike said, motioning Katherine toward the barrow with the muzzle of his rifle. "Go say goodbye quickly, and then we go."

John looked down at Tommy writhing like a worm under the black bags. His dead white eye blinked furiously through the tears.

As they approached, John knelt over his son and, with his right hand, pinched the bag right below the duct tape seal connecting the two bags and gave it a quick tug, separating the seam just enough to see Tommy's hand. "You know what to do," he whispered, standing straight again and stepping away.

Mike and Katherine approached. The horrible hissing and moaning and scraping and howling of the approaching Striker horde was nearly deafening. "We don't have much time," John said. "Say goodbye, Katherine, and then let's go."

Katherine knelt beside her son, tears streaming down her face. He dared reach out and put her hand on the bag near his head. "I'm sorry this happened to you," she whimpered. "I'm sorry. I'm going to miss you so much."

John's instinct was to go to her and console her, comfort her as she wept. But they were not married anymore, and Mike was standing nearby with a rifle. Would he care? John wondered. They were giving a final goodbye to their son, together. Surely even a man as arrogant and self-absorbed as Mike would give them a moment to be together to grieve the loss of their son.

Loss? Nope... not yet.

Mike had drifted closer to the barrow than perhaps he had wanted. His curiosity to look at Tommy all bundled up in that barrow was more powerful than perhaps he wished to admit. Like slowing down in traffic to witness a car crash. John did not know how close his son and Mike had been. Cordial, at least. But... perhaps not cordial enough.

Mike lowered his rifle and stepped closer. John took a step toward Katherine. Mike leaned in to watch Katherine pat her son's covered head.

Tommy's arm burst through the seam and grabbed Mike's leg. He wasn't strong enough anymore, nor were his nails sturdy and sharp enough to pierce Mike's denim jeans, but the move startled him. He jumped back with a howl and reflexively raised the barrel of his rifle.

John moved, almost leapt, across the barrow and into Mike's chest, knocking him off balance. He followed with a shove. Mike fired his rifle again into the sky as they tumbled across the asphalt.

Mike struggled to keep control of his rifle. John punched him again and again in the face.

"We're taking my son, damn you! You hear me? We're taking—"

"John!"

John turned toward Katherine and saw the Striker horde behind her, closing fast.

He stood up, collected himself, and went to Tommy, whose grab of Mike's pant leg had pulled him out of the barrow. He lay now on the asphalt, face down, his loose arm trying to pull him towards the station wagon. "Help me with him!" John called to Katherine. "Grab his legs."

Together they pulled and dragged Tommy to the wagon as Strikers reached Mike. Mike screamed, pleaded for help as he disappeared beneath their weight, claws, gnashing teeth.

John opened a back door on the wagon and hoisted Tommy inside. Katherine pushed her son's legs in all the way and shut the door behind him.

"Let's get out of here!"

They barely managed to climb in themselves as Strikers hit the wagon and rocked it back and forth.

"Drive!"

Katherine fumbled the keys, recovered, slammed the key into place, and turned the ignition. She gunned the engine, slammed it into *drive* and tore away, pushing and knocking and running over Strikers trying to bar their path and hold on to the hood.

She floored the pedal and slid across the bank parking lot and found a seam between the horde and the road out of the lot. She took it, knocked a couple more Strikers away, turned the wheel right, and squealed out of the parking lot and onto the road.

And where would the road lead them? John wondered as he settled into the seat, removed his heavy gear, and allowed his breathing and heart to slow. It didn't matter where; just away from here was all that he cared about now.

Katherine was crying. John let her do so as he turned around and stared at his son lying in the back seat, still writhing, and twitching under the now worn and badly scuffed black trash bags. Tommy had not tried to free himself from his modest restraints, despite the tear at his eye or the larger rip near his arm. He just lay there, like he used to do as a child, having fallen asleep on long drives to the beach or to their vacation timeshare in the mountains.

Despite the near-death experience from which they had escaped, despite Mike being left behind to be torn apart by Strikers, despite everything that had happened, John allowed himself a smile. They were together. How long that would last, he did not know. Perhaps only as long as the gas remained in the station wagon's tank. Perhaps longer. It didn't matter. Right now, they were together. They were a family again.

And that, more than anything else, mattered in a zombie apocalypse.

END

ABOUT THE AUTHORS

Robert E. Waters has sold over 85 stories and nine novels, many of which have been published by Winged Hussar. He has written several stories set in Eric Flint's Alternative History series, "1632", including two Baen novels co-authored with Eric Flint (*1637: The Transylvanian Decision*), and Charles E. Gannon (*1636: Calabar's War*). Robert's story "Ill Met in Mordheim" was published by The Black Library in 2007 (*Tales of the Old World*). Robert has also written two Dreadball novels set in Mantic Games' Warpath universe (*The Last Hurrah & The Final Rush*). Robert has worked in the gaming industry for 30 years as writer, designer, producer, and voice-actor. He currently lives in Baltimore, Maryland.

Jason M. Waters is a recent graduate of Stevenson University with a BA in English Language and Literature and a minor in Film and Moving Image. His poem, "Glasses", was published in Junto, Franklin High School's 2017-2018 Literary Magazine. Jason has also published two highly regarded stories, "Dinner" and "Skelly Ton", in Stevenson University's Literary Magazine, The *Greenspring Review*. Jason helped co-author a script for the annual student led 72-hour film festival, "Stevie U 72", where his group won first place with their short film *Genesis Sequence*. Jason recently completed an internship for Lexington Books where he worked as an assistant acquisition's editor. He currently lives in Baltimore, Maryland.

The Rewards of Our Father
By David Guymer

"30th March, 1869.

"Father Patrick Healy,

"I hope this letter finds you in good health and that the boys at Saint Columba's Home for Destitute Boys are treating you better than my year ever did. As you will have already discerned from the postage mark, I have neither died nor taken ship to Australia. I have, in fact, received every one of your letters since my return from Europe, I have simply lacked the means to reply to them until now; I do not know how a humble priest finds the 12p to write to one of his boys twice a week, or enough gossip from the old school to warrant the letter, but know that they aided my convalescence immeasurably.

"In answer to your many questions regarding my health, you can be assured that I am well. I hope that even the limp might fade with time. I have even moved out of Chelsea Asylum! The Regiment actually intended to dock food and linen from my invalid pension; can you believe that? I have since been lodging with a Mrs. Fowler on Milk Yard, doing tuppeny jobs around Spitalfields Market where I can get them.

"Anyway, all your sermons warning us boys about the dangers of London have turned out to be quite true. It is not like Liverpool or Belfast, where I grew up, or even Sevastapol after the war with the Russians; it is hot and filthy and dark; every crooked lane finds its way to another, such that one begins to feel that the city must go on forever and that no road leads out. It is a veritable Gehenna-on-Thames, Father, a colony of Hell where Lucifer can transport his poor and unwanted.

"The slums of Whitechapel where I am lodged are some of the worst in the city, and as dire as any battlefield I ever saw in the East. It makes as many orphans too. If anything, it is worse, because the children are left here underfoot rather than folded in with the mud of some faraway country. If there is one thing I will say for this part of London it is that the rats are small and nervous; you would be too, Father, if you had to share a home with these children.

"Now that you are fully caught up on the delights of London, I will get to the purpose of my letter.

"I put in for the job that you wrote of in your letter to me last week. They must have been desperate to fill it, too, because it was later that same day that a boy called in at my lodgings. In fact, and now I think on it I have no idea how he did it, I was still making my way back from the agency when he called. Mrs. Fowler later described the lad to me as haunted and pale ("*As though he'd the Devil on his shoulder*," she said, and made the sign of the Cross as she did so). The boy had left a note, which Mrs. Fowler, though illiterate herself, rather hesitantly passed on to me.

"The first thing I noticed was how crumpled it looked. I did not think much of it then, but it reminded me of the small photographs and the last letters from loved ones that I had so often pried from the grips of dead soldiers: things so important to a person that even the grave cannot make him part with them. Forgive me, Father, but I digress.

"The note, once uncrumpled, was a simply written invitation to interview, along with the address of a tearoom on the Strand and signed at the bottom by a Mr. William Styles. I did not know the place. As you will no doubt imagine, the Strand is a smarter stretch of town than I am accustomed to. It has actual shops with windows and doors as opposed to shifty-looking lads moving produce from the backs of barrows or old women selling cress from their front porches. A girl was sweeping the cobbles as I turned in from Waterloo Bridge, and I saw a constable ambling up the street; he was alone, which surprised me, as in my bit of Whitechapel they always come in fours.

"The tearoom itself was a little place between a chop house and a cobbler's. Mr. Styles was sitting at a table by the window, a glazed but contented look in his eyes as he watched the carriages go by. The agency must have given him my description because he stood up and called me over as I walked in. He was a big fellow, smart, but trying just a little too hard at looking respectable in a black coat and necktie. He did not offer his hand the way a proper Englishman would have and given the grief I have taken from Englishman over the years I decided that Mr. Styles and I were going to get along grand. He ordered a pot of tea for one; it's a little thing, I know, but I remember thinking then that whatever brought him to this work it was not his sense of charity. I waved the waitress away. Not that I would not have loved a sip of tea, but I had given my last penny to the shoeshine boy on the corner of Embankment.

"While Mr. Styles waited on his tea, we talked.

"He asked about my experiences as an orderly to Major Francis Earle in Crimea, and even my time with you at Saint Columba's in Liverpool. In fact, I am sure that it was your reference more than anything that won me the job. Heaven knows, I have little charm of my own. *The work will be hard,*" he warned me, to which I replied that work worth doing often is. One of your old sayings, Father. I told Mr. Styles that so long as I was not pulling young lads from battlefields while they screamed for their mothers then it would be better than where I had come from. He looked at me oddly. "*You are,*" he told me, "*just the sort of man that Miss Grimcroft is looking for.*" He left tuppence for the tea and no tip for the girl.

"I start on Thursday.

"Shane Kelly."

"30th March, 1869.

"Dear Mrs. Fowler,

"I will be moving out on the first of June. You will find my last week's overdue rent in the desk drawer. You can keep the rat.

"Shane Kelly."

"31st March, 1869.

"Father Patrick Healy,

"Two letters in as many days? I know what you must be thinking: either someone has died or it is Christmas. Well, nobody has died, but with two idle days and two weeks' advance pay in my pocket it does feel a little bit like Christmas. Even after a cooked breakfast of ham and eggs and a proper set of half-decent clothes (at London prices, mind you) I still have a little money left and decided to take it with me to Gravel Lane to see the orphanage.

"The building had been an abbey, though I am told that it burnt down in somewhat mysterious circumstances just before the turn of the century. Protestantism, eh Father: the gift that keeps on giving. It is difficult to tell from the outside how much of the original building remains intact and how much of its red brick frontage is new. It still feels old. The sense of peace around it is almost eerie, particularly for a school, and comes in no small part from the lack of waifs and vagrants that usually infest the East End. Sanctity has a weight to it, do you not find? It persists even after the lasts saints are martyred and the last witches burned.

"It is obvious to me that the estimable Miss Grimcroft does good work here.

"Shane Kelly."

"P.S. if you could please address your letters to *Miss Grimcroft's Orphan Asylum, Gravel Lane, Whitechapel, Tower Hamlets, London.*"

"15ᵗʰ April, 1869.

"Father Patrick Healy,

"Mr. Styles (or Bill, as he insists I call him) was lying to me, although I am not certain I could explain exactly how. He warned me that the work word be hard, but in hindsight I think he was being less emphatic than he could have been.

"Allow me to explain…

"For the children the day begins at a quarter to six o'clock. For the orderlies it starts half an hour earlier so as to get the children up, dressed, and breakfasted. Breakfast is the same each day: bread and oatmeal, with table beer for the older boys and tea for the girls and youngsters. We orderlies do not get to eat until the children are fed and this we do in shifts, meaning that on some days we might not have breakfast until it is almost time for dinner. Our food is not much grander or more substantial than theirs, though Miss Grimcroft has been known to bless us with a piece of hard cheese or a knob of butter to scrape across our bread.

"That the children are miserable is obvious. The sight of children weeping in corridors and dormitories is so commonplace that no one comments upon it. I am not sure why it occurs to me to make note of it now except to give you the fullest account of life here. They are hungry too, and will fight over food like a murder of crows. Expecting them to say grace before a meal is like expecting it of a rabid dog; the other orderlies don't even try and I too gave up soon enough. Forgive me that, Father.

"And yet what little the good Lord deems fit to provide, it is clearly adequate because most of my duties between six o'clock and bedtime amounts to the quelling of mischief. I remove malingerers from corridors. I break up fights. I stand watch over kitchens and water closets, and even the library of all places, because there are children here who will steal the donkey from beneath the Virgin Mary. I fetch those children as are summoned by Miss Grimcroft or Mr. Styles, though to what purpose I have not asked and am yet to be told; such children are invariably difficult for me to find, and tend to put up a fight when I do. I have taken as many bruises over this last fortnight than I did in two years in Crimea. I exaggerate, but only slightly. As evidence, let me tell you about this black eye that I received from a lad named Cooper. The other boys, who are somewhat in awe of him, know him as Punch.

"Not bad for a twelve-year-old.

"Was life this hard for us at Saint Columba's? It seems astonishing to me that I could forget something like that, but I have seen firsthand in Europe how horror fades from the memory, like panning for gold, leaving only the good and the pure, however small, behind.

"I wonder sometimes if that is truly a blessing.

"Mr. Styles asked me later about the black eye. I told him it was nothing and he took the dismissal so readily that I had to ask if he had not seen battle himself. He told me he had never left England, but there was something about the way he said it that made me disbelieve him. He has a look in his eyes, a way of walking, that advertises a person who has witnessed things that others have not.

"The orphanage is much larger on the inside than it looks from Gravel Lane. There must be a thousand attics and garret rooms, and mile upon mile of crumbling cellars that no doubt belonged to the old abbey. And what I have seen must comprise barely a fraction of the place for every other corridor, it seems, ends in a closed door locked even to me.

"What lies behind them I cannot help but wonder, but no one has yet been able to give me an answer.

"At the end of my first day, I pointed out to Mr. Styles that none of my duties had taken me in the vicinity of a chapel. Mr. Styles again wore that look of wearied despair, of comfortably worn-in horror, and explained to me that Miss Grimcroft's school, alas, has no chapel. This struck me as odd, but there is not nearly enough work for crippled soldiers in London, so I said I would simply nip out to St. Annes on my Sunday morning off. We argued over that point, or at least I did, saying something to the effect that even in Sevastopol we had a Sunday morning off.

"He said I could accept Miss Grimcroft's conditions or I could leave.

"I agonized all that night, but as you've no doubt deduced already, I am still here.

"Did I do right, Father?

"When Sunday came, I understood the lack of a morning off. This is a war of sorts and the guns are never silent. For every child we see off to India or the Americas there are fifty more waiting to be taken in off the Whitechapel slums. There are simply so many more of them than there are of us.

"Of Miss Grimcroft herself I have seen little so far, though she seems to be a very driven and imperious lady, well accustomed to getting things done. For all this institution's small faults, I can tell that she has a great passion for her mission here.

"Shane Kelly."

"17th April, 1869.

"Father Patrick Healy,"

"And I tell you, you are Peter, and on this rock I build my church,"

"Thank you for your words, Father, and for the quickness of your reply; they reassure me that I made the right decision in staying here. God has a way of sending us into the darkest places, but there is nowhere so dark he cannot see, so far that he cannot hear.

"And it's not as though I do not have a priest to call on when I need one.

"Shane Kelly."

"To whom it concerns, rinse the dregs from the teapot when you get to the bottom,

"SK."

"12th May, 1869.

"Forgive me, Father, for I have sinned.

   "I helped a boy today.

   "I may need to explain…

"In my last letter I wrote a little about my routine here at the orphanage. Reading those words back to myself now, I can see that while they are accurate, they are also somehow… incomplete. They can be read as though Miss Grimcroft's school is no different to any other workhouse or asylum in London. Believe me, Father, that it is not so. I cannot explain it, not even in my own thoughts, but I am beginning to feel it. I sense that there is no place on God's Earth quite like Miss Grimcroft's school.

"The children here are kept busy; there is a library, a room for sewing, a herb garden to be tended, floors to be scrubbed, and no end of dishes in the kitchen to be washed or vegetables to be scrubbed, but in terms of education, moral or otherwise, there is little. Miss Grimcroft believes in those virtues that arise naturally from hard work and austerity. Between bed and meal times then the children are left mostly to themselves and the hierarchies of the slums duplicate themselves here; the weak dominate the strong, the oldest boys lording over the dormitories like petty tyrants. What they long for is a clip around the ear and there are a few (that Cooper lad, for instance) to whom I long to administer it. Mr. Styles, however, insists that I am to leave them be. *'Miss Grimcroft,* he says, his brash cockney accent becoming wheedling when quoting our proprietress, *"believes in rectitude from hard living."*

"Anyway, the boy... He came to the school yesterday morning.

"There was nothing particularly exceptional about his arrival. There are more orphaned children on the streets of the East End then there are families for them in the Empire. At least, that is how it can feel. Miss Grimcroft tends to consciously take in the worst of them too: the pickpockets and the bullies, the serial-escapists and the hopelessly delinquent, youngsters who are already better known to the London police than charitable institutions like Miss Grimcroft's school. This one stood out to me because he was different. No hardened slum urchin, this lad. He looked dazed. You could tell from the hang of his face that he was still half-expecting, half-hoping, for his parents to turn up and pull him out of there, gushing to us all that there had been a terrible mistake.

"Brendan O'Donnell, his name was; Irish boy.

"I wonder if that is what made me feel for him.

"I did my best to keep an eye on him, but it was only going to be a matter of time before a good, grieving boy like that ran afoul of one of the dormitory toughs. I do not know what he did to deserve it, but I had to practically scrape the poor lad off the floor before carrying him to the infirmary.

"Miss Grimcroft hires a mortician, another old soldier by the name of Walters who had fought across China and New Zealand before his retirement. He stops by on Mondays and Fridays. Is Miss Grimcroft's school unusual in keeping its own morgue? I had not wondered about that until now. In addition to his more morbid duties, Walters also dabbles in basic surgery, which mostly amounts to treating the bruises and scrapes that we orderlies tend to accrue over the week. Believe me, Father, it would have to be quite the bruise that would make me trust that old soak's medicine over a coin toss from the Almighty. The children, of course, are expected to swallow whatever the Lord metes out and be grateful.

"I picked up a thing or two from the Army doctors in Crimea however and, although Miss Grimcroft's morgue is an unprepossessing infirmary even by the standards of what I saw in Sevastopol, I decided to see to young O'Donnel myself. Walters, as you will probably deduce from my low opinion of the man, is firmly of the old school; he believes that a good scream is cathartic and neither he, nor presumably Miss Grimcroft, holds much with the modern theories of Lister and Morton.

"I did the best I could with the facilities I had. I rinsed his cuts in clean water. I set the break in his arm with as much gentleness as such a thing can be done. I prepared him a mild dose of opium, and made him as comfortable as I could in that cold, lightless morgue.

"And for that, Father, I ask God's forgiveness.

"Shane Kelly."

"7th June, 1869.

"Father Patrick Healy,

"I have been on punishment duties today and not for my mercy towards the O'Donnell boy. At least, I do not think so. I told the other orderlies what happened, and I honestly do not believe that they cared. Not because they're monsters, but because they are men making the best out of Hell. The brawny old giant, Saunders, does charcoal drawings that he sometimes pins up in the children's dormitories. Mayfair bought a cricket bat and ball from his own purse; however hard the week, he always manages to put a match together in the colliery yard on Saturday. And I adopt the little Irish stray.

"We deal with the horror in our own ways.

"There had been a few of us orderlies in the tearoom when it happened: Williamson, Hendricks, Ambrose, and me, all sharing a pot of tea and some fruitcake that Saunders' sister had baked for his birthday. Our conversation had turned to Miss Grimcroft.

"You might imagine we speak of her all the time, a gang of semi-literate hard men like us, beaten senseless by middle age, and her a mysterious, unmarried young lady of obvious means, but you would be wrong. That would be to assume that ours is an ordinary workplace and Miss Grimcroft an ordinary woman.

"We all knew better.

"I cannot recall exactly what I said as Mr. Styles walked in. I am certain that I was simply wondering aloud about where Miss Grimcroft's money comes from, but I have never seen a man turn to anger the way Mr. Styles did over so trivial a question.

"He was angry, but more than that, I think he was also a little afraid. He loves her, Father, of that I am now quite certain; not in the way that a man might love a younger woman, but the way he might love his queen or his God: a Catholic love so tinged with guilt and fear and shame it is a wonder we still call it love. I think he feared that if he was not angry enough, and seen to be angry enough, that word of it would get back to Miss Grimcroft and earn her reproach.

"And this is why I have spent the day since scrubbing blood and what looks to me very much like burnt-on meat from one of the old bedrooms on the fourth floor.

"I can't for the life of me think how they got there.

"And you know what, Father?

"Suddenly I am scared too.

"Shane Kelly."

"2ⁿᵈ August, 1869.

"Father Patrick Healy,

"I saw a strange man on my rounds of the corridors last night. It was no one that I recognized, and definitely not one of the other orderlies on duty that night. He was taller than any man working at the orphanage, as tall as any man that I have ever seen. Have you ever sat on a night train and seen a scarecrow on a distant field in the dark? Or maybe caught a glimpse of a telegraph pole against a rag of moon? That was how he looked to me. Like something that I was not meant to see.

"I called out a challenge, but the man made no answer. I moved to apprehend him. His clothes were clearly those of an important gentleman, a frock coat with tails and a top hat, but no gentleman had any proper business in that corridor at night. I have been in and out of enough institutions in my life to know how many wealthy men there are whose charitable services mask a predilection for small children. He disappeared around a corner and I followed him at a run.

"And do you know what I ran into around that corner, Father?

"Nothing.

"Just another one of the orphanage's innumerable locked doors.

"I tried the handle. It was locked, of course, as I'd known it would be, despite the fact that this was clearly impossible. The gentleman must have had a key, I reasoned to myself, but unconvincingly, for surely the man could not have found the correct key, unlocked the door, opened it, shut, and then locked it again, all in the space of the few seconds in which he was out of my sight. He could not have done it. I tried the handle one last time before continuing on my rounds, trying to tell myself that I had imagined the whole episode: too little sleep and too little food.

"But I am not in the habit of imagining gaunt gentlemen in black.

"I shared all of this with the orderlies at the breakfast table the following morning, and there is little in this world that will return the surreal to the workaday like an airing in cool August sunshine over oatmeal and bread. "*It was*," they told me, "*The Foreign Gentleman.*" It was not what they said or the manner in which they spoke it, but the fact that they said it all. *The Foreign Gentleman*: the bogeyman whom the children whisper of when the lights go out and on whom blame for any mysterious disappearance or untimely death will fall. "*Who is he?*" I asked. It seemed likely that this *Gentleman* was nothing more supernatural than a patron or a benefactor, perhaps even the mysterious source of Miss Prendergast's income. That no one here knew his real name was simply testament to the fact that he knew his Matthew: *Be careful not to practice your righteousness in front of others to be seen by them. If you do, you will have no reward from your Father in heaven.*

"The looks on their faces told me more than what they actually said. Or did not say.

"This is something else that I learned in the Crimea. Men who are merely afraid will talk as though there is something they desperately need to say and have not the time left in which to say it. Men, on the other hand, who have grown so accustomed to the drudgery of fear that they wear it like an overcoat, say nothing at all.

"The orderlies said nothing.

"The little that I was able to get out of them led me to conclude that he was one of the new breed of industrialists, a self-made man whose interests would summon him for long spells to all corners of the Empire. To this, Ambrose broke his self-imposed silence to cite as evidence the Gentleman's lengthy absences and the tendency of Miss Grimcroft's children to disappear to the colonies on those occasions when he returned. *"Probably living in a grand house somewhere in Canada,"* he said.

"I am not sure I believed him. I am not sure he believed himself.

"Something about this is very wrong.

"Even the children feel it. They are unusually subdued and obedient today as, I am told, they always are when the Foreign Gentleman visits. Even that toe-rag, Cooper, who christened my first day with a black eye, called me Sir as I passed him and his gang in the corridor.

"It is a Monday and Walters is visiting the morgue.

"Eight children disappeared last night.

"Cooper was one of them.

"Shane Kelly."

"5th August, 1869.

"Dear Dr. Lyndhurst,

"I am an orderly at Miss Grimcroft's Orphan Asylum, formerly an orderly in the King's Own and a man of some medical experience. I have in my care a young lad of nine years suffering from bruising, sepsis, and delirium resulting, I believe, from an altercation that occurred exactly thirty days ago. I acknowledge that my expertise does not stretch particularly far, but there is no resident physician here at Miss Grimcroft's. I do not have much with which to pay you, but I implore you in the name of simple human decency and hope there's some Christian charity left somewhere in this town.

"Please tend to this matter promptly. I fear the boy does not have long.

"Shane Kelly."

"9th August, 1869.

"Father Patrick Healy,

"How did you even make the acquaintance of Miss Grimcroft in the first place? What manner of Hell have you got me into? Let me be frank now, Father, I want out. It was your recommendation that got me this job and now I need for you to help me get out of it.

"I could just walk out, of course, like Mr. Styles advised me too that first day, but then what – there is still not enough work for crippled soldiers in London? I would be just another lame beggar on the streets of Tower Hamlets, too old even for charity. Even Satan had to be thrown out. He did not leave of his own accord.

"Miss Grimcroft does not strike me as the sort to write glowing references for those who leave her employ. I cannot even recall anyone ever speaking of orderlies who have worked here in the past and moved on.

"Who did this job before I started in April?

"Where is he now?

"At this point, I would even go back to the Army if I thought for one second they would have me. I read in the *Daily Telegraph* that they are shipping men out to the Gold Coast. A second Ashanti War, they say. And Africa does not sound so bad. Milder than Crimea, at least.

"Maybe I really am going crazy.

"I have been practically daring Mr. Styles to fire me. I have not been attending to my duties. Not today. Not yesterday. Not the day before that either, I think, although I am starting to lose track. I have taken to sitting in the morgue with the O'Donnel boy where there are no windows. You remember him, don't you, Father? Have you been reading my letters at all? You have sent me no reply since I wrote to you about my sighting of the Foreign Gentleman in the corridor. Two letters a week, every week, for almost a year since the end of the war, and now that I actually want to hear from you, I get nothing?

"I need you to tell me that I am not insane. Or that I am. I am unsure at this point which diagnosis would comfort me least.

"Poor Brendan has got no better. In fact, I daresay he has got worse.

"It is an infection, I think, and Heaven knows I saw enough of them in the East. The next man who tells me that carbolic is bad for a growing boy's character will be getting my fist through his teeth. I do not care anymore if it is Miss Grimcroft herself.

"I have not been sleeping. In my dreams I am patrolling the corridors in my old foot private's tunic, an 1853 Enfield rather than the usual night stick in my hands, but there is something worse than Russians lurking there in the dark. God alone knows what I plan to do if I ever catch whatever it is I am hunting in those dreams.

"Or is it hunting me?

"I find myself thinking more and more about the Foreign Gentleman. I have seen him twice now, since that first encounter, but come no closer to apprehending him than I did that first night. On that third and final occasion, I pursued him onto a flight of stairs. At the top, while I struggled red-faced only halfway up, he turned to look over his shoulder and for the first time I caught a glimpse of his face. I wish to this very moment that I had not. The smile he bestowed upon me was wholly dispassionate, an incision cut into dead flesh to reveal rotting yellow teeth. Then he doffed his tall hat to me, a face that was as cold and unearthly as moonlight briefly allaying the darkness of the landing and turned to walk away.

"I pursued him no further that night.

"If it is not the Devil himself stalking these corridors for children then it is surely one of His unholy creatures. All I know for certain is it was no living man that I saw that night.

"I no longer speak of it with the other orderlies. It is my secret. They have made their own peace with this place; they have counted their silver and accepted it.

"What happened to the man who filled this job before April?

"No one ever speaks of him, or of anyone who had worked here before and then left to work elsewhere. There are no visits from old colleagues. No postcards or letters.

"Did the Gentleman take them the way he is said to take the children?

"The thought does not appal me as it once might have. As old soldiers will always say, it is the waiting and the not knowing that is the hardest part.

"God, when did I last sleep?

"Three days, I think. Maybe four? I dare not close my eyes for fear the Gentleman will come for me while I am sleeping.

"All I know for certain is that O'Donnell does not have long left for this world.

"The Foreign Gentleman will come for him soon.

"He talks sometimes, when the fever dips enough to make him lucid. I do not think it is me he talks too though; he calls me father, speaking to me of people and places I do not know and begging me for stories of an old county I scarcely recall myself. I gather from his feverish talk that his family came from Monaghan. Just like mine.

"He tosses and turns.

"*The Gentleman is coming*, he says. *He is in the corridor.*

"*At the door…*

"I don't know if it is me he's telling or the ghost of his father. I don't know whether it is a warning to me to leave or a desperate plea for my help.

"But I cannot leave.

"I see the handle turn, but the door does not open. It is locked and I have dragged Miss Grimcroft's heavy Eastlake medicine cabinet in front of it. I tell myself that I am unsure what possessed me to do such a thing, but that is a lie; I know why.

"The handle turns again.

"That is the real reason I am here, Father, writing what I expect to be my final letter. I have been unable to apprehend the Foreign Gentleman, but with O'Donnell here I knew that all I needed to do was wait. The Gentleman has come to me.

"I do not know if I can shield the boy from the Devil, or if I simply mean to go with him. I have had enough of not knowing, enough of living in fear of it. I mean to find out what kind of man I am, Father, and I will know no peace in this world until I can say that.

"It cannot be long now. The O'Donnel boy is barely breathing.

"God help me, Father, he is coming in! The legs of the Eastlake scrape across the hardwood floor, though I see no hands upon it. The sound of it goes through me like dead men's bayonets on church glass.

"The door inches wider.

"A pale hand reaches through.

"I wish I had my Enfield with me now, if only to support the lie that this is a dream.

"I must go now, Father. God have mercy on us a…"

About the Author

David Guymer is a former academic with a PhD in molecular biology and now writes fiction full time. His debut novel was the David Gemmel Award nominated, *Headtaker* and he has since written over twenty-five novels, primarily in the science fiction and fantasy genres, with publishers including Games Workshop and Marvel. He has written for computer games, and for roleplaying games such as *Age of Sigmar: Soulbound* and *Traveller*, but continues to devote most of his time to his fiction.

335 Evergreen Street

by Chris Noonan

"Healthy emotional development is marked by a gradually increasing ability to perceive, assess, and manage emotions."

- Health and Human Services, HHS.gov

Childhood

335 Evergreen Street remembered dimly, as consciousness came into being during the last weeks of construction, of being called a "Victorian" style house by the many craftsmen who adorned her with fine paints and intricate woodwork. As their voices became more than strange music to her, she started to feel their dull footsteps on her teak floorboards, or the sharp hammer strikes on her deep plum wine wood exterior. The sensations interested her in a strange, visceral way and she reached out, hungry for more.

Gradually, she began to sense more of her larger, three-story structure. Her consciousness extended itself slowly through the rough wood of the joists and rafters, then outside to her large front-facing gable and covered porch. The intricate spindlework on the columns there, along with the white crown molding that decorated her eaves made 335 feel very attractive. But that wasn't even the best thing.

From the pointed circular roof of her large tower, the house found that she could see past her small world here at the intersection of Evergreen and Main and into the grand, larger world of the neighborhood. There were all kinds of houses. It was exciting, but terribly fearful. They didn't seem very friendly, or even very alive for that matter, so she returned to safety of the craftsmen.

They would often speak of her beauty amongst themselves. She didn't always understand what the words meant, but when she heard herself described in that way it sounded so beautiful and elegant. It made her feel special. The men would spend long days working, lovingly showering 335 with care and affection, but then they would leave when the darkness came.

She began to experience a new emotion during those long, frightful hours in the dark. Loneliness. She contemplated on it, as hard as she could, but being as young as she was it was terribly difficult to understand. It must have something to do with the craftsmen who visited her during the daytime. The house wasn't lonely when they were within her.

The next day when the craftsmen showed up early in the morning for work, 335 watched them very closely. There were many different men and many different names, but she found that they all came to Victor when they needed to know what to do. He was a large, powerful man with a rough, sandpaper chin and broad shoulders. When he finished with the other lesser craftsmen, Victor would go back to doing the work of two of them. There was a strength about him and the way he cared for her that made the house feel safe. He might be the one to stay and protect her during the long, lonely nights.

As the crew began to wrap up for the day, the house knew that she needed to act now. She didn't know how to speak, but she did remember rattling the wooden shutters on her windows in infantile anger at the darkness the previous night. Maybe she could just force him to stay? It seemed reasonable, although the details were a little fuzzy. She hungered for companionship.

Her consciousness followed Victor as he packed up his tools for the day and collected the men. He was big. She might be able to hold her doors shut with one of the others, but it would not be so easy to stop him from leaving. Thinking this deeply on something was still quite difficult, almost painful in fact, but then she got an idea.

As the craftsmen were about to exit her front doors, she rattled the brass handle on her upstairs library door. It was a small sound — she hadn't spent much time with her doorknobs yet — and at first it seemed as if they didn't hear. Several of the men walked out into the growing twilight outside, leaving only Victor and another smaller man. The house panicked and rattled the handle as hard as she could. The dull thud of Victor's boot upon her circular staircase calmed her a little. The plan was working, so far.

She waited until Victor came upstairs to check her library, buzzing with growing anxiety and anticipation until he finally turned the knob and entered the room. Three steps in, 335 toppled one of the large, heavy, mahogany bookcases on top of him. It landed with a sickening thud. To her disappointment, he only gurgled some nonsense and then expired, leaking a viscous red liquid all over her fine teak flooring. That would not do, and on top of it they would have to hire someone to clean this mess up.

However, to her growing surprise she found herself sipping at the liquid through the floorboards. It had a strange energy to it that filled an appetite that the house didn't know she had. She sat full and contented that night, smiling back at the darkness.

Adolescence

It took almost five years after Victor's death for her to be finished. A new crew was finally hired, as it turned out the original crew was too frightened to return after his dead body was discovered drained of blood. 335 found that somewhat disrespectful. Any craftsmen worth his salt should yearn to contribute to her beauty. She sated her growing hunger on the small squirrels and birds that deigned to tread upon her glorious frame. And waited.

Henry moved in several months later, bringing with him something that he called his "family". The word sounded threating and alien to her, and the house quickly found she didn't like either the tall, frail mother or the small, annoyingly precocious daughter. It wasn't their looks or manner — it was their connection to *him*.

He was unlike Victor, much smaller and slighter of build. A pair of thick-rimmed glasses sat slightly askew on his lean, angular face. Coupled with his chronically unkempt mop of brown hair, the man was a not much to look at. But there was something in the way Henry smelled — an intoxicating mix of wool, wood, and sweat — and the way he caressed her walls and woodwork with the firm, but gentle touch of his hand. 335 began to feel a new emotion. Love. It made her feel like she needed to tear up her teak floorboards and wrap him in a deep embrace. Unfortunately, the house hadn't developed that ability yet, so she thought long and hard on it as she watched Henry and his wife sleep.

The dark had become 335's special place. She found it easier to think when it when the world was quiet and dead. And so, in her master bedroom, watching them slumber peacefully through the sheer linen canopy on the large, four poster bed, she came up with a solution.

She reached out and touched Henry's mind. The house had started to receive little snippets of thoughts from him and his family as they went about their day, but they were disjointed and random. Now, she let a long, dark tendril of consciousness crawl down the wall and across the pillow to the source. It was challenging at first, but gradually she made the connection and overcame the disorientation. There were far too many thoughts of his wife and daughter in there. She had only wanted to plant seeds for herself, but soon it became evident that some weeding was needed before they could have a chance to grow. That was just basic gardening.

335 contemplated simply crushing the pair of them beneath a bookcase or sending them tumbling down her twisting, circular staircase to the hard marble of the foyer, but she feared it might drive Henry away. Maybe the answer was to have *him* drive them away? Or worse. It had been long years of subsisting on squirrels and birds.

Henry began to thrash about in his sleep as she showed him things. Unspeakable, alien things. The darkness had taught her well.

The change was immediate. He became verbally abusive towards his wife and daughter, alienated his friends, and then left his job a week later. He began to spend long hours sitting cross-legged on the cool, dirt floor of her basement, talking to 335 in a low, lover's whisper. His wife and daughter would try to open the basement door, tearfully pleading with Henry to come upstairs, but the house would just rattle the doors on her kitchen cabinets until they ran screaming and hid beneath the bed.

Then those two had the audacity to demand that they all moved away. Leaving her behind like some useless, throwaway fling? Well, that would not do at all. That night she showed Henry her true self. He screamed wildly, clawed out his eyes, and took an axe to his wife and daughter. The house was thrilled, and eagerly supped at the splattered blood on her walls and wood floor.

But then to her horror, Henry began hacking parts off of himself. She was fine with the gore -- he tasted even better than he smelled – but she didn't want to be alone. He was to be her companion. Her love.

Soon, she knew it was over. It wasn't that what was left of the body hadn't moved in a while. There just wasn't anything left to drink.

Adulthood

Things were busy for a while after the incident with Henry. 335 had never been so full of people before. Their voices echoed around her interior in a chaotic whirlwind. It took some serious concentration to filter out the noise so the house could focus on the few she was interested in. The ones in the blue uniforms would huddle together and speak in whispered tones, but she could hear them as if they were speaking aloud.

Murder suicide. She didn't fully understand the words, but 335 knew that meant they didn't think she was involved. There were a lot of questions she expected about the missing blood, but she was genuinely surprised by the questions about her furniture and decor. Of course, she had cleaned up before having so many new guests. That was just proper manners for any self-respecting house.

Victor first, and now Henry. She seemed to have bad luck with men. They were a little too squishy for her tastes but filled with a delicious liquid. It made it hard for her to navigate the complicated feelings that she experienced around them. Love so far for her seemed to be a fleeting moment of anxiety and uneasiness, tinged with a strange excitement, followed by a meal and straightening up her living room.

She sat alone and unused for years after Henry and his family were laid to rest. 335 could hear the whispers as people crossed to the sidewalk on the other side of the street to pass by her. *Haunted. Cursed.* She felt embarrassed, even a little humiliated, but she still let dirt and cobwebs collect all over her fine exterior. It felt right to let herself go, she wasn't ever going to be as popular and full of people as the other houses on the block. Depression was a warm bath to pity herself in.

That was until the Reverend moved in.

The Reverend was different. He looked like other men, although he was clothed in all black with an odd white collar. He even smelled similar. But when he entered 335 that first day, she could feel his eyes upon *her*. It was rather unsettling. No one before had noticed her presence without her making it known. The house was suddenly mortified that he was seeing her interior covered in a thick layer of dust and grime.

She felt that strange excitement and uneasiness again, like with Victor and Henry before, and cursed it. 335 wasn't going there again. She told herself she'd rather be alone and neglected. In a fit of anger, she rattled her cabinets and threw furniture around the room. But the Reverend just smiled and waited for her to finish. Then he descended into her basement, sitting cross-legged on the cool, dirt floor, and spoke to her in a low, lover's whisper. And just like that, she was in love again.

The Reverend said he was on a mission from his God. He spoke at length about it, but it was all pillow talk to 335 until the first night he brought home a new convert. He said her name was Rose. The woman was incapable, being unconscious when they arrived. He tied her up down in the basement and covered her mouth with duct tape. After drinking from a bottle of some brownish liquid, he began to preach in frenzied, chaotic bursts to his prisoner, chastising her for her sins. Then back to the bottle. Then more preaching. It continued for hours until he collapsed from exhaustion and inebriation.

335 reached out and touched Rose's mind. She wanted to know why this woman was with the Reverend — her eyes only registered complete terror. Tendrils of dark, twisting consciousness squirmed across the dirt floor and implanted themselves in her head. The house saw what he had done to Rose before bringing her to the basement. Things that made the house feel embarrassed and angry. He spoke to the woman in low, lover's tones and did strange things to her body. This would not do at all.

The house groaned audibly with jealousy as she writhed in her foundation. Men were squishy inside, too. He was to be hers alone. Now, no one would have him. 335 showed Rose her true self and the bound woman spasmed in terror and madness. She greedily ate through the duct tape on her mouth, her bottom lip, and most of her right arm before the Reverend drunkenly stirred on the dirt floor.

He scrambled to his feet to quiet the screaming, but 335 wasn't finished. She had been saving this for just such an occasion. The dirt floor of her basement shook as a swarm of insects broke through and began to slowly engulf the

Reverend. He tried to beat them off with his hands, screaming wildly until they filled his mouth and throat. Once he had stopped moving, the house sent them for the crazed woman while she fed.

Men — at least they were good for something.

Middle-Age

335 watched the other houses, with their new, flashy exteriors and their insides full of people. In the interminable span of time she had sat alone and empty, it became her only real activity. Watching. Envying. It was easier to live through their experiences than admit her life had turned the other way.

The pointed, circular roof of her tower leaked now and many of her windows were cracked and missing glass. Even 335's one-glorious frame now sagged awkwardly in the stone foundation. She wished that she could feel footsteps upon her dusty teak floorboards again, or that she cared enough to clean up the mess she had become. But it was easier to watch.

All she wanted was a little attention, but slightly more dignified than partying teenagers. One had even urinated in her living room. In a fit of anger and revulsion, the house finally discovered how to control her teak flooring and used it to rip off the poor fool's member before tearing him limb from limb screaming. Now even the teenagers didn't come to visit.

So, day after day she watched the other houses and the people that came and went. After a while, she began to notice a gnawing feeling inside of her, similar to her hunger but different. 335 didn't really want to look like the other houses, all uniformly colored and lacking real curves, but she needed to feel life move around inside her again.

It was during the dark time, the world quiet and dead, that the urge became something more. 335 had forgotten what it was like to be young. Something in the darkness reminded her. There was pain, but she pushed anyway. The urge was all powerful now and she felt intoxicated by its grip. Her entire structure felt like it was burning. Consciousness failed somewhere during the ordeal.

When she awoke the next morning, the house was amazed at what had happened. The dirt and dust were gone, and not even "after cleaning" gone

It was as if they never existed. She looked like the day that construction had finished — even her sagging frame stood strong and proud. With her many windows intact and gleaming now, she looked out over the neighborhood and waited. Someone would come.

There was quite a stir among the neighbors when Stanley's car pulled up in front of 335 Evergreen Street. They stopped what they were doing and watched slack jawed as a tall, thin young man with short blond hair spent a moment looking around the property before ascending the front steps and entering the house. Like she was the only house on the block. The attention was thrilling.

She liked Stanley already, although he was a little young for her tastes. He was desperate, just like her. The house could feel it on him as he looked around her first floor. It was in the way he moved, the way he went to his phone when it rang like it was his last chance calling. 335 wanted to know what could make one so young desperate, so she reached out and touched his mind. Easier this time — she had learned her lesson over the years. He never noticed the long, pulsating tendril that cunningly slipped down from the shadows around the crystal chandelier and entered the crown of his head.

Stanley was a real estate agent. Or at least that was his title. He hadn't sold anything yet, and he was about to lose his job, along with his apartment. 335 bristled a little at the thought of being bought and sold so openly. Her past residents had all seemed to just show up one day. She wasn't some seedy lady of the night that should have to march the corner here, selling her wares, but he seemed so innocent and eager. She planted a seed.

Sitting cross-legged on the cool, dirt floor of her basement, Stanley listened as the house told him of her life. If he was to play matchmaker, then she thought he needed to know the whole story. She wanted to show him her true self but held off. He still had work to do, so she brought forth the swarms of insects and pleasured him until he passed out.

Golden Years

Although Stanley was never able to get her sold and they eventually gave up trying, those years were the happiest of 335's existence. All of the failures before with men had taught her something. She could finally see the arc of it all down the long hallway of her memory. They were all different. Stanley was as much like Henry or the Reverend as she was like the Ranch and Colonial style houses that surrounded her. It was about finding the right one.

They didn't speak down in her cellar anymore. Stanley's knees had trouble with that many stairs these days, so the house spoke to him softly as he dozed in his wooden rocking chair on her porch. His thoughts were simple and calming to her, free of the hunger that clawed at her insides.

Stanley had asked her about the missing repairmen on occasion through the years. He would call them to work on her plumbing or roof, but when he went back to pay them, they had disappeared. It wasn't like she was unfaithful to him, she just had needs. The insects took care of what was left when she was finished, so no one was the wiser. 335 couldn't imagine feeding on Stanley, but she was also scared he would leave when he eventually found out. He didn't. He admitted to her that he had known all the time, dumping the abandoned work trucks in the swamp to keep the police out of their lives. The house brought out the swarms to pleasure him, and everything returned to its wonderful normal.

When Stanley finally passed, 335 sat dark and alone. Empty. She had the insects bury him beneath the cool, dirt floor of her basement so she could hold him forever, but it wasn't the same. She spoke to him as if he was still there, and it helped a little, but the house needed something more. She needed change.

She began watching the other houses again to help fill a little of the void she carried inside. Their lives seemed so much more complete and fulfilling than hers. 335 was amazed at how effortless they made it seem. People always coming and going. She began to imagine what it would be like to *be* one of those houses, to be something different than she'd been her whole existence.

In particular, she watched a white, two-story Colonial just next door. There was a little girl that played in the front yard, and 335 felt something when she watched the child. *Free*. She wanted to feel that way all the time, not the emptiness she felt when she spent another night alone speaking to a dead Stanley.

That night, when the world was quiet and dead again, she got an idea. 335 always got the best ideas at night. She reached out, thick tendrils of consciousness boring their way through the dirt beneath her lawn until she touched the house next door. There was pain, but she let it flow into agony. There was nothing left for her here. She could feel her walls and ceilings cracking under the pressure. There was a moment of unconsciousness, followed by a peaceful calm.

She looked at the abandoned, partially collapsed Victorian house next door and smiled.

#

Julie Slater likes her new house. There is a big yard out front to play in, and she doesn't have to share it with the other kids like she did back at the apartment complex. Plus, Mommy seems happier here. She stopped drinking and the scar on Daddy's face is healing up okay. This is their "brand new start", as they had put it to her.

But the other day, things changed. Now, furniture moves around on its own and she can hear a strange voice in her head at night. Even worse, Mommy is drinking again. Julie sits in her room after school and listens to Mommy scream and cry at Daddy. He spends all of his time in the basement these days.

End

About the Author

Chris Noonan writes stories about the horror inherent in daily life from his suburban house in Mount Holly, New Jersey. His loving wife, Christina, and two children, Zachary and Ella, put up with his regular flights of fancy. When he's not writing or slaving away at his day job, Chris plays guitar in the band Groovepocket [https://groovepocketband.com/] and co-hosts a D&D podcast, 3 Wise DMs [https://3wisedms.com/].

Shot Game
By Duane Burke

After this the descent into Hell is easy. On the pale, white faces which the great billows whirl upward to my tower I see again and again, often and still more often, a writing of human hatred, a deep and passionate hatred, vast by the very vagueness of its expressions. - W. E. B. DuBois

I've never been a religious man. I wouldn't even say spiritual. But after one eventful night in a Manhattan bar, I began to change the way I looked at a lot of things. It was clearly the beginning of the end. Or maybe it was the end of the beginning. I guess it all really depends on the perspective. Either way, the world hasn't been the same since. The brisk evening air of early November in New York nipped at the nape of my neck. I shivered slightly as the heat inside met meet me at the door of *The Hemline*. The large television to the left of the main bar displayed political pundits espousing the virtues of this candidate over that one, gratefully muted. This time of evening was usually busy for the haunts of the Fashion District -- that witching hour between the exits of the close-to-retirement building engineers and the entrances of the eternally optimistic designer hopefuls. But it was election night in America, and there was plenty of space in the bar.

The owner of the bar, James Hardley, rushed by me mumbling a *hello* and clapping me on the shoulder abruptly as he hurried through the door. He was an athletically thin man, obsessed with running as far as he could as fast as he could in any contest he could find in the five boroughs. His skeletal appearance was perfect for this time of year sliding gracefully with the changing season from Halloween to Christmas carols. He stopped just shy of closing the door behind him and yelled an unintelligible instruction to the bar staff, then went on about his business without waiting for confirmation.

I surveyed a few pockets of patrons scattered about, sharing potables and I imagined some passionately debating the early reports of polling results. There was one such group I recognized from a start-up fashion company at a nearby four-top table. Past conversations with them revealed their youthful naivete usually overshadowed sound reasoning somewhere around the third round of mezcal margaritas. I noticed a couple on what had to be a bad first date, she was desperately trying to get and hold his attention and he only seemed to be interested in checking his social media feed or possibly even checking for a new date partner in the area. Some variance of these scenarios played itself out in other dimly lit parts of the bar and I was not particularly inclined to get too close to any of them.

The front bar area was exceptionally empty, but when I saw the imposing figure seated dead center the abundance of seating made a little more sense. I am not a small man, and he was almost my height sitting down, so I pegged him to be about six feet eight inches tall. He had the back and shoulders of a laborer who spent the last thirty years commanding a jack hammer, and the waist and legs of a prepubescent boy. In my mind I saw one of those top-heavy weightlifters, a barrel of chest and arms that never heard of leg days and chuckled inside.

I saw a shadow of a large ring on the crown of his bald head like someone had burned his scalp with an extremely large cigarette lighter. His skin was the color of roasted cinnamon and he smelled faintly of gasoline, not uncommon for many of the workers who kept the lights on in the city that never sleeps. He might have stood out more if this wasn't New York City. The parties might end in October for other cities, but costumes were welcome here year-round particularly in this fashion-focused part of the city.

The Hemline had become the favorite of my regular bars, and I had seen plenty of standouts over the years. I had no problem walking up and taking a seat keeping one chair between us, as is common "single man at a bar" etiquette. His head was bouncing back and forth between the two televisions, and I caught a glimpse of his face in the poor lighting most NYC bars offered. He wore a grizzled scowl and incredibly dark eyes. I thought it was the lack of light but there seemed to be darkness there. The polar opposite of the cloudy-eyed cataracts you might find on someone completely blind.

The bartender Kayla served me often over the last five years, and she smiled in recognition of my arrival. I quickly surveyed the rest of the bar while a generous pour of Jameson and a pint of Guinness was set in front of me. I raised my rocks glass to both her and my neighbor in mock toast and knocked it back in one hard swallow letting the cool burn from the Irish Whiskey wash over me. Kayla was heavy handed with her pours. Excellent customer service in her mind was making sure her customers left the bar drunk, whether they wanted to or not. I took a long drought of the stout and glanced at the television towards my right.

I had developed a reputation for making small talk with random visitors. I could keep to myself and let everyone continue our nights in silence, but there was never any fun in that. On nights there was a game on one of the seventy-inch televisions at either end of the bar, I was all but guaranteed to get into a heated -- but friendly -- debate. Not everyone responded favorably and not all debates ended well. I opted to press my luck.

"Weather's not bad for this time of year, right?" I asked.

"Definitely seen worse," he mumbled. He didn't stop his intent observations of the events playing out on the televisions or pay much attention to my attempt at cordial conversation. It was about right for a typical NYC bar. I wasn't offended or deterred.

"After the Olympics, election day is my second favorite thing to happen every four years. I do a shot every time they do an update and at least one state flips and double if it's more states going from red to blue. California just came in, and Florida should report in soon. At this rate, I hope to be dead drunk by the time the polls close," I chuckled.

"Come again?" he snickered.

"Yeah, man, I love shots. I mean, I care about issues, but it makes this whole election night thing a hell of a lot more entertaining. The coverage can drag on and on just looking at numbers and colors, and honestly half the people on tv are talking out of their ass. So, I started doing shots based on the results every time they call a state."

"And double for red to blue, huh? You putting a lot of faith in what's her face to have a chance to win, aren't you?"

I almost choked on my beer laughing. "A chance? Have you seen the alternative? Bro, it should be a bloodbath."

"If only we could be so lucky." he snickered again, but it seemed somewhat odd this time. There was a weird timbre to his voice that I couldn't place. Like trying to listen to someone on a plane after your ears pop. I motioned to Kayla for another round.

"Well, who do you think is going to win?" It wasn't sports, but my father always said a healthy debate is always good food for the soul regardless of the subject matter. My neighbor turned to face me more, and the weathered face looking back was noticeably older than I originally thought when I sat down.

"First of all, we could give two shits who wins."

"Could have fooled me the way you couldn't take your eyes off the screen."

"We care only about the aftermath. The chaos that would likely ensue on a worldwide scale regardless of who wins."

"Damn, dude, that's dark." And a little bit creepy.

"But since you're so confident, why don't we bet on the next state that reports. Loser buys."

I expected another snicker, but none came. Nothing came. I tried to search his eyes for some sign of -- well, anything recognizable. I found nothing in his voice or his eyes. Those obsidian orbs. I probably would have been spooked if I hadn't been already tipsy before I got there. Kayla startled me when she appeared suddenly, replaced my drinks, and then went off, back to her cell phone games and web videos. Liquid courage in hand, I regained my focus.

"Sheeeet, I'm definitely a gambling man, especially when the odds are in my favor. You're on."

"Excellent." That weird feeling was back when he spoke again. I couldn't help but picture Mr. Burns from the Simpsons grinning eerily with hellfire in the background. Yeah, I was officially a little tipsy.

"So, you really think that dude is a better choice for the country?"

"Again, we don't much care."

"You one of those people that are still mad about Obama? Get over it, bro."

"Nah."

"Ok, you must be some kind of anarchist or something."

I thought I saw a light in his eyes flicker with an impression of massive structures burning. I blinked instinctively, but the voice on the television broke my concentration. The newscaster cleared his throat and continued. "Ladies and gentlemen. The poll results are in for Florida, Pennsylvania and Ohio," I looked over at my compatriot with a confidently smug smirk and picked up my shot glass to resume drinking to my success on his tab. When did Kayla turn up the volume on the television?

"And, yes, it is confirmed..."

I turned to face him directly and started my celebratory chair dance. I started looking towards Kayla to signal it was time to re-up.

"In a shocking turn, the Republican challenger has carried all three key states," the reporter continued, "and is looking strong in a few other states that have historically voted Democrat for the past two decades."

I choked as the whiskey and air mixed in my throat in disbelief and dismay. He snickered again at first, and then laughed more hardily. I took a few sips of Guinness to try to get everything going back down the right pipes.

"HA! We like this game!" he said, and this time he was the one to get Kayla's attention, flashing up three fingers for shots."

"Ohhh, I get it now. You're a veteran, right?" I tried not to stare at his hand. "You still upset with the Democratic base's insistence on pulling out of the wars in the Middle East. I don't agree, but I get it. Where'd you serve?"

"Told ya before, we don't give a shit. It's all a game to us."

"Right, right. You don't have to be a jerk about it." My reaction brought out the first smile I had seen on him tonight.
"Your emotion has given us an idea. Shall we make this more interesting?"

"So you're all in with the shot game now, too?"

"Indeed," he nodded. "We are."

"Ok, I guess. I did say that I was a gambling man, and hey, the more the merrier. Who's here with you?"

"We do not understand."

"Where are your friends? They must be here somewhere since you keep saying 'we' and 'us' and you are the only one I'm talking to."

"Ah, we see now. You would not understand." He said this as a matter of fact, and it triggered another reaction from me.

"Hey, I'm as liberal as anyone you'll ever meet. So, if this is about how you gender-identify, I don't give a – "

"We should have said you cannot understand."

"Man, now you're just being rude. Ain't no need to talk down to me and call me ignorant. You don't even know me!"

I turned back around in my seat muttering to myself how much of an asshole he was being.

"Singularity can't define us as you typically do. We keep forgetting about your kind and your sensitive emotions."

I turned around, fully prepared to investigate the 'your kind' comment with violent thoroughness when he continued.

"We are a higher being. What you humans would call an angel."

I was the one who was laughing then. "Get the hell outta here. I ain't that freaking drunk."

"We told you that you were not capable of understanding."

"Buddy, this is New York City. Half the people you meet on a daily basis don't believe in any particular higher being, much less angels. You gotta do better than that. First you insult me, then you insult my intelligence. Whatever."

"Look at me and listen."

Before I could protest further, I heard distant choral singing emanating from inside my head, and then it was all around me at the same time. For the second time tonight, there was a hint of light in his eyes, but this time it was comforting. The circle atop his head emitted a faint glow. All of this was imperceptible to everyone else in the bar, but I was certain all of it was real.

"Ho-ly shit. Holy shit." I kept repeating the phrase over and over. That's all that would come out. I couldn't help but stare, but he didn't seem disturbed or even surprised. "But, but... How?"

"You humans are so vain. You may have been given dominion over this world, but that does not mean remotely that you inhabit it alone. There have always been and will always be others amongst you."

I downed the glass of whiskey in front of me and tried to get a grip on what I had just discovered. He was right – I couldn't understand. I mean it's one thing to believe there's life on other planets, but angels in bars in New York City? That was just too much.

"So why do you care so much about this election? I thought you all weren't supposed to interfere in human things and such."

"We don't care about the particulars - this election or that one. They are all the same, all over the world. We care about the potential for chaos after. You were given everything, a limitless world of potential with the free will to explore it all."

Here he paused to let that statement sink in. "You were given a world with a clean slate, cultivated civilization and culture with a path to greatness. Then mindfulness for the well-being of the masses yielded to full scale exploitation of the same. You seem mostly content to use a fraction of the brain power and that free will to do anything productive that does not lead to wars and violence against your own kind. In the vast cosmos of things in existence you are all more alike than you could ever be different, yet all you do is concentrate on the minuscule percent of traits that separate you."

I don't know if he paused again for effect or if I just focused intently on what he had just said and zoned out for a second pondering the "vastness of the cosmos".

"So in a nutshell, you get off on the pain that is the human experience?"

"Again, so short-sighted." When he sneered this time, I heard it in full stereo with my ears and my mind. I guess there was no need to hold back with me now that I knew what he was.

"Well, what then?"

"You humans think everything is all about you! You believe when you're done with this world everything will be destroyed and then you just get to inherit Heaven? After the terrible jobs you've done as a steward of this place? What intelligent creature would believe that?"

"Yeah, yeah, I'm not even sure I believe in heaven." At least I didn't really until tonight.

"Oh, it's real. And when we say you could not understand, this time we really mean there is no way for your human mind to comprehend. Your laws of science - biology, chemistry, physics - simply do not apply. The things humans will learn in the next millennium still will not help you grasp the beginning of the reality of Heaven."

"Ok, I get it. Puny humans. So again, what's in it for you?"

"We - in the plural sense you are used to using in conversation - get this world. All of it. The faster you humans finally ruin it for yourselves, the faster we get to finally enjoy it without needing to heed warnings of intervening in human affairs. You all are like a disease ruining the experience of this world for all other creatures - the ones you know about and especially the ones you do not. The sooner you are gone, the better for everyone else."

I didn't know if I was ready to believe in the pearly gates, but I wasn't ready to give up on the only world I did know. Sure, there could have been life on other planets. Hell, now I knew there was other life on this planet. But as far as I was concerned it was our planet - Earth - and I wasn't ready to envision an Earth devoid of humans with every other conceivable creature joyfully dancing on our corpses.

"If it's so bad down here and you hate us so much, why don't you just go back to Heaven."

I sensed something different in their eyes at this question. It was loss. It took my breath away as if he had punched me in the solar plexus. I felt the loss as much as he did, and it was hurting inside me just as much as him. He continued.

"Not all of us can. So, we wait out your existence until we can at last claim this world. More chaos, more fear, and endless frustration will all lead to your ruin. As those things rise your contempt for each other rises with it, all moving you closer to your own self-destruction."

He didn't have to pause this time for me to get the full brunt of it.

"So, are we going to make this more interesting? You said you are a gambling man, are you not?"

"Huh?"

"We have some election news to watch and some shots to be had, and maybe more to be wagered."

"I kind of feel like this is a suckers bet since you already know what's going to happen."

"We know a great many things, but we do not know the future. Remember, humans have free will and their decisions cannot be foretold. We do not yet know the outcomes which is why we watch."

"Yeah, maybe. Still. I somehow feel like the stakes have already changed--"

"Not for us," he asserted.

Before I could respond with the value of humankind, the newscaster was back."

"We can now report - Michigan, North Carolina, and Wisconsin have all gone to the Republican underdog! Honestly, the way this night is going, I don't know how much longer we'll be able to call him that."

There were groans from random tables in the bar, but a few claps mixed in indiscriminately. The Democratic pundits on set with the newscaster were shaking their heads in disbelief while the Republicans smugly nodded "I told you so". At each cluster of patrons, people tried to apply reason to the current state of events, and once again the bar was soon awash in top 50 pop and hip hop waiting for the next update. I swallowed the rest of the Guinness in my glass and motioned to Kayla.

"What did you have in mind?" I asked nervously.

"Your wife is a politician, yes?"

"How did you--" I cut myself off, remembering to whom I was talking. "What does that have to do with anything?"

"Well, we could find many uses for a person with power in this country. It could prove beneficial to us in the future."

I chuckled. "She's just a local politician. More title than power."

"That is the case now. But many things can change."

"And if I win?"

"I'm sure you could find use for our powers in this country, yes?"

The obsidian eyes were back accompanied by a sinister grin, as well as the tingling hairs on the back of my neck. I tipped my empty glass and nodded in his direction in acceptance of our bet.

"Yes. Excellent! We like this game a lot!" He shouted loudly enough for everyone to hear keeping up the appearance of an exuberant drinker. "Shots for the bar on us!" he exclaimed. The divisions ceased to exist long enough for enthusiastic cheers of "Shots! Shots! Shots, shots, shots!" He smiled widely.

And now I fully understood why he was smiling. I started to change the way I looked at a lot of things.

I was sure this was the beginning of the end. Or the end of the beginning. Guess it all depends on the perspective.

About the Author

Duane Burke was born and raised in Newark, NJ with parental roots extending to the beautiful island nation of Barbados. He is the author of *Shot Game* and other short stories, and he is an avid consumer of all genres of fiction, especially speculative fiction and urban tales from around the world. His favorite movies are *The Princess Bride* and *Marked For Death* – a combination only a twisted mind could love. A contest on Reedsy.com "Write your story from the perspective of an outsider watching something or someone change", provided the prompt that inspired this story. He has to say that for legal reasons - so there it is.

Look for more books from Winged Hussar Publishing, LLC – E-books, paper-backs and Limited-Edition hardcovers. The best in history, science fiction and fantasy at:

https://www. wingedhussarpublishing.com

https://www.whpsupplyroom.com

or follow us on Facebook at:

Winged Hussar Publishing LLC

Or on twitter at:

WingHusPubLLC

For information and upcoming publications

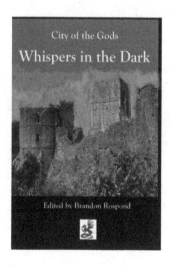

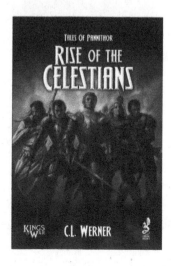

ZMOK
BOOKS